# DISTANT
# STARLESS
# NIGHTS

# DISTANT

# STARLESS

# NIGHTS

*A fictional memoir by*
Myriam Ullens

*Translated by*
Sam Alexander

This book is a work of fiction. The characters, incidents, and dialogue are drawn from the author's imagination and are not construed as real. Any resemblance to actual persons, living or dead, is entirely coincidental.

DISTANT STARLESS NIGHT.
Copyright © 2017 by Myriam Ullens

FIRST EDITION

Jacket Designed by Karen Horton

Interior Designed by Cathleen Elliott

*To my husband and children,*
*who never stopped believing in me and*
*supporting me in all my projects.*

# Prologue

*October, 2009*

Usually, Mansfield Manor is a comfort to me. From the granite walls that surround the estate, perched on a hill outside Dinard, France, there is a view right out to sea. The 18th-century Breton manor, and the surrounding land all the way down to the beach, once belonged to my godfather, Uncle Oliver. I remember how comfortable and convivial the house was, how conversations ran long into the night, how laughter rose and fell and got caught up in the music that played there. I remember the large sitting room with its enormous open fire, and the endless hours he spent with his guests, sipping cups of white tea brought all the way from China – Emperor's Tea, he called it – or perhaps a glass of fine old cognac.

My godfather's personality is indelibly stamped on this place. Lord Oliver Ashbury – polo player, epicurean, lover of life, lover of women, collector of precious stones, old seadog par excellence – always returned to Mansfield Manor to recover after his adventures. And it was here, with him, that I spent my holidays as a child.

Today, more than fifty years later, the manor belongs to me. I have kept up all his old ways, and kept on the person who most embodies the spirit of the place: Leo. Leo is four foot ten of pure

Chinese benevolence: a first-rate chef, valet, advisor, and longstanding family confidant. And today he's worried. He's worried about me.

We've been here so long together I can imagine what he is doing now. A few moments ago, I put on a record of Fauré's *Requiem* in the study adjoining my bedroom on the first floor. Loudly. Leo is bearing it as best he can by concentrating on the *gâteau aux trois chocolats* he is making for Kenya and Vittorio, two of my grandchildren. In two days' time, the children – well, young adults now, at fourteen and fifteen years old – are due to arrive for the midterm holidays, and Leo's chocolate cake is their absolute favorite.

I open the windows of my study, but the music and the blast of cold air still aren't enough. "Come on, Mozart," I call to one of my three Labrador retrievers. "We're going outside."

~

I walk along the sea's edge, water up to my ankles. Mozart trots alongside me with a stick in his mouth, waiting for a game that won't come.

The tide is rising, and the wind has picked up; it's biting cold now.

For several weeks, my strength has been slipping away. I've been finding it difficult to leave my room, except to walk the dogs. I can't seem to shake this terrible cough, and my appetite has vanished. I don't know what to do. So, I've come to find the sea. It has always given me a taste for life, a taste for the fight.

My steps are getting shorter. I'm searching deep down for something to make it all worthwhile again. The waves are crashing over my boots, the salt air fills my lungs, the wind lashes my face. I search and search within and I find…nothing. I collapse to my knees. Water seeps into my clothes. Small, forgettable words pass my lips: a prayer to the God we only invoke when everything has gone wrong.

"Why did you put me through it *again*?" I ask. "We'd found a sort of peace, hadn't we?"

A bigger wave knocks me off balance, and begins to tug me out to sea. I let myself be carried along, calmer now that the water is taking me.

A sharp pinch on my arm jolts me back to life. Mozart's powerful jaws grip tightly. I struggle to find my footing, and am surprised to feel sand beneath my feet. Drenched and groggy, I lie washed up on the beach, nuzzled by my dog.

Back to my feet again. My clothes, weighed down by the water, are heavy and make it hard to walk. I get to the boathouse, fling open the doors, and lurch toward my little sail boat.

Outside, the rain is falling in sheets. I look around for Mozart, and realize he's not with me anymore.

A few minutes later, I'm standing proudly atop the boat when I hear a familiar voice yelling, out of breath:

"Marsie! You're mad!"

In spite of it all, I smile when I see my granddaughter, and hear my nickname. Perhaps I look like a naughty child caught in the act; Kenya certainly sounds angry. "You're not even thinking about going out in this weather, I hope," she says.

I reply blankly: "I just wanted to see that everything was ship-shape...in case we felt like going sailing, the three of us...I wasn't expecting you yet!"

Is she fooled? It doesn't matter.

Kenya runs to give me a hug. And then Vittorio arrives, breathing hard, dogs yapping cheerfully around his ankles. Mozart must have led them to me. Vittorio envelops me in a blanket and wraps his arms around me. And, for the first time in months and months, warm tears trickle down my cheeks.

~

Trying to get warm again under the shower, I picture Kenya and Vittorio sitting by the fire in my study, on the huge sofa piled high with cushions. I know they're waiting impatiently. Just as they always did, as grandchildren do. They used to wait for endless, fabulous stories: tales of pirates and princesses, abandoned little girls and long-lost mothers, palaces made of sweets, red-faced witches, child-eating ogres, and fairies casting magic spells. They used to wait for our special reunions after one of my far-flung voyages. Kenya and Vittorio saw wonder in everything I brought back. They would rummage through the trunks, discovering spices and fabrics, breathing in the objects' foreign smells. They would sit with me, surrounded by half-unpacked suitcases, engrossed by my stories, clutching at a little secret hope: perhaps they would never have to go back to boring old school and the dull daily grind.

When I'm dressed, Vittorio tells me that Paul Le Kern, the family doctor, will be here at seven o'clock this evening. Leo has probably told them I have been refusing to see a doctor for a while.

All three of us sit around the little study table, and I try to wash down a crêpe with one of Leo's hot chocolates. A reassuring warmth spreads over me. I look at them both, and it makes me want to cry.

My two grandchildren, cousins, have been thick as thieves since they were toddlers. They were always careening around together and getting into scrapes, to the consternation of their parents, my own William and Alissa. When the time came, they even chose to go to the same school: Los Angeles's prestigious Harvard High School. Kenya's fiery temperament primes her for action, Vittorio has an extraordinary capacity to keep his cool – this intense balancing act has caused occasional bouts of arguing punctuated by periods of deep friendship.

At seven o'clock on the nose, Paul Le Kern comes to examine me in my bedroom. He leaves looking upset, even neglecting to shut the door properly behind him. As I get dressed, I can hear him talking to Kenya and Vittorio.

"Listen, I'm very concerned. Your grandma has a temperature of a hundred and four, and she's wheezing badly. I want her to have a chest scan tomorrow. It's your job to remind her to take her pills, and make sure she eats and drinks, all of which she seems to have forgotten. But her mood's worrying me most, and there's nothing we…." His voice fades away as they walk down the hall.

As he's leaving, I overhear him say: "Look, bottom line: I'm counting on you two."

My study is like Ali Baba's cave. A refuge or, rather, a sanctuary. So many objects from so many countries have wound up here that visitors don't know where to look. On the desk sits a Fat Lady – a little painted clay figurine, all the rage in the 7th and 8th centuries. They were placed on Chinese graves to accompany the dead into the afterlife, and usually depict the Consort Yang Guifrei, the beloved of Emperor Xuanzong of the Tang Dynasty, who was lauded for her beauty.

In a little alcove, candles are arranged around various religious icons and photographs of family members past and present. As a little boy, Vittorio found it terrifying to contemplate these characters. They seemed to look at him knowingly, as if offering a glimpse of life after death. I remember him visibly shuddering in front of them, poor boy. Kenya, on the other hand, used to daydream serenely in front of these fantastic candlelit dolls. I suppose it depends on how you see the world, how you're put together.

Now the three of us are in my study, like the old days. Vittorio stands in the middle of the room; Kenya is shivering slightly. Instinctively, she asks her cousin for a lighter, and goes over to the candles that haven't been lit for…who knows how long. Her shin brushes against something sticking out from under my desk.

She crouches down to have a look, then pulls out a large quilt strewn with objects I have sewn onto it. I know she'll recognize the teddy bear she gave me when, at age eight, she decided she could sleep on her own at last. Her hands pass over several other items attached to the quilt: a baby's rattle, a medal, letters, a passport....

"Is this a new hobby?" she asks. As she handles the quilt, dozens of little bells sewn to the edge jangle at once. Vittorio helps her spread my strange creation out on the floor, so they can get a better look. It is almost as large as a Persian rug, almost as thick as a tapestry, and adorned with ornate hand embroidery in rich, jewel-like colors. My grandchildren turn to me with wide, questioning eyes.

"My memories. I've sewn all my most precious things onto it. My life story...basically." My voice sounds hoarse and my breath comes in tight bursts. I don't know how to talk to them. I'm frightened, frightened of hurting them. "I hate coffins. When they bury me, I want you to cover mine with this. The sound of the bells will be me winking at you." I expect them to let this sink in. They don't.

"Hang on, Marsie, you're not going anywhere!" Vittorio says indignantly. "What are you...sixty-something? You'd be better off packing your bags and going around the world again. You can bring us back a few more souvenirs."

"And have you thought about *our* kids?" Kenya pipes up.

"Yeah, who's going to tell them stories?"

"Who's going to have pillow fights with them on stormy nights?"

"Who's going to be waiting for them with a hot chocolate after skiing? You're not allowed to get all dark on us like this, it's not fair," Vittorio protests.

Their barrage convinces me: Time to come clean.

"I don't know how to put this, my darlings," I begin. "My spirit, my body…they're tired. Sad. They're not working together anymore. It feels like I'm falling into some bottomless black hole."

Vittorio breaks the silence that follows, his voice calm and serious. "Marsie, this might shock you. I think it's time to talk about what you're leaving us."

I look up at him. What on earth is he saying? "No, not that!" he says, reading my expression. "The best legacy you can give us is your life story, told properly – the bad parts as well as the good."

Kenya looks at her cousin. She is dumbfounded for a second, then suddenly catches on. "Brilliant idea! Right, let's go and get cozy in your bedroom."

And now, I can't help but smile. I'm amazed by my grandchildren's grown-up, matter-of-fact way of talking. They may only be fourteen and fifteen sixteen, but they make me feel I must do as I'm told.

"Leo has made a beautiful dinner, and I'm dying of hunger," declares Vittorio. "I'm going to take a shower, and then we'll meet downstairs. Coming, Ken?"

Outside the door, they stop for a moment before heading downstairs. It doesn't occur to them that I might have gotten out of my chair and that, with my ear to the door, I can hear them talking.

"That was perfect!" says Kenya, clearly excited. "Did you get that from *Arabian Nights*?"

"Huh?"

"You know, Scheherazade tells stories so the prince won't kill her."

"Something like that. We get her to tell us her life story, to stop her from thinking about dying."

"Brilliant! I just can't imagine life without Marsie."

"Neither can I. That's why I've come up with another idea. It's a longshot, and I can't tell you yet, but you'll like it."

"Come on!"

"Wait, just give me time. You'll see."

After supper, all three of us settle down on my bed, surrounded by cushions. I feel as though I've gone ten years back in time. When they were little, these two would refuse point blank to go to bed without a story. And now, here they are again. Waiting.

My hand brushes one of the objects sewn onto the quilt: a military medal. "This was awarded posthumously to Uncle Travis. You never knew him, of course…neither did I. But all you need to know for now is that he was my mother's best friend. Well…she met him just after she came to Britain for the first time. Later, Travis introduced her to his brother, Gordon…my father, of course…."

I trail off, short of breath. Or perhaps short of ideas, and not yet sure where to start. I breathe out, then smile at Kenya and Vittorio, because I don't know what else to do. Their eyes sparkle back at me. They look patient, calm, as if they've got all the time in the world. "Let's take things slowly. The objects will be my guide." And the words just come.

# PART ONE
# 1943-1961

CHAPTER 1

# Medal

In the winter of 1942, victory was still a long way off for the Allied forces. Hitler and his followers had their hands on most of Europe. London wasn't glitz and glamour then, not the city you two know. It had been ravaged by wave after wave of German bombs. The neighborhood where my parents-to-be lived looked like the "capital of the moon." That's how the writer Elizabeth Bowen described it. Know her work? ...No, of course you don't.

In spite of the Blitz, in spite of the uneasy wait for more destruction, Londoners weren't in the least bit cowed. No, every day they showed ingenuity, solidarity and courage. A sort of coolness tinged with humor that would so impress the world in the years to come. You know about that, at least.

Gordon Rochester, my father, was desperately disappointed never to see active service. His dreams of becoming an army officer had been shattered in the thirties, when he broke his back in a parachute accident at Sandhurst. No more military school for him. He had to make do with a career in diplomacy. When war broke out, he was still wearing a back brace, so joining up was quite out of the question.

That was left to his brother, Travis, who joined the navy. But I'm getting ahead of myself already.

In 1942, Gordon's war – "doing his part" – consisted of government work in London. He joined Winston Churchill in his Cabinet War Rooms. What an extraordinary place that was: a secret bunker buried deep beneath Whitehall, from where Britain dared to plan her victory – by no means sure, at that point, that America would come to the rescue. My father wasn't right at the top of things, but his job was important all the same. He never talked about it to anyone, of course. The very existence of the Cabinet War Rooms was hush-hush. After all, as the posters said: "Careless talk costs lives!"

You two will remember that Sarah – I was never entirely at ease calling her Mother, much less *Maman* – was French. She had been living in England for more than seven years at the time, and she opted to stay in London with my father. The influx of French refugees answering General de Gaulle's call to arms gave her a new role as guide and interpreter, knowing, as she did, about London life during the war.

My mother usually took a room at the Connaught Hotel, the favorite haunt of the English aristocracy – well, the high born who wouldn't be seen dead at Claridge's, and preferred a Bentley to a Rolls. She chose the Connaught for three reasons. Firstly, when he wasn't at his house in Hampstead, Charles de Gaulle occupied Suite 103. Secondly, she liked the fact that she could have a proper dinner there without breaking the law.

…Yes, Vittorio, I expect it does sound ridiculous to you. You click your fingers and get whatever you want, but rationing was severe during the war, and afterwards, too. There were two ways around it for the well-off – and my parents qualified on that score: They could either make use of the black market, or eat in one of the restaurants that were still open, and could still produce a decent menu – which the Connaught could.

The third reason? Years later, I found out that there was a less pragmatic motive for Sarah's visits to the Connaught Hotel – but I mustn't leap ahead. Where was I?

…Ah, yes, thank you. It was late autumn, 1942. The fate of my Uncle Travis – so dear to my mother's heart – was soon to be decided. He was an officer in the Royal Marines, and ready to serve. He didn't know it yet, but his name had already been raised in meetings about a top-secret mission.

Churchill had been informed that the port of Bordeaux, France was home to a fleet of German ships known as the Blockade Breakers. All day, these vessels unloaded cargos of rubber from the Far East, and, more worryingly, took on weapons to be delivered to Japan. His general staff considered bombing the port, but that would amount to signing a death warrant for countless Bordeaux citizens. Unthinkable.

So, a special mission was conceived, code-named Operation Frankton, but also known as Cockleshell. The plan was to dispatch a division of twelve men in specially-designed foldable canoes, called the Cockle – the Cockle Mark II, in fact, I think it was. A British

Navy submarine was to drop the men at the Gironde estuary. The marines would then advance upstream, paddling by night, hiding out by day, until they reached Bordeaux, where they would attach limpet mines to the German vessels. Their mission accomplished, the men were to make for the village of Ruffec, a hundred miles away. From there, members of the French Resistance would help them get home. Sounds easy when you say it like that, doesn't it?

Travis Rochester embraced the mission enthusiastically. He knew what he was getting himself into, all right, as did the other eleven. Gordon was so proud of his brother, you can't imagine how proud....

At the time, Sarah was pregnant. The baby—me—was unwanted. And now her beloved brother-in-law was being sent off on a potentially fatal mission. For her, it seemed like yet more evidence that the heavens were hostile.

As it transpired, things went wrong from the word go. HMS Tuna – I think I've got the name right – arrived at the estuary on the evening of December 7, 1942, and straightaway, six canoes became five as one got damaged before it even hit the water. Then, a second canoe disappeared in the powerful cross tide, and a third capsized. The strong current carried the three remaining canoes toward a fleet of German frigates. Two managed to slip through, but one was discovered, and its marines were captured.

Two canoes carrying four men, including Uncle Travis, did accomplish phase one of the mission: on December 11, 1942, at around nine o'clock at night, they managed to attach magnetic charges to six enemy vessels. These exploded early the next morning. Although the ships stayed afloat, they were unusable. Of course, the marines were long gone by then. Decided not to hang about, I imagine.

Then came phase two of the mission: getting to the resistance at Ruffec. Walking a hundred miles at night in the middle of December, in occupied territory, can't have been much fun. They got on all right at first but, on December 14, Uncle Travis and the marine he was traveling with were captured. They were taken to Paris, imprisoned for three months, and tortured. We learned later that of the twelve, only two men made it home, after a long and arduous journey via Gibraltar.

At ten o'clock at night on Monday, March 23, 1943, my mother, seven and a half months pregnant at the time, learned that Travis had been executed. My father, himself quite devastated, told her the news. He had found out from his friend Anthony Eden, the Foreign Secretary, who had followed the operation from the start and passed on information to my parents when he could. My mother collapsed in shock, and her water broke.

So, I came into the world the day my uncle left it; and this medal is the only memento I have of his life. For a long time, I thought my mother had never forgiven me – until the day I discovered that the truth was altogether more complicated.

# CHAPTER 2

# Silver Rattle

"She's so ugly…"

My mother didn't dare say it out loud, of course, as she stood over the crib. But she was thinking it so hard that it was possible to decipher the brain waves. Margaret Black, the nurse looking after me in the maternity ward of London's St. George's Hospital, was certainly under no illusions. She had noticed the French woman who never asked a single question about her baby – quite the opposite from all the other new mothers.

I'd been fighting for survival for three weeks. Born prematurely, then swaddled with only my face peeping out, I lay there without making a sound – much to everyone's astonishment. Mind you, I was lucky. No bombs fell on the hospital while I was there. Londoners had the Eastern Front to thank for that: the Luftwaffe had their hands full. At that time, St. George's was located near Hyde Park Corner. Even during the bombing, very few doctors and nurses had wanted to leave. This was their frontline.

Amidst the power cuts and water shortages, the makeshift wards and make-do nursing, the adversity and the courage, I arrived – quickly and noiselessly, as though making my apologies for being early, for only weighing five pounds, for breathing the same air as the woman who had brought me into the world against her will.

Yes, Sarah Rochester had done all she could to get rid of me. Deliberate tumbles from her bicycle, frenetic gallops in the saddle, scalding baths – she had tried pretty much everything, though she was careful to keep on the right side of the law. An abortion would, she feared, get her husband into trouble.

In the face of all that, I demonstrated quite singular stubbornness. I wouldn't budge. And for three weeks in St. George's, I hung on, although at times, it was touch and go.

The day they came to fetch me, I still weighed next to nothing, but after three more weeks, I was finally out of harm's way. My mother was dressed like the proper French woman she was. Her outfit had been carefully assembled to combine shades of almond and green that complemented the colors of her eyes perfectly. That's right, I did say "colors."

On a beautiful spring morning, my mother walked toward Margaret Black with the determination of a would-be conqueror. Nurse Black had decided to personally oversee my discharge from St. George's, and held me tight in her arms, as if frightened to let go. She walked toward my mother until she was close enough to hand me over. Sarah Rochester reached out without even looking at me, her eyes fixed on the nurse, who angled her head away slightly to avoid the disconcerting sight of one green eye and one brown. A beautiful face and different-colored eyes; it must have been quite a shock, especially since the face displayed not a single trace of kindliness towards her. Margaret Black had seen it all before. She had something to say.

"Are you aware that a man came to see your daughter every day? He spent hours just standing there, with his forehead pressed against the glass, not a care for anyone else. Sometimes, it was very late. Then yesterday evening, he asked me if he could hold her. For once, the little one cried, and he began to tell her a story with such a soothing voice that she went back to sleep again. The nurse on duty told me he was here all night, but when I got here this morning he had gone. He left this silver rattle beside her. Do you know him?"

For a moment, Sarah looked thrown. She quickly composed herself, taking the proffered rattle and stuffing it into a pocket.

"Yes, of course. He's my late brother-in-law's cousin." And, perhaps because Margaret Black looked baffled at this, my mother felt duty-bound to add: "I say cousin, but more than that, they were lifelong friends. My brother-in-law was shot by the Germans the day my daughter was born. She must have taken on a peculiar significance in his eyes."

With this, she turned on her heel and marched toward the waiting car, whose black doors swallowed her up. I was handed to the newly-employed nanny on the back seat as though I were a dirty bundle of linen that my mother could quite happily do without.

"Take me home," she said to the chauffeur, Max, with a sigh.

Nurse Black stood still, watching the car disappear from sight. She didn't believe a word of what she had just been told, but you never would have known it to look at her. She simply nodded once, turned around, and walked back into the hospital and back to work.

≈

"Marsie, who told you the story of the rattle?" asks Kenya.

"Why, Margaret herself. I found her, you know…a few years later. I'll get to that," I promise, and I find that I meant it. I am already feeling a little better, beginning to put my past into words. "Keep talking, Marsie," says Vittorio.

≈

Having arrived at my new home, the nanny carefully carried me – Kimberly Rochester, aged six weeks – up to the family bassinet. The lace-festooned heirloom from Alsace, passed down on my mother's side, was waiting for its latest occupant in my bedroom at 11a

20

Belgrave Square. The white three-story house, just opposite Wilton Crescent, was part of an impressive collection of buildings erected on the Earl of Grosvenor's land in the 1830s, in what is now called Belgravia. My paternal grandfather bought the lease from the Earl's descendant, the Duke of Westminster.

When my father saw me in the arms of the nanny, he shuffled toward us. My mother stopped him halfway, wanting to know if he had been to see me at the hospital. He replied that he had, unable to wait for me to come home. Sarah shrugged her shoulders, and then, believing she had made enough effort for one day, took refuge in her room.

A little chap, four years old, appeared at my father's side, apparently from nowhere: blond, skinny, and dressed immaculately in a dark-green velvet suit. He couldn't stop himself from jumping up and down.

My father spoke calmly: "Charles, allow me to introduce your little sister, Kimberly." A broad smile lit up the boy's face. He tugged at the nanny's skirts to make her kneel down to his level, then snuggled up to me as best he could.

"She's for me, isn't she?" he said, with a bubbly mix of joy and pride.

Against all expectation, it wasn't long before Nurse Black reappeared on the scene. As I began to find my voice, it soon became clear that the nanny my parents had hired was not up to the job. My brother discovered me gagged, a bandage wrapped around my mouth. The "specialist in child development" had, it seems, found my crying exasperating. Charles screamed bloody murder. The nanny was fired on the spot. My mother, not knowing where else to turn, approached Margaret Black, who accepted a domestic position at once.

Had she become so attached to such a small person in those few weeks spent at the hospital? Did she know, even then, that her care and affection would provide the love I needed to grow up?

# CHAPTER 3

# Navy Blue Beret

*October*, 1949.

My trunk was almost bigger than me. It was as black as I was pale. Six years old, dressed in a navy blue uniform, a beret perched on my head. I was a tiny little thing lost in the courtyard of a huge nineteenth-century building. In front of me was a massive door, where the chauffeur had left me with a goodbye nod. I hadn't dared ask him to take me home again, or somewhere else entirely…anywhere but here.

I know, six years old seems young. But that's how it was done in those days.

I crossed the threshold all by myself, walking past the female warden, who barely glanced my way. She knew who I was. I'd already been a boarder for a year here at St. Augustine's Convent School near Namur in Belgium. My parents sent me there when I was five-years-old, shortly after my father was named British Ambassador in Brussels.

He gave us the news one evening in July, 1948. I remember it well, because that morning, my mother had given me an earful.

Perhaps I'd stained the organza dress she's ordered for me, or maybe my shoes were badly polished. I can't recall; but I'll never forget how strident her voice sounded. It cracked like a whip. She called me *gourde* – halfwit – and plenty of other French words I didn't know.

I ran into the arms of Margaret Black, who was never far away when my mother got angry with me. Margaret brushed my hair away from my face, and straightaway I calmed down. I had run away in the middle of my mother's tirade, and now she threw open the kitchen door, marched over to me, and grabbed me by the collar of my dress as if picking up a naughty puppy by the scruff of its neck. The next thing I knew, I was in a heap on the floor, trembling all over. She barked at Margaret: "See me in my study! And you," she added, pointing a finger at me, "go to your room, and don't come down until suppertime."

Later on, when Father got home, he told us he had been posted to Brussels. He looked anxiously at my mother for her reaction.

"What a marvelous opportunity!" she replied. "Just what Kim needs. Her spoken French is very limited, I find. A few years in a Belgian boarding school will do her good. What's more, Margaret left us this afternoon."

The ground beneath my feet gave way.

"Margaret's gone? Without saying goodbye?"

"Yes."

"Why?"

"Because that kind of woman doesn't get attached to anyone. They go where the money is. Quite simply, she must have been offered more elsewhere. Or she decided you gave her too much work. Who's to say?"

"But she loved me." I was in pieces. I curled up into a ball in my chair.

"It's time to grow up, Kim. You're too old for a nanny, anyway."

And so there I was, pushing open that heavy door to begin my second year at what I called "my cage of Crows." The Crows were enormous. Ugly. Mean. They were all dressed the same: long, dark habits and angular headdresses that hid their faces and gave them a sort of beak. They cawed instructions that I rarely understood, and I frequently got the feeling, when one of them got too close, that I'd be gobbled up. Those nuns were frightening, all right.

I continued toward the dormitory to drop off my suitcase before going to chapel for Benediction. In my pocket, I carried a lucky charm that I held onto tightly: a photo of my family all together for the holidays, everyone smiling at the camera. Then, up the stairs to the dormitory. This huge room with a high ceiling had been divided up with partitions into narrow sleeping quarters: one long corridor down the middle and little corridors at the sides linked these individual "rooms." I came to mine: minuscule – seven feet by seven feet – four flimsy wooden walls, no ceiling. A curtain where a door should be. The furnishings consisted of a bed, a wardrobe, and a table with a bowl and a jug of water on it. There was a crucifix on the wall, and that's where I hid the photo – the first place that came to mind. Behind Jesus. Safe and sound. Then I unpacked my suitcase and went down to the refectory for supper.

One evening, like any other, I moved the photo, wedging it between the crucifix and the wall. That way, I could look at it whenever I wanted, and it wouldn't fall down. On my knees, before Jesus, I prayed. After all, Jesus had a reputation for miracles; the Catechist Crow told us so in our Scripture lessons. Jesus sees everything and hears everything, so why shouldn't he see and hear me? I put my hands over my eyes so I could really concentrate, and murmured as quietly as I could.

"Jesus, can you make me work harder in class, so perhaps my mother will be proud of me and have me at home again?" I let a few seconds go by. Perhaps useful to explain. Did Jesus know what I meant? "I know it's tricky. The other day, you must have seen, I got hit with the ruler, but it's not easy, Jesus, writing with your right hand when you're left-handed, just because it's the devil's hand and we're not allowed to use it – we have to use our right hand, that's the rules – but the thing is, if they tie my hand, how am I supposed to write in the exercise book? Without making smudges, I mean? I have to do it ten times over sometimes, and then later, the Crow in charge of discipline put the dunce's cap on me in front of the whole school, in the middle of the refectory, so that everyone could see I'm a bad pupil and a bad Christian…Oh, Jesus, I promise I'll do everything I can to be kind, but please, help me!"

I jumped up on my bed and kissed the photo as hard as I could. I was totally caught up in all this when, suddenly, something yanked me by the collar of my nightgown. The Discipline Crow. With her free hand, she whipped the photo away, crumpled it up, and threw it and me to the floor.

"Do you realize you are committing blasphemy?" What a complicated word...then a sudden change of tack. "Dirty little spy! You were trying to peek through the wall, weren't you?" The slap she unleashed might have woken the whole dorm. Not knowing what was going on, half concussed and completely terrified, I felt the Crow dragging me out of the dorm and into a dark room I'd never been in before. I was put up against a wall and made to kneel on a thin metal ruler with my arms up in the air. "Not a word out of you," squawked the Crow, "or you'll get another slap."

Two warm tears trickled down my bruised cheeks – the only warmth anywhere on that freezing night. Left alone in the dark, my jaw set tight with rage and a sense of injustice, I hardly dared to breathe. My face was burning. I was shivering in the cold, my feet were freezing, and my knees ached. Luckily, that evening, I had put on my nightgown; otherwise, I would have received a double punishment. Sometimes, you see, to keep warm at night, I slept with my clothes on. It was very practical in the mornings, too.

Three long hours later, I was allowed back to my room. Standing in front of my bed, I felt the anger bubble up inside me. I turned the crucifix around to face the wall.

"If I'm punished, you can be, too!" I picked up the photo, tried to smooth it out, and, once in bed, held it tightly against me. I fell asleep, woozy with misery.

# CHAPTER 4

# Mousetrap

Luckily, I had my friend Lucie.

I found her during one of my nocturnal missions. At nighttime, instead of using the bucket provided, I often flouted the rules and slipped through the dark as far as the toilet. I would leave my room without a sound, and quietly walk the maze of corridors which, all of a sudden, turned into secret paths. The partitions became trees in a forest. The floorboards creaked – covered with twigs and moss, you see – but an ancient Sioux Indian spirit showed me where to step to avoid the traps. Friendly animals and hundred-year-old trees cast shadows onto the walls, and my own shadow danced with theirs. At night, while the Crows slept, my senses came alive. They couldn't stop me living anymore. In the half-light, at last, I existed!

One night, after an uneventful excursion across the dorm, I heard a small squeak. Where was it coming from? There? No, there! In a broom cupboard – I knew that because I had once taken a wrong turn on a night expedition and ended up inside. I crept up to the cupboard. Another squeak. I listened with all my might; a Crow could swoop down on me at any moment and carry me away to tear me to shreds. But, no. There was no one around. I opened the door of the cupboard as delicately as I could, and bent down to get a look at the little thing wriggling about, its tail caught in a trap. I tried to free it several times without getting my fingers pinched. It wasn't easy. In the end, I had to leave the tip of the mouse's tail behind – nothing else I could do – but how exhilarating to hold it, alive, in my hands.

Back in my room, trembling, I hid it in among the clothes in one of my drawers, with a nice little piece of biscuit. I whispered: "I'm going to call you Lucie."

From then on, every evening, I brought her food to eat. I talked to her and pampered her. I told her about my day, my hardships, my fleeting joys. She was my only friend. Now I know, of course, that Lucie means *light*.

A month went by. Then, one Sunday, I was called to the parlor. I could only think of one thing: the Crows must have found Lucie during one of their surprise inspections. My worst fear. Apparently, there were more and more mice in the building – hardly surprising with all the food I was sneaking in – so I had reason to worry.

In fact, I was told I had a visitor: my godfather, known as Uncle Oliver by the whole family. I loved him. He was the only person who ever came to visit me in my cage of Crows, even though my parents were in Brussels, a lot closer than London, where Oliver lived. Once a month, he made a special journey to see me.

There he was, coming through the parlor door toward me. He picked me up for a hug and boomed: "Right, off we go!"

I climbed into his beige Aston Martin and collapsed into the soft leather seat next to him. Bliss. Uncle Oliver was magical. He collected old cars, and in his country home, the corridors were lined with family portraits of men on horseback, about to go off to war or to hunt with their dogs. His real passion, though, was precious stones. Every time I saw him, he had pieces of carefully-folded paper in his pockets. Inside each one was a little colored rock. I couldn't wait to see what he had with him that day; I knew he'd show me, and tell me how and where he had come across it.

Outside the town, we came across a nice-looking spot. Right in the middle of the meadow was a tree with enough leaves left to offer us some shade. It was still terribly warm, I remember, although it was the end of September. Uncle Oliver stopped the engine at the edge of the field. He handed me a small wicker basket, then picked up a large bag in one hand and a tartan blanket in the other. We set off. At the foot of the tree, we laid out the provisions. What a moment that was. With great ceremony, he produced pâtés, ham, egg salad, roasted chicken wings, fruit salad, and chocolate cake. It was all so carefully planned. There were china plates and glasses, into which he poured wine for him ("taste that; go on, it's part of your education!") and apple juice for me.

The intense pleasure I felt at tucking into these dishes went up a notch when, a few minutes later, he gently tipped a superb red stone into the palm of my hand. The sun's rays leapt from it. Uncle Oliver had found it on one of his trips to Burma. He told me about the lengths to which he had gone to obtain it. I loved listening to his stories. They provided an escape route to a land far away, where there were no Crows.

The sun began to set, and it was nearly time to say goodbye.

◠

January, 1950. On the last day of the Christmas holidays – spent *en famille* in England, my father insisted on that – we went to visit a cousin who lived in Dorset. Elvira Maugham lived in a magnificent house by a stream. It was a lively family gathering. Everyone was there – except my brother, for some reason, I can't remember why. I soon got bored, so Sarah told me to go for a walk around the grounds. I didn't need much persuading; I loved to wander by myself, away from adult eyes.

I passed through the kitchen, breathing in the sugary smells. The cook, recognizing a *gourmande* when she saw one, gave me freshly-baked shortbread, still warm, and I stuffed them into the pockets of my cardigan.

It was cold outside, and I had forgotten my coat. Good – perhaps I would catch a cold, and not be made to go back to the cage of Crows. Or perhaps I'd be sent to the infirmary, the only place in the whole school where pupils were pampered.

In the courtyard, I came face to face with a vicious-looking dog. His barks were ear-splitting; thank goodness he was tied up. I decided to be daring and get a bit closer. He growled and bared his teeth. I got the message, all right: another step, and he would have me for lunch. We'd see about that. I knelt down to his level – not too close – and got out the shortbread and threw him a few little pieces. He gobbled them up. Then I sat down cross-legged, and started to talk to him. Not much at first. Then, little by little, I started to tell him about my life. To my astonishment, after what seem liked half an hour, his barks changed to friendly yaps. He wanted to come closer to me, but his chain wouldn't let him. So I took him off the chain. He licked my hand, and the two of us went off to explore. As I walked, he trotted alongside. The grounds were lovely. A long line of oaks led up to the house; there was a vegetable garden here, an orchard there. Because it was midwinter, nature was fast asleep, but it wasn't hard to imagine how splendid it would look in spring. I kept on talking to the dog as if he were my best friend in the world. Perhaps he was, too.

We came upon an aviary full of magnificent, colorful birds who seemed to be fighting each other. I glanced around: no sign of any food, no water, either. Perhaps that was why they seemed intent on tearing each other to pieces. A few minutes later, we went past a shed with live hens piled on top of one another. Same story. Further on, we found sheep huddled together in a fold: the smell was foul.

"It's sad to have such a beautiful property and lock everyone up, isn't it?" I remarked to my companion. He shook his tail. Nothing else for it; I decided to free all the animals. "Operation Freedom!" I flew here and there, opening doors, windows, and gates, with the dog yapping cheerfully and bounding alongside me. "Come on, everybody out!"

Mission accomplished. I felt really proud. I took the path leading back to the house, singing all the way, with the dog leaping around and panting at my heels. It was dark by four o'clock, and from some distance away, I could make out my mother, standing on the front steps, illuminated by the porch light. Her voice rang out clearly. It would be fun to tell her all about my walk.

Suddenly, I heard the cousin's husband yelling: "Who unchained that bastard dog?"

I stepped forward proudly. "It was me."

"You're out of your mind. He's dangerous, he bites!" Furious now, he grabbed a stick and marched toward the dog, who started to growl. The man raised the stick and shouted: "Get back, you little bastard, or you'll get it!" I rushed to shield the dog, then took him by the collar and attached him to his post. He lowered his tail compliantly.

I kept my head down, and murmured through my teeth: "Your place smells; it's dirty. When you've got animals, you should look after them, and love them." Quieter still, I added, "It's like having children." Then I stormed off toward the car, opened the door, and slammed it behind me. A big knot stuck in my throat. Though I wanted to cry, I found I couldn't.

There was a deathly silence on the way home. As I sat bolt upright in the back seat, I thought of a conversation I had heard some months previously. My grandmother was talking to a friend of hers. I listened from the next room, following as best I could. I had a feeling they were talking about me.

"The little one is a bastard child, you know."

"Oh, I see…well, that explains why your son has packed her off to a boarding school, poor thing. How sad. A millstone around his neck, I imagine." I didn't understand any of that. Why was I a millstone?

It was pitch black outside by now, and the motion of the car was making me sleepy, but a nagging thought was kept me wide awake.

I decided to break my silence. In a small voice I asked: "*Maman*, what's a bastard?"

"A very naughty animal." Her voice was taut with anger. I was none the wiser. Did that mean I was naughty?

On the telephone later that evening, the cousin complained bitterly to my parents about the sheep wandering free, the aviary emptied of its exotic birds, hens pecking around all over the place, and peacocks perched in the trees. My father immediately declared that the pocket money I had been saving to buy a dog would be confiscated. What he said next hurt even more: "Because of you, those birds will die. They're not used to fending for themselves."

I went to sleep telling myself that it must be true, that I really was a bastard child.

It was almost a relief to return to my cage of Crows the next day. After the usual long and boring journey, I arrived at Namur. With only one thing on my mind, I headed straight for that drawer in my room. Where was Lucie? There was the packet of biscuits, still intact. My stomach tightened; I should have taken her with me.

Gradually, the panic subsided, and I thought more rationally. If she wasn't there, I would have to look for her. That meant waiting until everyone was in bed, asleep. I slipped on my nightdress, brushed my teeth, and hung on for the all-clear: the sound of snoring coming from the Crow on duty. I didn't have long to wait.

I drew back the curtain and headed out into the corridor. A full moon lit the way. When I reached the broom cupboard, I opened the door and knelt down. In the half-light I saw a mouse, its body caught in the trap. Lucie? I brought it over to the window to get a better look. The end of her tail was missing.

If I could warm her up, perhaps she'd start to move. I took her out of the trap and blew hot breath on her, then held her, whispering, "I won't leave you ever again. I'll take you with me wherever I go. You deserve a friend, a real friend."

Cupping Lucie carefully in my hands, I brought her back to bed with me, just as I had done four months earlier. She was stiff and cold. Was that how death was? Tears streamed down my cheeks, and I rubbed my eyes with the back of my sleeve. "I'll give you a burial, a proper burial," I promised.

It took me five days to make her little coffin. I drew flowers on it, and hearts, birds, butterflies, and kites. I slipped a picture of me inside, too, cut out from the class photograph, so she wouldn't feel lonely. I didn't know where I was going to bury her, but there would have to be a special Mass. Next Sunday, then.

That Saturday, I raised my hand when they asked for volunteers to get the chapel ready for Mass. The following day, before leaving my room, I delicately placed Lucie in the little coffin and slipped it into my pocket. I had been thinking of the funeral rites given to people, which I had witnessed at my great-aunt Celia's funeral: the coffin in front of the altar, people coming up to pray. There may have been little chance of all that for Lucie, but I had an idea.

Arranging the flowers at the altar for Mass, I took my time, my face a picture of concentration. When no one was watching, I gently placed the little coffin on the edge of the altar's marble base, right underneath the bottom of the altar cloth. No would notice, but it meant Lucie would get her funeral service at the altar. The first stage of the mission was a success, and my heart swelled with pride. The tricky bit would be getting the coffin back afterwards; but one thing at a time, I thought.

I took my place on the chapel pews with everyone else. When it was time to take communion, I found myself at the front of the line, walking right behind Discipline Crow. Her long black veil trailed on the floor ahead of me. All of a sudden, the urge to step on it came over me. Just to see what would happen. I couldn't resist; I had to do it. With each step, my toe got closer to the Crow's tail. She was parading through chapel, holding her head high and smiling, when my shoe came down on the veil.

Chaos.

The Crow's unkempt hair was revealed for all to see, and she twisted this way and that, completely panic-stricken. Her black wings flapped wildly as she tried to get the veil back on her head, but it was still stuck under my shoe. The choir stopped singing. Pupils waited, petrified, anxious to see how the headmistress would react. Some began to lose their composure: there were sniggers, and then, row by row, gales of laughter. Several nuns rushed to help the

Crow recover her plumage. Pandemonium broke out, and the bird of ill omen raced out of chapel, escorted by her colleagues. My only concern was how on earth I was going to recover Lucie.

Two days later, inevitably, I was summoned to the headmistress's study. What would she decide? No less than three months' detention, I guessed. More than that didn't even bear thinking about. To my great surprise, when I entered the room, my parents were sitting at her desk, utterly motionless. They had come all the way from Brussels. I rushed over to my mother, but she put her arms up to resist my embrace. As for my father, he didn't even look at me.

I stood up straight, my head held high, and listened to the headmistress's sermon. Seated beside her, the Discipline Crow scarcely bothered to hide her delight. The sentence was pronounced. I would not be allowed out of school before Easter: no more walks, no more visits, no weekend activities. And I would have to make a public apology. I just couldn't! And more besides: I would have to stand on a table during supper with a sign around my neck saying *I have behaved badly*. I would also have to pick up litter on the playground and get chapel ready for Mass. Ah, now *that* was a bit of luck: I'd be able to get Lucie back. That sounds very flippant, I know. The truth was, I was extremely upset. I have never forgotten that scene, or the Discipline Crow smiling broadly as the punishments were read out.

The headmistress told me to kneel down and apologize. My trembling, six-year-old self replied, "No." She looked me straight in the eye. I held her stare.

"Bow your head, you impudent child. Get down on your knees, and do not ever forget that you are the servant of the Lord."

I refused point-blank.

My parents stood up and left without saying a word, without so much as a glance in my direction.

Every cloud has a silver lining, they say. From then on, the older girls took me under their wing. They helped me bury Lucie in the corner of the vegetable garden by the rosebush. They made sure I was never left by myself during my detentions, and that my snack box was never empty. After all, the notoriously pitiless Discipline Crow was loathed by everyone, and I was the girl who had taught her a lesson. The incident in chapel had given everyone such a thrill that it soon became a school legend.

∾

"I think Kenya got a bit of your feisty character, Marsie," Vittorio says, grinning.

Kenya throws a raisin at him, and we all laugh. I notice a little admiration in my grandchildren's eyes as they look at me, and even as tired as I am nowadays, I can't help but feel a little younger remembering the fiery little girl I sometimes was back then.

# CHAPTER 5

# Pheasant-Shaped Tiepin

"Look here, that mouse of yours didn't die because of you," Uncle Oliver said during one of my trips to England. "She just preferred the cheese in the trap to your biscuits, that's all."

That hadn't occurred to me before. "Do you think?"

"And a mouse's life is very short, I should say. Two or three years or something."

Life with Uncle Oliver always seemed lighter somehow. We were sitting on our tartan rug overlooking some magnificent countryside, sheltered by one of those kindly oak trees you find in Belgium and England, eating cucumber sandwiches. It was like taking tea at the Ritz. It did me a world of good to eat delicious food and speak English again, particularly since this was the first time I'd been allowed out of school for three months. "Thanks to your mouse, you made a friend. You gave her your time, your love, all that sort of thing."

"What about the dog?"

It was a sort of game, this to-and-fro of questions and answers. It had always been that way. He would ask what I was doing, and I kept nothing from him – well, virtually nothing. I knew he would never try to twist my words. Quite the opposite; he received them in a jumble, and seemed to put them in the right order. We only saw each other once a month, but each time, thanks to his way of putting things, I felt calmer.

"You were a bit foolhardy there; he could have bitten your leg off. But you opened your heart and treated him like the next man…the next dog. And, though I happen to know you were looking forward to eating that shortbread, you gave it to him instead. Then you took the time to have a little chat."

"And he didn't bite me!"

"You know, lurking somewhere behind an aggressive manner, you'll often find a good egg. It's the circumstances life has thrown at him that have made him naughty. Not a bad thing to take your time to get to know someone before making them your friend or deciding to ignore them."

"And do you think the birds did die?"

"Some of them will have learned to fend for themselves, I dare say. Others are bound to have returned to their cage out of sheer habit. Look here: the point is, it wasn't up to you whether they were free or not. They didn't belong to you! Don't make other people's decisions for them."

That was typical of Uncle Oliver. He always wanted to teach me things. I didn't tell him I was worried about that word: *bastard*. Perhaps it was too shadowy; perhaps there were too many thoughts that I didn't know how to put into words.

We finished eating in contented silence. Then Uncle Oliver took off his tiepin. I had always admired it, because it was decorated with a brightly-colored pheasant. He bent down and attached it to my pullover. "Here you are. A medal."

"What for?"

"Heroism for lost causes."

Before I went to sleep that night, he offered to tell me the Chinese legend of the seamstress and the cowherd.

"I can only tell you this tale when the sky is clear, and we can make out all the stars in the sky. And, one day, you'll be able to pass on this marvelous legend – but only when starless nights are far away and forgotten about. On clear nights, you'll be able to see two stars that shine much brighter than the rest. Come and have a look out of the window; we can sit on the sofa."

Night was falling, and there wasn't a cloud in the sky.

And so, once again, I was transported into Uncle Oliver's world of stories: pernicious women who laid traps for simple, honest men; temples stuffed with treasure; a land of perilous legends and magical encounters.

This one was about a cowherd and a beautiful young seamstress who weaves pretty clothes. They are in love, but cruelly separated. Eventually, they are granted permission to see each other for just one day every year. The rest of the story would have to wait: I had fallen asleep before he could get properly started, my head slumped on his shoulder.

And then it was back to my prison for four long, dreary weeks. Normal life was quite impossible. There was always a Crow on hand to call me out on my shortcomings. And which Crow gave me the hardest time? The one I disrobed that memorable day. She kept her eye on me, you could say. She had me in her sights. My punishment did not go far enough, she maintained, and whenever she could, she reprimanded me with a slap. Always with an open hand, best not to leave a trace. "It's for your own good," she claimed.

One Saturday in April, 1952, the day before a visit from Uncle Oliver, the Discipline Crow's hand strayed. Miraculously, she actually left a bruise.

"Uncle Oliver, am I really naughty?" I asked him.

"Whatever gave you that idea, sweetheart? You're a wonderful little girl."

I looked at the ground. "That's not true. I get everything wrong. I'm bad even if I try really hard to be good!"

Uncle Oliver came right up close, and lifted my chin with his big hands. "Come on, my dear, don't get downhearted. In two years, you'll go to a different boarding school where you'll have more freedom. In the meantime, I know it's hard, but you're learning lots here." Suddenly, he frowned and lifted my chin so he could get a better look. "What's that bruise?"

I told myself I shouldn't say a word, but I couldn't help it. I told him everything: about the Discipline Crow, the punishments, the unfair treatment, the beatings, the humiliation. The words poured out. He didn't interrupt.

When we got back to school, he asked to see the headmistress. I waited outside her study on the bench as I'd been told. After ten minutes or so, the Discipline Crow approached, hurried and puffed-up as ever. She gave me a look full of disdain. The door closed behind her. I heard Uncle Oliver's voice, raised in indignation, and the women's whispers. No, not whispers; hushing. The door opened once more, and out walked the Discipline Crow, not in the least bit hurried now. She stole a glance at me out of the corner of her eye before setting off for the refectory, keeping close to the walls as she walked.

One hour later, I was outside with my suitcases.

"Is it forever?"

"Forever."

"Where are we going now?"

"I'm taking you to Brussels. To your parents."

I had trouble containing my excitement. Not only had I left my cage, but on top of that, my long-held dream was coming true: I was going to live with my parents. 1953 was off to a fine start.

# CHAPTER 6

# Champagne Cork

How are dreams fashioned? What are they made from? From what we hear or read, from what we see or want; a sentence stays with us, a picture in a children's book haunts us by night. For as long as I could remember, I had dreamed of receiving a kiss from a loving mother as she tucked me into bed. A mother who would tickle me until I agreed to take a bath; who would wait for me at the school gates with warm donuts for tea; who would listen as I talked about my day; who would understand.

∾

Uncle Oliver entered the drawing room, preceded by a maid dressed in black with a white pinafore. I hadn't ever seen her; she must have been new.

He and I both sat on the ornate eighteenth-century couch upholstered in white. We were like two strangers, hardly daring to say a word. The door flew open and my mother appeared. She was furious. Uncle Oliver got up to greet her, intending to kiss her hand, as he always did. She didn't let him. Nor did she sit down.

"What is she doing here?" Sarah demanded.

"I'll explain."

They left quickly by the far door. I stayed put on the couch, worried stiff. I could hear them in the distance, speaking French. I couldn't make out the words, but the tone of their voices kept rising. Then a door slammed. And a second one. A minute later, my mother returned to the drawing room and marched over to where I was sitting.

"You're nothing but a filthy, spoiled little *gourde!*" she raged. "Your uncle tells me you were given a slap."

"Yes."

"Well, I imagine you deserved it. You should have thanked God for being accepted in such a prestigious boarding school, and left it at that. You have been good for nothing, not there, not ever in the course of your short life, and now you want to come back to my home? And all because someone has given you a little slap?"

Sarah lapsed into silence on the other end of the couch, looking straight ahead, her eyes in a daze.

Slowly, she turned to face me. "You want to stay here? Well, so be it. In any case, I have no choice. But do not believe for one moment that you are going to be lazing about."

I didn't reply. What was there to say?

Before leaving the room, she turned around and barked, "Go up to your room, and don't come out 'til suppertime. Maria will call you."

Uncle Oliver had left without saying goodbye.

Not long after this episode, my parents enrolled me at the local school. I made some friends there, but my spirit and my energy were taken up with the torment of my home life. I existed in an emotional desert surrounded by domestic staff. My brother was off at Eton, and doing incredibly well there. I missed him enormously.

Every evening, my parents went out, as my father's position demanded. My mother was always very beautiful, thin, and flamboyant; and, as such, the object of many admiring glances. Her elegant outfits and jewels, the way she carried herself, and her strange, striking eyes made her attractive to men and women alike. She knew how to turn on the charm in the company of men. Perhaps each of them imagined, if only during the conversation, that one day she might choose him. If so, they did not know my mother. Seduction was a pastime of hers like any other. With women, it was a different story as soon as they met: looking into those eyes was like locking horns with the devil. I exaggerate, perhaps? Barely. Several women have since told me of the appalling impression my mother left on them. More than one has since admitted to feeling exposed, despised even, by this peerless woman who made their blood run cold. Some never forgave her. I know what she was capable of, and I can't say I blame them.

The general atmosphere at home could not exactly be described as joyful. At mealtimes, conversations would quickly degenerate if an effort wasn't made. Mother would get cross at the drop of a hat, leave the room, and lock herself away upstairs. I remember being seated at a long table that seemed immense to me – just colossal. At the other end, facing me, but a long way away, sat my father, who was totally engrossed in his thoughts, doubtless work-related. He responded to my efforts at conversation with monosyllabic grunts. There we were, waiting for Maria to serve the second course. I wanted to shake him so he would listen to me, but didn't dare, of course.

Even Jesus had abandoned me. I no longer felt anything when I spoke to him – I didn't even say his name anymore. I put that down to "growing up."

Sometimes, toward the end of the day, my mother would put on a white glove and mercilessly run her finger over various items, bend down to inspect the baseboards, glide a hand over the tables and armchairs with the express purpose of checking whether the maid's work had been carried out satisfactorily. Upon seeing the dust that never failed to stain that immaculate glove, she would grimace and summon the poor girl, and none of us would hear the end of it.

From time to time, she would pay a trip to my bedroom while I was at school. When I returned, I would find the clothes all over the floor, drawers emptied out, the whole place upside down. On what grounds? "It's untidy!" The first time, I was shocked, then I got used to it – if it's possible to get used to such things.

She would disappear for days at a time without warning, and we would gather from a phone call that she was visiting friends in London.

As for Father, he seemed to take refuge in classical music. Delightful notes from various symphonies and operas wafted from his study. I let them carry me far away.

Happily, the loneliness of the school holidays was tempered by Maria, our cook. She looked after me and took me for walks or on trips to the finest patisseries to eat cakes. She brought back a distant memory of my nanny Margaret Black, whom I still missed.

Then there were the receptions at the embassy, with mother in the principal role, Maria as her long-suffering foil, Max the chauffeur as doormat, and, finally, Father as prince consort – despite the fact that *he* was the ambassador, not his wife.

I loved these occasions, because it was the only time my mother would deign to look at me. I got to wear a beautiful dress and a new pair of shoes, have my hair brushed at least ten times by the maid, my ears inspected, my nails filed. It made my heart soar when my mother looked at me with something approaching satisfaction.

Every detail of the evening was finely tuned – no wrong note would be tolerated – and, there too, I knew how to make myself useful and find favor with her.

When the guests arrived, I would tuck myself into a corner by the window to admire their finery. I liked to listen in on their conversations, and imagine all I could about each person's life based upon what I had overheard. It was a helpful little exercise, similar to making up a story. Uncle Oliver sometimes asked me what I wanted to be when I grew up. I usually answered: "a storyteller." Tucked up in bed, I would amuse myself by trying to recall the tiniest details from the party. Smiles, faces, conversations…they could all set my dreams alight.

However, austere habits soon took hold again, and the evening would fade to a hazy memory, just another fantasy little girls are wont to concoct as they lie in bed at night.

After two years of living at home, the only real joy in my life remained Uncle Oliver. He came to fetch me from Brussels in August. Since their argument, he and my mother had not set eyes on each other. *Maman* made sure she was elsewhere when he arrived.

The first year, we drove down toward Bordeaux. He wasn't taking me on holiday – oh, no. This was a "voyage of discovery." I climbed into his gleaming automobile and listened to the revving of the engine. It sounded as eager to get away as I was. Uncle Oliver had stowed my suitcase in the trunk. Once he was happily driving, he began asking me questions. The weather was sublime, and I was so happy to be talking that I didn't pause for breath. It didn't matter; it was *our* time. Judging from how often he turned to snatch a look at me, and how he smiled at what I had to say, I felt pretty sure his enjoyment was equal to mine.

Every day, we stopped at a different hotel, which Uncle Oliver chose according to two strict criteria: luxury and gastronomy. For the duration of the trip, I became Taster-in-Chief, delighted to savor the increasingly sophisticated dishes that were put before me. Uncle Oliver said he was very proud of my "gustative ability"; I simply gave free rein to an instinctive talent I had for eating! The pleasure of spending time with him helped, too.

The following year, he decided to raise the bar, and we went crisscrossing through the Champagne region, visiting the famous wineries. After that, I could babble on about champagne for hours. Did you know that its ancestor was called *tranquille*, and was a *vin clair* popular with French monarchs as far back as Clovis, King of the Franks? No, didn't think you did.

"You know what champagne's for, don't you?" asked Uncle Oliver the first time he took me around a wine cellar in the region.

"I've seen some at home – people use it for cocktails?" A good answer, I thought.

"And on your birthday?" Uncle Oliver suggested.

"On my birthday?"

"Champagne is for celebrating, for parties…don't they let you have a little taste?"

"Not on my birthday, no…"

"Come on, we're going to open a bottle," he announced. "And you can keep the cork as a souvenir of happy days!"

The smell from the cellars was enough to make me tipsy. I loved exploring these dark, mysterious places. Once, when we were wandering through a particularly gloomy *cave*, Uncle Oliver took my small hand in his, and a thousand blurry memories came back to me. Had he always been there, close to me? I looked up at him, and was astonished to see a tear trickling down his cheek. "Are you sad?"

"No, not a bit. Very happy to be with you!"

Much later, I learned that his wife, Lisa, and twelve-year-old daughter, Beatrice, had died in a car accident in the Alps that summer; but at the time, Uncle Oliver never said a word.

At the end of the summer holidays in '54, my father announced that he had been posted to London to work in the Foreign Office. Mother was delighted, and quickly set about finding me a new boarding school.

# CHAPTER 7

# Little Box Decorated with Shells

Mid-September, 1954.

To this day, I remember my first impressions upon seeing the school's gray stone buildings with elaborate stained-glass windows, Victorian gothic architecture at its finest. I recall the impeccably mown lawns, the squeals of delight as classmates reunited after the holidays, the friendly atmosphere around me. Compared to my last school, whose sad walls still haunted me, it was paradise. My most distinct memory, the one that comes right back to me when I think of my first day at Cheltenham Ladies' College, is meeting Alicia for the first time.

I walked down from the top of Parabola Road, where Max the chauffeur had dropped me off, toward St. Austin's, one of the oldest houses at the College. The place felt right. From the path leading to the front door, I could see roses climbing up the walls. "That bodes well; I do like roses," I said out loud.

I left my two suitcases by the front steps and walked across a hallway, the floorboards creaking beneath my feet. A lovely, waxy smell hung in the air. Girls were dashing around on all sides. I had a quick look in the sitting room, where a group of pupils were chattering excitedly, then into what must have been the music room: a parlor grand piano had pride of place, and there were several pieces of sheet music scattered on its lid. I felt at home already. This would be quite a change from the cage of Crows.

Fifty-four girls of all ages who are due to spend the year together are likely to make quite a noise, but the hubbub suddenly died down. Our housemistress, Miss Shipman, called out our last names, and the matrons allocated rooms. The older girls showed us where to find them. I was led up some stairs and onto a landing.

Just then, a girl with the blondest hair I had ever seen popped up out of nowhere, dragging a suitcase behind her. In a murmur I could only just make out, she asked me if I knew where her room was. Her striking blue eyes were riveting. She showed me a piece of paper, upon which was written "Mozart."

"Imagine that, we're sharing," I said. "Follow me."

All the bedrooms were named after famous composers. Music was clearly taken very seriously at Cheltenham. In the middle of the main corridor was a little door that led to our room.

"We lucked out," I said, "being in a room for two. We could have wound up in a four-bed or a six-bed." I had a look around, which didn't take long. There was a bunk bed, two bedside tables, and two little desks.

My new roommate quietly asked if she could sleep up top, saying she would feel safer.

I held out my hand. "Hello. I'm Kim Rochester."

"Alicia Cunningham," she murmured.

When I finished putting all my things away, I noticed that my new friend was still only halfway through unpacking. What a funny character. I offered to give her a hand. After all our belongings were stowed away, we sprawled on the bottom bunk and chatted for a while before Alicia climbed the ladder. I read aloud from the little leaflet that had been placed on the pillow:

*Cheltenham Ladies' College was one of the first girls' schools to be founded in the 1860s, at a time when the notion of educating young women from prosperous families was considered to be nothing short of fantasy. Not long after its inauguration, Dorothea Beale, a passionate mathematician, became headmistress. Her teaching and strong sense of moral duty would leave an indelible mark on the school. She oversaw the construction of the College, the design of which was influenced by medieval architecture. Classes are given there to this day. Later, when Cheltenham began to welcome boarders, Houses needed to be found in the vicinity of the College.*

"That explains why Saint Austen is a walk away from the main building," I said, putting down the leaflet. Then I popped my head over the bed rail. "Shall we turn out the light? A good night's sleep will do us good before our first day of lessons."

Alicia hesitated. "Do you mind leaving it on? I don't like sleeping in the dark."

"Do you want me to lie down next to you until you fall asleep? Oh, and I've got a little flashlight I can give you."

"You'd do that for me?"

I leapt up the ladder and dived onto her bed. We both burst out laughing, and then she took my hand in hers and whispered, "Thank you."

Once Alicia had fallen asleep, I got back into my own bed and listened to the sounds outside. It had been a long, long time since I had known peace and quiet like this. As I ran through my first day in my mind, I thought more about Alicia, whom I had observed carefully during the few hours we had spent together. Her words, her movements, her gestures, her behavior, everything seemed self-contained, silent. She made me want to look after her. I drifted off to sleep, soothed by the sound of Alicia's breathing in the bed above me.

The next morning at breakfast, I noticed that she didn't eat much at all. I frowned over my cereal bowl. "You're not going to face the day on three oats, are you?"

She looked sheepish.

"Come with me," I said. "I'll show you how to make delicious scrambled eggs." In the kitchen, I opened the fridge door, took out some eggs, and threw one at Alicia, who promptly dropped it. Cue hysterical giggling. We had to clean up the mess quickly, before a prefect turned up.

I fixed us toast and eggs for breakfast. Alicia astonished me by wolfing down the whole plate.

"I'll make you a proper breakfast every morning," I promised. "You'll be the right shape with a few extra pounds!"

When we'd finished eating, we put on our woolen coats, picked up our canvas satchels, and walked down Parabola Road, two by two. As we passed through the College's grand entrance, I felt rather proud to have been accepted here. And I knew, for once, that I had my mother to thank for it.

~

Just before nine the next morning, accompanied by our teachers, we made our way in silence to Princess Hall, the heart of the establishment. It was an immense space: a three-tiered auditorium with carved wooden balconies. On the stage stood an organ, and in the center, a table decorated with a crucifix. This was to be our first encounter with Miss Bonham, the headmistress. I felt her positive energy and strength of character straight away. Her smile was charged with charm and purpose. The sight of her upright, imposing figure, alongside our teachers in their black gowns, left us in no doubt as to who was in charge.

The organ played as we took our places, each holding a small prayer book. Standing at the lectern to the right of the stage, the Senior Prefect read out a passage from the Scriptures that encouraged us to reflect on the day ahead. She finished with the School Prayer. We said it out loud all together, and it gave me goosebumps. "Lord, look after our College, remove all that might destroy order and camaraderie…" After that, we sang some hymns. Hearing our voices in unison thrilled me.

A pleasant routine set in. Between math, physics, French, English, swimming, tennis, fencing, and so on, we were kept delightfully busy; but I soon realized that Alicia tended to opt out of games. I usually knew where to find her: reading in the library, or, more often still, sitting at the piano practicing her scales. So as not to disturb her, I would walk on tiptoe and lean against the wall behind her, listening to the crystal-clear notes tumbling from her hands.

Sometimes, I would sit alongside her, and she would give me my first music lessons. Gradually, I picked up the basics, and even began to take real pleasure from playing.

A few months into our first term, after an English lesson, I headed for the library, confident I would find Alicia there. I had resolved to convince her to come to a swimming lesson with me; so far, she had appeared allergic to the very idea of sports.

I saw her seated at a desk, surrounded by open books, scribbling notes into an exercise book. She was concentrating so hard that she didn't even hear me approach. When I touched her back, she leapt out of her chair. Shaking all over, she asked me never to make her jump like that again.

Her reaction surprised me, but I didn't let on. Instead, I said, "Sorry," and gave her a hug to calm her down. She collapsed back into her chair, and I joined her, reverting to plan A.

"Are you allergic to sports?" I asked.

"No, not really…."

"Well, I've decided that from today onward, you're coming swimming with me. It'll do you a world of good."

She seemed on the verge of tears; and, almost like a guilty child, admitted, "I can't swim."

"Doesn't matter, I'll teach you."

Her face lit up. "And why don't you come to art class with me?" she suggested.

"Tell you what; we'll make a deal. I'll teach you to like water, and you can teach me to like paintbrushes."

We sealed our pact with a wink.

The swimming pool at College was an important place at the center of the girls' education. Swimming soon became my thing at Cheltenham: I had finally found a way of pushing myself as far as I could go. Regular competitions against other schools were held, and I always took part. I was particularly fond of the butterfly; I could totally empty my mind doing that stroke.

The first time I took Alicia over to the main pool, her body tightened and her eyes widened in complete panic. I took her gently by the hand, and got her paddling in the shallow end. Then I asked her to hop, then to blow bubbles on the surface of the water. For the final quarter of an hour, I put a rubber ring around her middle, and we paddled from one side of the pool to the other, chatting and giggling as we went – though I could tell she was still on edge.

After a few months, nothing gave me more pleasure than seeing Alicia dive off the small board and frolic around in the pool. I doubted she would ever be a strong swimmer, but at least she was starting to relax in the water. After a swim, she was less prone to those bouts of chronic fatigue, which had been known to leave her paralyzed for hours.

Sometimes, she would announce that she didn't want to get up in the mornings because she had a migraine. I would drag her toward the shower, make her get dressed, and virtually feed her breakfast like a baby. Some nights, she would ask me to lie down beside her, and tell her a story; on others, I heard her crying in her sleep. I just couldn't get to the bottom of this mysterious behavior. But she was gradually starting to find some peace – at least, that was the impression I got.

To keep my part of the deal, I took up art. Or rather, I took full advantage of Elizabeth Lilly, a remarkable woman who taught us calligraphy. I had thought that my handwriting was a total lost cause; but I soon took to writing upstrokes and downstrokes with nibs of all widths and sizes, in ink ranging from gray to sepia to deepest black. This art form had been inspired by manuscripts created by monks, years and years ago, Miss Lilly told us, and often appeared alongside illuminations. Every so often, for inspiration, we were allowed to look at an eighteenth-century French manuscript that was kept in the library under lock and key.

"Did you know that calligraphy has been practiced in China for thousands of years?" Miss Lilly asked me one day, brandishing a strange scroll of paper in her hand.

"No, I didn't." I loved reading the book of Chinese stories and legends that Uncle Oliver had given me a few years previously, and had noticed that calligraphy featured in it, but I had never associated it with the monkish art we had been taught.

"It's quite simple. Because Chinese handwriting is formed of ideograms, writing it is almost like painting a picture."

"It's beautiful, all right, but it looks so complicated," I replied, gazing at the scroll as she unrolled it. It was decorated with bamboo shoots and various Chinese symbols.

"You're not wrong. There are over forty thousand characters that can be used to form words."

"Gosh, and it's hard enough for a left-hander to learn our measly twenty-six!"

Miss Lilly grinned.

"I know some Chinese legends," I told her, "especially the story of the Last Empress."

Miss Lilly began to tell me how the Dowager Empress Cixi loved to spend time in her huge summer palace. "That's the one that was looted by the English and the French!" I piped up.

"How do you know that?"

"Oh, my uncle is always going to China, and he tells me all about it."

We were talking in the art room, and Alicia, who had gone off to fetch some supplies from the bursary, now joined us. Miss Lilly seemed impressed by my interest in China, and Alicia was astonished, though she didn't let on until later that evening.

"How do you do know about China?" she asked when we were back in our room. "Have you been there?"

"No, but I'll go one day."

"Tell me about it."

"Why? Are you interested?"

"One day, I'll go there, too. With you."

"All right, then!"

And that's how our joint passion for the Middle Kingdom was born – a passion we would foster in the years to come, thanks to all the amazing books Miss Lilly dug out.

∾

Back in Cheltenham after a weekend spent with our respective families, I could tell that Alicia was a bundle of nerves. She couldn't get to sleep; she was so anxious that I went to lie down beside her. Once I had told her a story, she fell asleep hugging Felix, her soft toy rabbit – as if she didn't ever want to grow up.

Alicia was a sister to me. I wanted to help her so much.

The next day, she turned to me and said glumly, "Do you love me?"

"Yes, and I'll always be your friend, but I don't know what to do when you're upset like this," I admitted. She shut herself away in resolute silence. How would I get her to break it?

Day after day, year after year, Alicia and I became as inseparable as the heroes of the Chinese legends. We became blood sisters, by pricking our index fingers and squishing them together. We declared in unison that from that day forth, we would be inseparable for life.

The most fun of all came during the midterm holidays. Oliver had agreed that Alicia could come with me to visit him every midterm. The days went too quickly. When we weren't on our bikes, we were out in little sailing boats, rain or shine, or in the kitchen baking a cake, or looking for shells on the beach. We fashioned different objects out of them, which we sold to tourists to fill our piggy banks, saving up for our trip to China. I did keep one little wooden box decorated with shells from those days, and today, it's attached to my quilt.

Not once did Alicia ask me if I loved her, and not once did she wake up in the middle of the night. And sometimes, we held hands in bed, just like two sisters who loved each other very much.

～

Moved, Kenya got up to fetch her favorite teddy, a brown bear who never left her side as a child. One day, she had announced that she was too big for her bear. But I could see in her eyes that this wasn't true—and from her rueful expression, that she knew it, too. The bear now lives at my house, so the two can be reunited from time to time. Seeing her, long-limbed and beginning to grow into a beautiful young woman, I feel a rush of protectiveness. I hope that she has at least one friend as kind and sweet and important as Alicia was to me. And I can't help but smile as I look at my quilt, full of objects that have sentimental importance to me, and my granddaughter, who is lovingly clutching a precious part of her own history.

# CHAPTER 8

# 45-inch Record Sleeve

June, 1958.

Alicia and I – fifteen by now – attended the end-of-year ceremony that took place in a packed Princess Hall. My parents were noticeable absentees, as usual. Once the list of prizewinners had been announced, I naturally went straight over to congratulate Alicia, who had snatched up most of them. Her brother and mother were with her, but neither seemed to have anything to say. To see Alicia standing beside Edward, who had never said more than two words to me, and her mother, Kate, who looked pitifully buttoned-up, I understood where my friend's acute timidity came from.

I first met Alicia's mother and father at one of my parents' cocktail parties. Her father, an eminent London surgeon, would doubtless have qualified as a guest of honor in his own right, but in fact, I was responsible for their invitation. Towards the end of one of our summer holidays, I had been really impatient to see Alicia again.

"Well, we'll see what we can do," Sarah muttered.

As it happened, she had been quite impressed by my buddy's parents (for once). "Henrik Cunningham is a decent fellow – charming, too," she said afterwards. "And he has a very good reputation. They say he's the finest surgeon in London."

In Princess Hall that day, Alicia's father was absent. The rest of the Cunningham family took me out for lunch in town. The sun was shining through a thin veil of passing clouds, and it warmed us as we walked the few hundred yards from the College to Queen's Hotel. When we got there, we sat down at a table and ate lunch in a slightly strained atmosphere.

Alicia and I were wearing our uniforms: green skirt, white shirt, and tie. We kept catching each other's eye, suppressing the desire to break out in a fit of giggles in such a serious place. I stole a few furtive glances at Alicia's mother. Her shoulders were rounded, as if she had spent a lifetime digging a hole to hide in. She spoke so quietly you could barely hear her. Her blue eyes struggled to make contact with whomever she was talking to. I saw a certain likeness with Alicia – her slenderness, her pale coloring and porcelain-like fragility – but my friend was more beautiful and smiled more, though I noticed she had become more withdrawn in the presence of her family.

I was astonished when Kate suddenly adopted a cheery tone to ask me something over dessert. It was a bit forced: a pupil who has agreed to recite something, but expects to get called out by the teacher for the slightest mistake.

"We would be delighted if you would spend a week of the holidays with us at our house in the south of France." She stopped to snatch a breath, and then sort of sighed the rest: "Alicia talks about you a lot…thank you for being her friend."

I was perplexed at that last remark. As if it were somehow out of the ordinary to be friends with Alicia. Why was Kate so uptight? Although the invitation had been given in a slightly odd fashion, I accepted it, of course. When it came down to it, I was really happy to spend the holidays at my friend's house.

After the annual gastronomic expedition with Uncle Oliver, he dropped me off at Alicia's parents' home near Vaison-la-Romaine in southeastern France. His Aston Martin zoomed up the drive and into the impeccable gravel courtyard. On either side, 15th-century stone cottages bordered the main body of the house, which was flanked by two wings, one of which had once been a chapel. I hadn't expected such a large estate; Uncle Oliver couldn't help but give a little nod of admiration. He seemed delighted to leave me in such beautiful surroundings, and shot off straight after lunch. "I'll come and get you in two weeks, my dear. I'm going to take the opportunity to look up a friend of mine."

I had no doubt this friend was a woman. I'd never met any of them, but Uncle Oliver often talked of these "friends" of his. After a while, I realized that these friendships were as fleeting as they were mysterious.

At the end of the first week, it was Alicia's birthday. *That'll bring a little joy to the household*, I thought. Being around Alicia's parents did not make me feel relaxed; her father barely said a word, and her mother was anxious and pale. I loved her brother, Edward, on the other hand. He was gentle and sensitive, but athletic all the same, training hard each day – weightlifting, swimming, or running – as if there were a competition around the next corner. I did laps with him in the pool just thirty yards away from the house. One morning, we got a surprise when his sister jumped in with us.

While Edward was three years older than Alicia and me, he could have treated us like kids, but there was no question of that. It was the first time I'd met a boy who was so open to the way girls saw the world. He was a wonderful listener.

It was Edward who had the idea of throwing a party for his sister's birthday. His parents immediately threw out all sorts of objections, but he convinced them, eventually, by promising to organize the whole thing.

In the end, Kate offered to help out in the kitchen, and prepared huge bowls full of fruit, crudités, and salad. Alicia and I made dozens of canapés, little pastries filled with diced crabmeat or cucumber with mayonnaise. Edward decorated the stone terrace and arranged tables on it. He got his hands on a record player, too, and even gave me a 45 for a present: *La Chanteuse de Minuit*, a great tune by a young French singer caller Barbara. We all belted it out while I was making the cake. It promised to be quite a party.

Evening fell. Guests began to arrive in clusters. From the courtyard, they walked around the side of the house and straight onto the terrace. Everyone was bowled over by the Chinese lanterns that Edward had scattered around – the only source of light apart from the few candles that dotted the tables between vast dishes of food. The music, and Edward's atmospheric lighting, soon got everyone in the mood, laughing and dancing together.

Alicia and Edward's parents even came to join us for a glass of sangria. At one point, Henrik tapped me on the shoulder. "Will you dance, mademoiselle?" he asked.

I don't know what came over me. Perhaps it was the sangria I'd knocked back, or his rancid breath, or the strange need to assert myself that invaded me all of a sudden.

"I don't dance with my friends' fathers," I replied.

He shot me a look. I didn't know what to do with myself. When one of Edward's friends came to encourage me onto the dance floor, his hips twisting wildly to the music, I let myself be dragged away. Anything rather than stay next to that man. Luckily, I couldn't very well dwell on that unpleasantness, and concentrated instead on the flurry of complicated steps and sequences that my dance partner led me through. He whirled me around and spun me with grace and *savoir-faire*. When I was completely rock 'n' rolled out, I looked around anxiously. It seemed Alicia's parents had gone to bed.

As the evening wore on, little pockets of young people joked and flirted in the pool house, around an oleander bush by the pool, and by the little stone well in the courtyard.

At around two in the morning, only the diehards were still up: Alicia, Edward, one of Edward's friends – I can't remember his name – and me. The four of us talked and laughed and shared stories and debated until three: ideas we had, plans for the future, hopes…. Alicia and I took great delight in discussing our trip to China for the umpteenth time. We would go as soon as we had studied the language and set aside enough money.

Slumped amongst cushions in rattan chairs, we flapped ineffectually at the mosquitoes with one hand, and clutched our glasses with the other. The wailing of the crickets and the thousands of night insects was a melodious antidote to the blaring music of earlier on. So peaceful. We felt as though the world was ours for the taking. Someone said how clear the night sky was. We looked up and gasped in unison as a shooting star streaked across the Milky Way. It reminded me of my favorite story, as told to me by Uncle Oliver.

"Do you know the legend of the seamstress and the cowherd?" I asked. Everyone was craning their necks up at the sky, looking out for another shooting star. They didn't reply, so I went on. "It's about the stars, sort of."

It was still warm outside. Summer nights are like that in the south of France. Still, no one spoke. Perhaps they were hoping to be led like children through the mysterious twists and turns of a good story before they went to bed. The time was right.

"There are lots of versions of the story; they vary according to region and period and things," I continued. "It's ancient. All Chinese people know it. This is my favorite version. Here goes…. A young man by the name of Niu Lang has one friend in the world: the ox he looks after. One late afternoon, when he's leading his friend the ox to the lake to drink, the young cowherd sees seven sisters bathing. They are so beautiful that Niu Lang – who is twenty and not yet married – falls in love. But he knows that a poor cowherd like him has no chance of marrying one of the girls, for he can see they are high-born." When I stopped to draw breath, to my great surprise, Alicia's small voice piped up out of the darkness.

"Just then," she continued, "the ox says to Niu Lang, 'Take up one of the sister's clothes, then she'll have to speak to you, and perhaps you can persuade her to marry you.' Hearing a noise, the sisters get frightened, and they hurry over to their clothes so they can run away to the heavens – that's where they came from, because they are the daughters of the Emperor of Heaven. All of them flee except for one, the most beautiful: Zhi Nu, who tries to hide her naked body behind some tall grass. 'Give me my clothes back,' she implores. 'Promise to marry me, and you can have them back,' declares Niu Lang, urged on by his friend the ox. The beautiful Zhi Nu looks at the cowherd and her heart is moved: the young man's bearing is honest, and there is a kindness in his eyes. She accepts. Many happy years go by, in which time the pair have two children."

When Alicia paused for breath, it was my turn to jump in and carry on the story. I didn't hold back, and my voice became quite passionate. Was I moved by the story itself, or by the fact that my friend knew the tale so well? I never would have guessed she did. "But one day, the Empress of the Heavens discovers that one of her daughters has married a mere mortal, and she is overcome with anger. She sends for her and locks her up at the palace. Then she picks up her huge hairpin and draws a river of stars across the sky, separating the two lovers for all eternity. And that is how the Milky Way was made: there's the cowherd on one side – the Altair star – and the seamstress on the other – the Vega. They are both condemned: one to weave, and the other to look on from afar and tend his oxen in the company of their two children, the smaller stars Beta and Gamma Aquilae. By good fortune, the Queen of the Magpies took pity on them, and ordered all the magpies in the world to form a bridge once a year – on the seventh day of the seventh month – to reunite the lovers for one solitary night. In China, it is the Qixi Festival – the Night of Sevens – when all lovers dream of their future happiness together, and young women make a wish to find a good husband."

Alicia, in that quiet little voice of hers, said: "It's the seventh day of the seventh month, isn't it? Can you see them in the sky?"

How I wished I knew where to find those legendary stars in the sky. Perhaps I had known once. Perhaps Uncle Oliver had taught me. But that night, I couldn't remember, because by then, I was feeling tearful. Alicia had just given me a gift: her complicity. She made the story all the richer by telling it with me. It became a story about our friendship, too. From then on, the seamstress and the cowherd would also stand for her and me.

Edward and his friend were busily trying to guess where Altair and Vega were, but neither of them were budding astronomers. I glimpsed a movement in the darkness. Were they holding hands? I couldn't be sure.

It was late. We were so tired that our heads kept lolling and we couldn't stop yawning. We all went off to bed, our heads spinning with the magic of that night.

In bed, I tossed and turned and dozed a little, but couldn't seem to get to sleep properly. The slightest noise snapped me awake. At six o'clock in the morning, after a troubled hour or two, I decided that a swim would relax me, and more than likely banish my uneasiness.

Without making a sound, I headed off toward the pool in my bathing suit and bathrobe. As the pool was set back a bit from the house, I didn't run the risk of waking anyone up.

The water was cool and refreshing. Fifty laps of crawl and butterfly loosened me up. I caught my breath floating on my back. Time to get out. Now, perhaps, I would get some sleep.

I pulled myself out of the pool, the water gushing from me, and reached for my towel. My blood froze. In front of me stood Henrik. He stared at me coldly; there was no trace of the usual shyness in his eyes. I barely noticed how ridiculous he looked, with a bathrobe that was too small for him and his squat, curiously hairless legs. He was holding out a towel for me.

"Alicia's 'old man' has come to warm you up, so you don't catch cold," he said.

Even if anyone were awake, they wouldn't have been able to see us from the house since the pool hut stood between them. I felt panic rush over me. I replied as dryly as I could, assessing all the while what chance I had of getting away. "I'm old enough to dry myself, thank you."

My only thought: run as fast as I could back to the house, and lock my bedroom door behind me. I tried to get past him, and the next thing I knew, I felt the grass against my face, and a throbbing pain in my nose. I have no idea how Henrik moved so fast. He had knocked me off my feet, and was now straddling my back and shoving my head into the turf. I wanted to scream in pain, but no air could find its way into my lungs. I was paralyzed in the grip of utter panic. All I could hear was the blood pounding in my chest and temples. He grabbed hold of my hair and pulled my head back. At least it meant I could get some air.

"So, you think you can be rude to me? Forgotten you're my guest here, eh? Got to be polite! Now, you're going to do exactly what I say," he growled.

I remember being surprised to feel tears run down my cheeks, as if they belonged to someone else. Were they tears of fear? Of rage? I heard myself say in a murmur, barely audibly: "I beg you, please don't hurt me."

"That's more like it! Now you're being reasonable. If you are very good, if you do what I say, nothing will happen to you. You are going to roll over slowly."

I couldn't move. I was frozen.

A fist crashed into my back.

"You will do as I say!"

I struggled to turn myself over. I didn't dare open my eyes. He was still straddling me.

"Look at me."

I couldn't do it. The thought of seeing his eyes was worse than the violence. I closed my eyes tighter.

An uppercut straight to my jaw.

I pleaded with myself to find the strength to open my eyes, but I couldn't. He angrily ripped off the upper half of my swimsuit and grabbed my breasts.

A hideous cry rattled in my throat, and with it, my strength came back to me tenfold. Wild now, I struggled to sit up, then slashed at his face with my nails. He wrapped his hand around my neck, pushing me back down.

He started to strangle me. This determination came over him, every bit as strong as my own desperate desire to get away. A voice somewhere in my head said *move, do something*, but my strength had evaporated. My limbs wouldn't move. I was short of breath; my lungs were burning. I felt myself slipping away…but then I heard noises at a distance, a voice reeling off words that meant nothing to me. It was almost a shame when the feeling of floating disappeared. Then everything hurt again. The air rushed back into my lungs. Someone was stroking my face, I could hear crying, and the sounds got more and more defined. I glimpsed Alicia and Edward bent over me.

"Kim! Breathe, open your eyes, say something!"

My whole body started to shake. Someone put something soft

under my head. A glass was held clumsily to my mouth, and the water flowed down my throat. I sat up, supported by Alicia. Edward tried to explain, as gently as he could, what had happened.

"Mum came to wake me up to tell me something was going on in the garden. When I saw your empty bed, I woke Alicia up, grabbed my hockey stick, and got here before my father could hurt you anymore. I just kept whacking him on the back."

I listened to him as best I could. Now and then, I lost the sense of what he was saying. I was so grateful he'd done what he did. I tried to speak, but found I couldn't.

What he said next threw me completely: "I can't tell you how good it felt to hit him like that. I feel like I obliterated eight years of horror."

When I tried to move, every muscle in my body hurt. Alicia was crying. I managed to get some words out. "I want to go home."

Alicia was sobbing. "Don't go, I beg you. My father will leave, I promise you. Stay with us. Don't tell anyone what happened, I'd die of shame." A sick feeling came over me. I didn't reply.

"I'm so sorry. So sorry," she repeated, trying to look me in the eye. "Kim, say something, tell me you'll still be my friend. You and my brother, you're all I've got."

I did look at her then. The confusion I saw in her face made me shudder. How could I make any sort of decision right then? It wasn't possible after what I'd been through.

I turned away. I had to do something. Despite the intense heat of the early morning, I couldn't stop shivering. I knew I had to stand up. I hauled myself to my feet and walked toward the house. With every heavy step I was trying to bring myself back to life. That contact with the earth gave me energy again.

In the shower, I vigorously scrubbed myself as if scouring my body could expunge any trace left by that horrible man. I used a nailbrush and nearly a whole bar of soap. My skin was soon red all over. But no matter how hard I scrubbed and scraped, the images kept flooding my brain. I realized I knew nothing of what this family had lived through all these years. My mind was racing to put together the pieces of the puzzle: my friend's mood swings, her stunning bouts of fatigue, her melancholy, her attachment to Felix – I saw it all in a new light. Guilt crept up on me. Why hadn't I asked her more questions? What had happened to her, exactly? Would she even tell me?

Eventually, I dried myself, dressed quickly, and went back to our room. I found Edward and Alicia there, collapsed on her bed. They were waiting for me. "He's gone," Edward said. "I told him that if he so much as touched my mother, my sister, or you, I would kill him. As of today, he knows I could."

I understood at that moment that what I had imagined, without really believing it possible, stopped short of the truth. Edward began to pour out miserable story after miserable story in faltering, jolting sentences. He described what his sister and he had suffered at the hands of their father over the years. Sometimes, I wanted to block my ears, it was so horrible. Their childhood was a terrible nightmare. And I thought *I* was unhappy...

During this deeply disturbing confession, Alicia bowed her head and cried, then kept repeating "Sorry, sorry, sorry." I couldn't take it anymore. "Alicia, stop! Tell me this: what has your mom been doing all this time?"

"She's petrified."

"Well, then, speak to the police, or your grandparents, or what about Miss Bonham? You've got to!" I was incensed.

"I don't know if they'd listen. And even if they did, why should they believe us?" She added, almost solemnly, "Kim, I beg you, don't tell anyone about this. You remember last year, two weeks before Easter, when I was out of school because I had the flu?"

"I remember."

"I was having my stomach pumped. I'd taken a whole bottle of sleeping pills. For the first time, I had spoken to my father, threatened to tell people the truth. The state my mother was in when I got home…he had beaten her so hard. She's as terrorized as we are." Then, with a voice I could barely hear she said "I feel so dirty, Kim. Sometimes, in bed at night, I pray so hard. I want to die. I can't put up with what he does to me anymore. No other man will ever want me. My life is over before it's begun."

Edward, his face dark with grief, took his sister in his arms. It was unbearable to see them like this. Whatever I did, I couldn't make them suffer any more.

"It will be our secret. You can both trust me, I won't tell anyone. I'll stay with you, as planned, and I will never let you down," I promised.

Like frightened children, we took each other's hands and made a circle. Ideas flooded my mind. Why hadn't my friend confided in me sooner? What could I do to help them?

~

I take a sip of water. My hands are trembling.

"Are you all right, Marsie?" Vittorio asks. Kenya looks shaken.

"Oh, my darlings, it's embarrassing to tell you about this. I still find it so upsetting, to this day. It makes me feel ashamed…."

"But it's not your fault," Kenya insists, taking my hand. "Surely you know that."

I nod, weakly. But the feelings of powerlessness have come crashing back again. "Why didn't you go to the police?" asks Vittorio. I can see that he is angry, though not at me, of course.

"To keep my promise."

I think that it's time for us to take a break. Sharing the good moments with them gave me energy, but I feel more sapped than ever talking about the hard ones. I hope retelling my story won't do me more harm—or them. I hope they are old enough to hear these horrible things. I don't want to dampen their incredible spirits. But there is a part of me that must tell this story—for Alicia.

# CHAPTER 9

# Farewell Letter

"Why not?" I was on the verge of tears. I had told my mother that I wanted – no – I *needed* to invite Alicia to our house. After what had happened, I couldn't just sit back. I had to help her. But Sarah wouldn't budge.

"No means no! I don't have to justify myself. Mother's privilege." She couldn't quite lose her slight French accent, despite her impeccable English. Normally, I didn't notice it, but that day, it infuriated me.

"I'm going to call Uncle Oliver."

"Well, call him then! If you think that your godfather can grant all your wishes, you are mistaken. He's usually away at this time of year. And I'm sure he's got better things to do than look after two little girls, anyway."

Sarah was wrong. Uncle Oliver was in Brittany. And when he heard how anxious I sounded, there were no questions asked. Alicia and I arrived three days later at Mansfield Manor.

Alicia and I couldn't bring ourselves to talk about what had happened; awkward silences sometimes prevailed between us. As the days passed, I realized that it wasn't easy to pick up where we had left off. In the end, I calmed down by telling myself that perhaps it was just a phase in our lives together, one chapter in our story. How I wished that nothing had happened, and everything could be how it once was.

September. Back to school. I found out from Edward that Henrik was keeping a low profile.

"Hardly surprising. Since I smashed his face in, he knows I'm stronger than he is. All that working out didn't go to waste," he told me on the phone.

Yet again, I was struck by how much that family had gone through. It must have been agony for Edward looking on, powerless to stop its destruction.

At Cheltenham, things between me and Alicia clicked back into place. Nothing like familiar surroundings. For our second to last year, we were still at Saint Austen but moved to Senior House. We'd managed to luck into one of the bigger rooms and had beds alongside each other. Our nocturnal nattering soon started up again. In the evenings, we rehearsed *Much Ado About Nothing* for the end-of-year show.

Uncle Oliver was stranded in Thailand for the midterm holidays. He wouldn't be back for two weeks, but promised we could spend some of the Christmas holidays at his house. That meant Alicia and I would go to our respective homes for a few days.

London was awash with autumn gold. My mother dragged me from one social function to the next. I didn't mind: these were the only times I felt we were close. Alicia was never far from my thoughts. I suggested we get together, but she wanted to stay home and try to rebuild some sort of relationship with her family – which was working, by all accounts. I understood, and resolved to wait patiently for Sunday.

As soon as I got back to Cheltenham, I rushed over to our room to see Alicia. The autumnal chill I felt as I got out of bed that morning had given me a shot of energy: I could take on the whole world. I had decided, during the journey from London to Cheltenham, to persuade Alicia to tell Miss Bonham everything. I had to help her get rid of the wretched burden she was carrying around with her.

Surprisingly, our room was empty. Alicia must have already gone to lessons. I headed straight over to College with three other girls from our house. The day went on. Still no sign of Alicia. Not in class, nor at the pool, nor in the library or study room, where four or five of us often got together to work. She was nowhere to be seen. I was starting to worry.

Just before supper, the principal sent for me.

I was used to having to wait to see Miss Bonham, sitting on the little carved wooden bench in the vestibule outside her study. I'd been sent to see her for various misdemeanors. She was always very fair. It was in my character to be direct, and that prompted me to speak my mind to a teacher if I felt there were some injustice being done. Hence, my trips to the principal's study.

She would sit me down and assign me essays with titles like "How to Live Better," explaining she was "duty-bound" to punish me. What should have been penance very quickly turned to pleasure: once I'd finished my work, we would have a little chat. She would answer the numerous questions I asked, firing my imagination with suggestions of books to read, opening my mind to ideas I knew nothing about. I admired her, and became quite attached, too. It had gradually dawned on me that it couldn't have been easy supervising all those young women. It required a firm hand.

That day, I waited on the bench as usual for Miss Bonham to open the door. When she called me in, I could see how anxious she was right away. Her whole face, usually so serene, looked distressed. Her cheeks were swollen, her words faltering.

"Kim…you were Alicia's best friend."

*Were?* A lead weight crashed onto my shoulders, my heartbeat raced, and blood rapped at my temples.

Miss Bonham stood up, walked around her desk, and placed her hands on my shoulders. Her large blue eyes were dulled with the pain.

"I don't know how to tell you…the Lord has taken Alicia."

I couldn't swallow, as if something was stuck in my throat. I mumbled, "It can't be. You're mistaken." I could tell Miss Bonham was lost for words, and I stumbled on. "It isn't Alicia who's died, it's her mother. Alicia must have stayed behind to be with her…Please call and check. I'm sure I'm right. No, Alicia isn't dead. She would have called me if anything was wrong." I stood bolt upright facing Miss Bonham, who was perched on the edge of her desk.

"This is so difficult…." She looked straight into my eyes. "Alicia died this morning. Her mother found her in the loft of their house in London. She hanged herself."

I had to get out of that room. There was no air, I was going to explode. My brain was boiling. My heart was on fire. I spun on my heels and headed for the door. Before going through it, I screamed in rage, "A fine God, yours is! How can he afflict us with something we wouldn't even dare put animals through?" I slammed the door behind me.

I ran down the endless corridors and found myself in the street, walking blindly, wanting to kick everything in sight. Instinctively, I headed for the swimming pool, a few streets away. I picked up a branch that was lying on the ground and took out my rage on a lamppost, then a tree. The cold stung me. I wasn't wearing a coat. I just kept going.

I was stuck between pain, rage at not being considered a good enough friend, and guilt for not having done something before it was too late. I started talking to myself. One or two passers-by turned around.

"I'll kill him! Why didn't you call me? I was there to help you. I kept it secret out of loyalty to you!"

I got to the pool. It was locked, but there was a side door I knew would be open. I went to my locker and took out my swimsuit. Changed. Dove in. The water was cold. It was dark. I didn't ever want to stop swimming. After about a hundred laps, my anger subsided, like night falling. I dragged myself out of the water and sat on the edge of the pool. My muscles were burning. A terrible sadness came over me.

"Alicia, where are you? Give me a sign. Please, tell me that you are somewhere out there…tell me I'll see you tomorrow. Don't abandon me. We had so many dreams together."

I finally let my sorrow burst out. The sobs shook me.

My life would never be the same again.

When I got back to Saint Austen, Matron was there to welcome me, even though I'd broken the rules. In our room, I threw myself onto Alicia's bed. I grabbed a sweater she had left there, and climbed between her sheets. The sweater still smelled of her. I pressed it against me so it felt like she was with me.

The bedroom door opened, and without a word, Miss Bonham came and sat on the edge of the bed.

"Kim, I understand you're in pain. We are all deeply distressed. No one is responsible for the choice Alicia made."

"I'm responsible. If I'd said something, she'd be here now. In her bed next to me…."

I spilled out the details of the horrors Alicia had endured. A release of all that secret knowledge. Before leaving me, Miss Bonham held me tight, whispering words of comfort. Alone again, I thought of Uncle Oliver. I needed to talk to him. Then another realization: if we had gone to his house for the holidays, Alicia would still be alive. I sank into a fitful, haunted sleep.

*A thick glass windowpane. Behind the glass, Alicia is smiling at me. She looks like an angel. I suddenly notice she has a rope around her neck. "Alicia, don't do it!" She smiles, then vanishes in a sort of fog. With a huge stick, I try to break the glass, but I can't get through.*

I woke with a start. I had just dreamed the first in a series of nightmares that have continued ever since.

The next day, my classmates looked at me kindly and smiled. One of them gave me a record to listen to, another one asked if I wanted to play checkers. I didn't want anything. They were well-meaning gestures, but I felt so empty that I didn't even reply.

The following evening, I found a package on my pillow. It was addressed to me in Alicia's handwriting. I sat on the bed – my heart pounding – and tore it open. There was Felix, Alicia's toy rabbit. And a letter. I held him tight while I read.

*My beloved friend.*

*I know that you must be very angry with me. Please try to understand, and don't be upset. I can't bear this life anymore. He will always be there, waiting for me in the corner of a room, in reality or in my mind's eye. At last, I'm going to be able to sleep peacefully without being frightened, without my thoughts torturing me, without feeling dirty, without asking myself what will happen tomorrow.*

*Above all, don't feel responsible for my death. It's my own decision, and I don't mean to mix you up in it all. I love you too much. You are my sister, and you will be my sister in the next world. In this one, the only thing I'll miss will be our laughing fits, and, more than anything, your love.*

*Thank you for listening to me all those nights when I couldn't get to sleep. Thank you for your trust. You didn't give away our secret, I know. Now you can tell people. You must, in fact. Tell them what my father is, how he has abused us all these years. Show them this letter. Your word and my death will save my brother and my mother, never mind the shame.*

*I know that we will be together again one day. I know that you will always be close to me, and I to you. Remember the legend of the seamstress and the cowherd. Promise me that you will go on our trip to China. Be happy, I know you can be.*

*Forgive me. Take care of Felix. He will be a little part of me that goes with you.*

*Your friend who loves and will always love you,*
*Alicia*


The next day, the principal sent for me.

"Kim, the police are conducting an inquiry. They've asked me if Alicia had any close friends. I haven't gotten back to them yet. Do you intend to give evidence?"

"Yes, I do."

"I'm well aware that it's going to provoke quite a scandal, but I think you're right. You have my full support."

I knew I could count on that special woman.

∽

When Kenya heard about what happened to Alicia, she had gotten up and rushed out of the room. Eyes brimming with tears, Vittorio stayed beside me. Now, he stands. "This story of yours takes some telling, Marsie. I need some time out."

"Me, too," I reply. "Let's see where your cousin has gotten to."

We find Kenya in tears on the other side of the door.

"Come on, darling, let's have something to eat. We'll continue with the story tomorrow."

We don't talk about Alicia over supper, and all of us make an effort to try to lighten the mood.

# CHAPTER 10

# Dried Rose

*November, 1958.*

The funeral service took place at St. Mary Abbots in South Kensington. The Cunningham party was limited to Edward, two of his cousins, a few aunts, and friends. Kate, Alicia's mother, was not there, but lots of classmates had come from Cheltenham, wanting to honor Alicia's memory.

I sat with the family, in the front row next to Edward. My brother, Charles came, too, to lend his support. I had slipped Felix into my bag. Alicia's white coffin sat on trestles in the middle of the chancel.

Up until then, I had been able to keep up a sort of illusion, hidden away in our room in Saint Austen, recalling our days spent together. But there was no escaping that rectangular wooden box. I couldn't hold back my tears.

When the service was over, everyone headed to Brompton Cemetery. The cars were parked by the main gate, and we walked to the grave. One by one, the roses that our friends had given out were swallowed up by the earth. They dropped out of sight, heavy with sorrow and, in some cases, wishes, too: wishes for a life without suffering. If they knew the half of it....

At the end of the ceremony, the guests met at the house in South Kensington where Edward now lived by himself. I had never been before, because Alicia hadn't wanted me to. In different circumstances, 19 Kensington Court would have been an inviting house in an attractive part of London, with its red bricks, iron balustrades, and grand front door. Inside, the slightly worn carpet, the silverware arranged on the mahogany credenza, the mirrors and the sitting room with its sofa and matching armchairs – all testified to an attentive housewife and a top surgeon who was much admired. But in the air hung a vaguely rancid smell, as if the rooms had never been aired. Although the place was immaculate, desolation seeped into the walls.

Little sandwiches had been arranged in rows on a silver tray on the dining room table. A maid in black and white served the tea; a butler held a tray of other drinks.

Edward was unhurried in everything he did, totally at odds with his usual hyperactive self. His eyes were puffy, his expression weary, his complexion pale. I noticed his tie was askew, which was most unlike him. Once hands had been shaken and condolences expressed, once he had made sure that his guests were all right, and conversation was flowing again, Edward turned to me. He took me by the hand. We slipped away from the others into a small, chaotic study.

Fabrics from Liberty of London hanging from the walls, old paintings in gilt frames, an eighteenth-century escritoire, a pair of armchairs upholstered to match the fabrics: I knew at once that this was his mother's room.

He sat me in one chair, and collapsed into the other.

"Kim, I feel utterly responsible for Alicia's death." His words hit hard. I listened as he made his confession, which was broken by tears.

After the events of the summer and Alicia's departure for Brittany with me, the Cunningham family had quickly returned to London. Henrik appeared repentant. He swore to God that he would seek to cure himself, that he would go to see a psychiatrist. He had apologized to everyone, and talked about how ashamed he was, how the episode with me had opened his eyes. At first, the family reacted coldly; but gradually, doubt, then collective astonishment, set in. "He's changed," they said to one another in hushed tones. For two months, he was like a different man: going to therapy sessions and acting with ever-increasing consideration towards his family.

So when the weekend of midterm break came around, it seemed reasonable to go away, Edward thought. He picked up Alicia from Cheltenham, reassured himself that all was well at home, and went to visit a friend of his in Sussex, though not without giving his mother and sister a telephone number and strict instructions to get in touch with him if they were the least bit concerned.

With Edward out of the way, the snake struck for the last time. It was likely he slipped into Alicia's bedroom while she was in the bathroom. He must have hid in the wardrobe and waited for her.

Once his daughter was carefully locked in her room for the night, as her brother had advised her to do, Henrik came out from his hiding place.

"It's the only explanation I can find, piecing together what I know and what I could understand from Mom. Perhaps we'll never know the rest. My father fled. The police have issued an international warrant for his arrest."

"And your mother?"

"She's been admitted to a psychiatric hospital. She lost her mind when she found Alicia in the loft."

Edward's tears rolled down my neck as we hugged.

Henrik Cunningham was found some days after the funeral. After relentless questioning, he broke down and admitted everything. He was placed on remand. Edward called me at Cheltenham daily for the next few weeks. He needed my support…and I, his. Despite this contact with him, I couldn't pick myself up. Everything was an ordeal: eating, swimming, work. Miss Bonham intervened. She suggested to my parents that I might go home for two weeks to try to recover my spirits. They agreed.

Bad idea. At breakfast, on my first morning home, I found a newspaper folded on my plate. Its headline – *The Good Doctor?* – jumped off the page. I looked to my parents for an explanation.

My mother had something to say. "Your father and I want you to keep out of this affair as much as possible. There can be no question of this scandal affecting our family."

"*Maman*, I can't just keep quiet. I'm personally involved in the whole thing."

"I'm not asking you, I'm telling you."

I started to get up.

"Sit down at once!" Sarah barked. "We are going to address this problem once and for all. You want to get involved, but as usual, you haven't thought it through. As you know perfectly well, there is no smoke without fire. Who's to say your friend didn't provoke her father?"

I could not listen to another word. I left the room.

The next day, I was back at Cheltenham. The stay with my parents had barely lasted twenty-four hours. I had to rebuild my life far away from my mother's cruelty. Unfortunately, Uncle Oliver still wasn't back from his expedition. I needed his shoulder to cry on, his advice.

I turned to Miss Bonham, and asked her permission to stay at College permanently, even during the holidays. She gave her consent, and found me work over the summer. I needed to save up for my trip to China. Alicia and I had had a dream. I would make it a reality, alone.

Uncle Oliver returned from Asia two weeks later. When I heard his voice on the telephone, I broke down. Incapable of saying a word, I just sobbed.

"Don't cry, my darling I'll be with you in three hours." He hung up.

I could see he was exhausted when he arrived. He didn't seem to mind; he set about organizing everything so that we could see each other every day. He took a room at a hotel not far from Saint Austen. I greeted him as my savior, so relieved to have him close to me at last. We spent hours talking: he asked me questions, listened patiently and kindly. Not once did he criticize me for keeping quiet about the assault in France, or for promising to keep Alicia's secret.

Miss Bonham gave me permission to take all my evening meals with Uncle Oliver at the hotel. Afterwards, he often helped me with a tricky math problem, or we might read over my essays together.

Uncle Oliver returned to London after two weeks, promising to phone me every evening, which he did, no matter where he was. Life gradually returned to normal. Although I was still suffering a great deal, I decided to get back to my swimming, piano lessons, and art classes.

That was my frame of mind when I received a visit from a policeman. He asked if I would consider appearing as a witness in Henrik's trial.

"What good is the word of a sixteen-year-old girl?" I asked.

"It can do a great deal of good, as a matter of fact."

"Even if I don't have my mother's consent?"

"You don't need it. This is the criminal justice system, not a cocktail party."

I liked his reasoning. I said yes. I would go to the trial, and I would act as a witness. He thanked me, and assured me that his officers would be discreet. I kept it all from my mother. In any case, the trial wouldn't take place until the following year, when my studies would be nearly complete.

∽

Throughout the trial, the English press had a field day with sensational headlines about the duplicity of "the good doctor." There was a raft of articles alluding to Dr. Jekyll and Mr. Hyde, and drawing comparisons with various notorious cases. My name was never mentioned because I was a minor. I had made my decision known to Miss Bonham, who continued to support me. My brother, Charles, telephoned from Oxford, where he was studying law. "You can count on me. I'll be there," he promised.

The day before I was due to appear in court, I took the train up to London; Edward had suggested I spend the night at his house. I looked out of the window at the fields and woods flashing by. The English countryside was radiant in early June, 1959. The woodland floors were teeming with bluebells, streams sparkled, birds dove and soared in the air. I looked on, feeling the anxiety creeping back. At last, though, I was doing something positive to assuage the grief that had been gnawing at me for a year and a half. Not a day had gone by that I hadn't thought of Alicia.

In the house at South Kensington, everything seemed as bleak as ever. The same could be said for Edward. He had begun his architectural training, but his future was up in the air, he said. Was he going to continue living with his mother? Should they sell the properties in France and London? He was chain-smoking. The trial was clearly taking its toll.

We retreated into Kate's study, a haven of peace in the house. The fire crackled. Edward offered me a glass of port, and I accepted.

"Do you want to sleep in the spare room?" he asked.

"No, in Alicia's."

"Will you be able to?"

"Yes."

"Are you sure?"

I nodded. Edward went into the sitting room to put on some music. I didn't doubt my resolve for a second, from the safety of that armchair.

Edward chose Mozart's clarinet concerto. He sat back down again, and restlessly lit a cigarette. His hand was trembling. He was in a dreadful state.

"Are you not feeling well? Is it the trial?"

"No, it's not just that." He faltered. "What I'm...what I'm going to tell you isn't easy to put into words." He downed his glass of port in one swallow. "For some time now, I've realized that I am not attracted to women. They make me feel uncomfortable. Apart from you, of course. But that's not the same."

"Are you more inclined to be attracted to men?"

"Yes."

"This may seem funny, but I've never imagined you any other way."

"What?" Edward asked, relief flooding his voice.

"You remember when we were in France – four of us – sitting on the terrace, looking out for shooting stars? We all made a wish, and I saw your friend reach out and hold your hand. You didn't take it away."

"It feels so good to hear you say that. So, you accept me as I am? If everyone was like you, I wouldn't have to hide myself away…."

I told him about my past year at College, my daily struggle to separate my persona from the one I shared with Alicia, the kindness shown by Uncle Oliver, Miss Bonham, and my friends.

"I've been coping. Just," I said. "Enough to get my work done."

"I can't seem to be able to. Maybe when the trial's over…"

We realized, quite suddenly, that we had talked long into the night. Our tummies were rumbling, so we went into the kitchen to make a snack. Then it was time for bed; I needed a few hours' sleep before tomorrow's ordeal.

I climbed the stairs and stopped in front of Alicia's door. Would I have the strength to open it? I made myself. Her smell hit me full in the face. I just couldn't take another step. It was all too much. I turned around and nearly ran into Edward, who had climbed the stairs behind me. He took me in his arms.

"How is it she's still here?"

"Every week I bring her to life. With her perfume."

"Oh, Ed…we have to let her go."

"I promise you that when this trial is finished, I'll try. I'll sell this house, I'll do up the one in Little Wittenham. And you'd better come and visit!"

A taxi took us up the Mall, up the Strand, over Holborn Viaduct to Newgate Street, and we arrived at the Old Bailey, London's Central Criminal Court, at half past ten. The driver dropped us at the main entrance of the imposing building. I was about to go through the grand doors when I heard someone call my name. Uncle Oliver!

"Nothing was going to stop me from being by your side today," he announced, and behind his typical bluster, he was clearly quite emotional.

Edward headed off to take his place in the courtroom. Uncle Oliver escorted me to a special desk, where I had to present myself as a witness. I was shown into a little anteroom where I waited under the watchful eye of a woman with a most reassuring smile. After about fifteen minutes, she led me along various corridors toward the famous Court Number One.

I climbed some steps, and found myself standing before a wooden screen that was designed to hide me, as was the usual practice for child witnesses. I hated that arrangement. I needed to see the person who was responsible for Alicia's death. I turned to an usher, and asked him to remove the screen. He referred the question to the clerk, who referred it to the judge. I was clearly causing quite a commotion. After a brief conference – and to my surprise and great relief – the thin board was wheeled away.

It revealed a packed courtroom. To my left, on a podium, the judge sat on a sort of ornate wooden throne, with his wig and red gown. Behind him, on the wall, the motto of the British monarchy: *Dieu et mon Droit*. God and my right.

The jury was looking at me intensely, as if trying to decipher my every movement. At the back of the court, the members of the press were shifting excitedly in their seats. I looked around for Henrik Cunningham. In the mêlée of clerks and barristers in wigs and the abundance of legal records bound in green leather, I couldn't make him out for a few moments.

Then I saw him. He was sitting opposite the judge in the dock, protected by a glass screen. I almost didn't recognize him. He was emaciated and hunched. He looked shrunken, a shadow of the man I had met. He was looking straight at me. What had happened to those steely eyes of his?

The realization of what he had done suddenly bubbled to the surface, and I was instantly struck with fear. And doubt. I broke his gaze. Could I really be a witness? I didn't know what I had to do anymore, what to say. I began to panic. Suddenly, I heard the rap of a hammer.

"Miss Rochester, can you answer the question that has been put to you?"

I looked about for Edward, Charles, and Uncle Oliver in the crowd. There they were, sitting upright, perfectly still.

I had to speak. My heart was thumping. I was short of breath. I stammered at first, unable to find the right words, then, spurred on by a force I didn't recognize, I found my voice, describing my friend's ordeal and the attack carried out against me. I was carried along in a whirlwind of words. I didn't notice Edward or Charles anymore, or the barrister, or the accused.

At the end of my cross-examination, the usher led me out of the court and back to the waiting room so I could pick up my things. Uncle Oliver was waiting for me in the corridor. He put his arms around me, and only then did I stop shaking. I felt relieved, but a certain emptiness washed over me, too. I silently said to Alicia: *Rest in peace.*

That afternoon, Oliver took me back to Cheltenham. There was no way I was going home to face my mother's rage; she must have heard about my performance on the witness stand by now.

We reached the College in the early evening. Back home in Saint Austen at last, I was exhausted. A deep, deep sleep carried me far away from the court, away from it all.

The next day, I was called to the parlor for a telephone call.

"You are a little monster! How dare you make an exhibition of us like that?" Sarah hissed.

"Thank you, *Maman,* for being there for me during this very difficult time. I'm touched."

She hung up.

The next day I got a big surprise: a long letter from Margaret Black, my nanny for all those years. She congratulated me on my courage in openly facing the court. She told me she was there throughout the trial. I was astonished that she hadn't tried to find me afterwards, but perhaps the fact that I was surrounded by police had put her off. Deciding to reply straightaway, I sat at my desk and wrote long into the night.

In the letter I asked if she would meet me for a cup of tea during the holidays. So we did, and that was when she told me how I came into the world. We kept in touch after that.

Forty-eight hours after his trial, I learned that Henrik Cunningham had died. He'd been found strangled to death in his cell.

~

The Leavers' Ceremony—Cheltenham's graduation and announcement of honors—took place two years after that. The whole school crammed into Princess Hall, the floor and galleries teeming with uniforms and teachers' gowns. On the stage stood Miss Bonham, her mortarboard perched on her head and her glasses perched on her nose. As I sat in one of the wooden chairs in the main hall, waiting for my name to be called. I looked up and noticed Edward sitting on the first-floor balcony, smiling gently. He had made the effort to come and celebrate with me.

My parents were absent, of course. My father had shown solidarity with Sarah; mother and daughter had ignored each other for a year and a half. She wouldn't be at home when I returned that evening, Charles had warned me. He couldn't be at the awards ceremony either; his year-end exams at Oxford saw to that.

I ended up sixth out of twenty-five in my class, an honorable position. I couldn't really get excited; in fact, I suddenly felt very alone. They announced the special prizes for French and English.

Where was mention of Alicia, who had so excelled in those subjects? My eyes met Edward's. We were thinking the same thing. I was so lost in thought that I didn't notice when my own name was read out. My neighbor jabbed me in the ribs with her elbow. I came back to Earth to hear, "…wins the prize for creative writing. The panel congratulates you; it's the highest grade that has ever been awarded."

I went up to receive my award from Miss Bonham. That was when I noticed a tall, elegant man standing up and beaming from ear to ear. Uncle Oliver! He began to clap, and soon the whole hall joined in.

"You have a real talent for surprises," I said, giving him a hug after the ceremony.

"Pack your bags, I'm taking you away."

Before leaving, I wanted to say goodbye to Miss Bonham. I went to look for her in Christ Church chapel, a few streets away from College. It was the first time I'd set foot in the place since Alicia's death.

I slipped into the end of a pew and attempted an Our Father, but my mind wandered. I was so caught up in my memories that I jumped when Miss Bonham laid a hand on my shoulder. We left chapel, keeping step with one another down the stone path. The past six years had brought us together. We went down Overton Road without saying a word, just happy to be side by side one last time. At the entrance to Cheltenham Ladies College, the principal stopped and looked at me intently.

"You know, I don't like goodbyes, Kim, but I wanted to say this: I will always be here if you need me. With your creativity, you are bound to take many interesting paths in life. Some of them will be difficult. But because you always strive for honesty, I know you'll stay true to yourself." The corners of her mouth betrayed half a smile, and she added: "And if, on your journey, things are troubling you, drop in on us for a few days to talk it over and take stock. Now, go. Have confidence in yourself, and in what's to come."

She turned around quickly, though not quite quickly enough; I noticed her eyes were glistening with tears.

On the way back, in the car, Uncle Oliver couldn't hide his pride.

At Belgrave Square, I just had time to pack my suitcase and look in on my father in his first-floor study. He confirmed that my mother did not wish to see me for the time being. I couldn't summon up the insolence to tell him how delighted that made me.

"Under the circumstances," he added, "your idea of studying Chinese strikes us as completely appropriate. There's a very good school in Paris: *l'Ecole Nationale des Langues Orientales Vivantes*, or Langues O', as it's known. You've probably heard of it. A friend of your mother's, Laurence de Gastines, owns a small studio flat in Rue du Dragon. It's on the seventh floor overlooking Paris. I'm sure you'll be very happy there. You can move in after your holidays with your uncle."

It didn't matter that my parents wanted to get rid of me. I was going far away. That was all that mattered.

∽

"Come on, let's have a few oysters and get some fresh air!" I say to my grandchildren. It is their vacation, after all. "Oh, no, Marsie, don't stop! I've asked Leo to make up a tray of supper for the three of us," Kenya says.

"Why doesn't Leo join us?" suggests Vittorio.

"Good idea!" I agree.

Leo opens the door and bursts out laughing: there he is with a tray of food, and *four* plates already in place.

# PART TWO

# 1961-1965

# CHAPTER 1

# Student Card

My father was right: the studio in Paris was gorgeous, with a really comfortable bed. There was only one thing missing: an elevator! Converting maids' quarters into studio flats in the attic of these buildings was all the rage. "The kind of thing that appeals to foreigners," said my landlady, an elegant Parisian aristocrat dressed in Chanel from head to toe. The Rue du Dragon was relatively quiet compared to the buzzing area around the church of Saint-Germain, a few yards away.

Langues O' had been entirely dedicated to Oriental languages and culture for the best part of two centuries. It was ideally situated, as far as I was concerned, at 2 Rue de Lille, on the corner of the Rue des Saints Pères, about a minute's walk from my apartment.

On my first day, in September, 1961, I knew no one, though my father had done some research for me. He was able to get the lowdown on various professors because so many of his French counterparts had studied there. Diplomats were sent to Langues O' before going off to the so-called "exotic postings." Because of this, the atmosphere was a lot more professional than in Paris's other universities. There were no common rooms or student conviviality. People came to lectures armed with their student cards, then went home again. To get to know the other students, you had to go over to the Saint-Germain crossroads, to the Deux Magots or the Café Flore. You might even run into an existentialist – Jean-Paul Sartre, Simone de Beauvoir, and that crowd – knocking back *cafés crèmes* all day long.

The building that housed our gray classrooms seemed stuck in a prestigious and slightly pompous yesteryear. Compared with Cheltenham, the facilities were lackluster, though at first, I was so pleased to be a step closer to my goal that I didn't even notice. There were so few textbooks available that sometimes we had to make do with duplicated handouts for the whole lesson. Our learning resources consisted of sheets of paper stuck on the wall with thumbtacks, a few books, and lots of pencils. The only real inconvenience, though, was the cramped conditions.

The teaching, on the other hand, was of the highest standard. What's more, we were lucky enough to have language assistants, from China for the most part, with whom we set up little conversation groups. When the time came to collect our degrees in three years, we should at least know how to speak a bit, even if the mysteries of the written language might remain beyond us. East Asian calligraphy is as much an art form as a means of communication, so one couldn't hope to master it in such a short time.

I arrived at Langues O' with dreams, memories, and plenty of books. The first few classes made me painfully aware of my lack of knowledge. For as long as I could remember, I had been fascinated by the Middle Kingdom; but what could someone as disinterested in politics as myself know about China? Plenty about the past, but precious little about the present, was the honest answer. Mind you, we didn't have much news from over there, or if we did, it was badly twisted.

My passion for my studies couldn't mask the fact that I had very few funds at my disposal. The money my father gave me wasn't anywhere near enough (I suspected my mother had a hand in that). I was trying to figure out what to do when, one afternoon, I saw a postcard in the bakery in the Rue des St. Pères.

*Fifteen-year-old girl studying at the Lycée Victor Duruy seeks English-speaking tutor. Telephone Solférino 35 34.*

The day I walked through the door of 213 Boulevard Saint-Germain, I had no idea that what would happen next would change my life forever.

∼

Madame Lestrange took me on to give her daughter Françoise English lessons. "What a coincidence, you studying Chinese," she said when I told her what I was doing in Paris. "My husband trades with

China, and spends a lot of time going back and forth between Paris and Peking."

That was it. I couldn't wait to meet this husband of hers, and gather as much information as possible from him. I didn't know anyone who worked in China, much less someone who did business with the government there. I thanked my lucky stars. It remained to be seen just when I would meet the head of the household – he was always abroad.

Three months after being adopted by this young family – Madame Lestrange kept insisting I stay for supper – I eventually met him one early Friday evening. Françoise and I were finishing her English lesson when the door of her bedroom burst open, and a whirlwind spun over to my young charge and swept her off her feet.

"Françoise!"

"Papa!"

"I've missed you."

"You, too!"

A French Uncle Oliver! Once he had put his daughter down, he asked me all sorts of questions, fascinated to hear about my studies at Langues O'. His energy was infectious.

"How I would have loved to study there!" he said as I described the course. "Knowing a bit about ancient Chinese culture would make my life a hell of a lot easier, I'm sure. My Mandarin is pretty ropey, and I land myself in hot water sometimes. My Chinese counterparts speak virtually no French, and very little English. We have to use interpreters, and that always slows up communication. Mind you, slowing down isn't always a bad idea in business," he added with a smile.

"May I ask what type of trade you do with the Chinese?"

"I sell them industrial diamonds."

Whereupon I was invited to supper, yet again.

My other great pleasure was spending time with Uncle Oliver. He would take a room at the Ritz – Coco Chanel still lived there at the time – and stroll over the Seine to fetch me. Together, we would take a taxi to La Tour d'Argent, le Grand Véfour, Chez Maxim's, or some other trendy or fancy restaurant. He wanted to hear all about my studies, and I asked him about his trips abroad and his gemstones. Occasionally, he would take out one of his magic pieces of paper and pry them open to reveal the marvels within. I learned all about the size of the stones, their provenance, and their value, too. He sold some of them to a jeweler in Place Vendôme – for pretty ridiculous sums of money, it seemed to me.

"I don't understand, Uncle. You don't even need to work, so why all this haggling? It sometimes takes you months to make a sale."

"For the fun of it, my dear! It's a bit like those games of *Go* that the Orientals are so fond of. You move one of your pawns forward by a measly square, secure in the knowledge that the consequences of your move will be felt later on in the game. It wouldn't be nearly such fun if I needed to do it. And I don't expect I'd come out on top so often, either!"

The first six months went by peacefully enough. One day at Langues O', when our teacher, Monsieur Ruhlman, was introducing us to the arts of translation, the door of our small classroom opened and a brunette with long, shiny hair appeared. Heads turned. "Bonjour, my name is Manuela Barzini. I am very sorry to interrupt the lesson, but I have just enrolled…."

The teacher was torn between irritation at being interrupted and admiration for this gorgeous apparition with a sing-song accent. When she came and sat down next to me, I felt flattered, failing to notice that it was the only free seat. I had already fallen for her Italian accent. At the end of the lesson, instead of trudging back to my studio, I suggested the two of us have a coffee at Les Deux Magots.

"In St.-Germain," I explained to Manuela, "you have a choice: the Deux Magots clique, or the Café de Flore clique."

She smiled and replied in a gentle, almost timid voice: "I choose the Deux Magots. I have friends there."

I know beauty opens doors, but I quite thought that the part of me reserved for friendship was locked for good. How wrong I was.

Manuela's friends were "lefties," as my parents would say. Some of them even hung out with Sartre. One of them, Pierre, was a sensitive young photographer. His natural affinity with women quickly made him confidant to a whole band of female students, who worshipped him.

"But he doesn't make the most of it," Manuela said to me.

"Well, not all men prefer the Second Sex, you know!"

That made my new friend smile; I must have hit the nail on the head.

We were forever referring to *Le Deuxième Sexe*, Simone de Beauvoir's book that I had recently devoured. It brilliantly explained the role of women in our society, I thought, and the difficulties they have simply being. "If *Maman* could see me now," I kept thinking as I read. She would have chucked it into the fire. And she wouldn't have had much time for Pierre, not with those flowing, curly, black locks, flamboyant scarves, and beautiful silver rings on each finger.

Though Manuela never raised her voice, she seemed to be a figure of authority in her little group of friends, wreathed in a sort of halo. One morning, sitting in our favorite bistro, *café crème* in hand, she explained: "You know, I love the cinema of my country, and I am a very good friend with a journalist from Roma who is close to Fellini. I am sure that you have heard of him, no?" She didn't bother to wait for an answer. "When I arrived here, Luigi, an Italian friend, put me in contact with Georges, the cinema critic for the radio program on Paris-Inter called *Le Masque et la Plume*. You see?"

"No, I don't see at all."

"*Le Masque et la Plume*, Thursdays at ten o'clock in the evening? No?"

I loved Manuela's way of speaking. Every sentence was a mini-interrogation. I was still none the wiser about this program of hers. I can't say I listened to the radio much in England, never mind in France.

"Okay, I tell you. George asked me to help him to prepare this program. I contact people, I read the Italian press, and I invite the critics from my country. It's super fun. If you want, I will take you one day."

"And is Langues O' just for fun, too?"

"Ah, that is different. It is to cultivate my political sense!"

What I loved about Manuela was that you couldn't always tell if she was joking.

In a matter of months, I too was rubbing shoulders with left-wing intellectuals. They pricked up their ears when we talked about our Chinese studies. We sat at tables overlooking the Church of Saint-Germain, and the conversations really motored along.

"China! Now there's a country ahead of its time…you are so lucky to be studying Mandarin," Pierre pronounced one day after his third coffee.

"A hundred thousand communists died in the Long March of 1934, never mind all the others! Is that a country ahead of its time?" I replied.

"Whatever it takes to bring about the revolution."

"Deng Xiaoping is launching the most extraordinary political experiment of all time. The Great Leap Forward will revolutionize China's industries, and make it a match for Britain," Pierre said.

"You seem very well informed."

"Well, I'm passionate about it. When Mao launched the Hundred Flowers Campaign in June '57, and then denounced those who took part, I too questioned him. But with the Great Leap Forward, steel production has gone through the roof. Mao did well to get free of the Soviets, if you ask me."

Pierre's enthusiasm was, perhaps, unsurprising: he was taking his lead from France's infatuated intellectual elite who, disappointed by the USSR and Stalin, began to revere China. It made a good impression to say you were a Maoist. Manuela and I caught the bug, too, perhaps because our studies put us at the heart of such discussions. People often asked our opinion. At first, I was flattered. Then, I began to get more and more interested for my own sake.

From time to time, I went with Manuela to the Récamier theater to see the recordings of *Le Masque et la Plume*. I would find a spot right in the middle of the audience. I loved meeting the young critics who bad-mouthed the studios, but praised the Nouvelle Vague to the skies. I realized, listening to them, that the gulf between the generations was getting wider and wider all the time. Once or twice, I asked a question of the guest directors .

Manuela used one of my contributions to bring me to the attention of the show's producers, and asked if I could become a member of the team.

"Kim is English! She could be responsible for the British and American press, discover some good critics, make contact with directors...do *my* job, but in English, no?"

Thanks to her enthusiasm, I was taken on there and then. It was a huge commitment, but it supplemented what I earned tutoring, and, thankfully, Langues O' was not too demanding as universities go. I aimed high, and tried to bring Alfred Hitchcock over for the program. He was the favorite director of François Truffaut, a young filmmaker and critic we knew. I didn't quite manage that, but the experience I picked up working for the radio would prove decisive in a different way.

Summer came around. I spent July working. So did Manuela. I couldn't wait to see Charles and Edward, who were coming to spend two weeks with us. We had found them a little hotel which didn't cost the moon.

The boys had become close since I left. Sometimes, I'd catch myself thinking of them both as my brothers. They knew Paris already, but were delighted when Manuela and I took them to all our favorite haunts. In the evenings, they took us out to jazz clubs: *Le Caveau de la Montagne*, perhaps, or *Le Chat Qui Pêche* or *Le Blue Note* – we heard all they had to offer. By the end of the first week, I was having trouble keeping up, what with my workload. However, I saw clearly that my brother couldn't take his eyes of Manuela for one second. He always found some pretext to sit next to her. One evening, before going out, the two of us found ourselves alone, waiting for the others.

"Manuela is fantastic," Charles began.

"She's a friend of mine, what did you expect? Don't think I haven't noticed what's going on."

"Is it that obvious?"

"…that you like her? Uh, remind me, is the pope Catholic?"

Two days later, it was Manuela's turn to confide in me.

"He's very nice, your brother, but I have told him that I'm not ready. That I need some time."

This surprised me. "Not ready? Why?"

She wouldn't say, and I didn't push it.

At the end of July, once I'd finished tutoring, Charles, Edward, and I bundled onto a train bound for Brittany and Mansfield Manor. Manuela had to stay in Paris to show some cousins around.

For the whole of August, it was trips to St. Malo, strolls on the beach, and regattas. The three of us, each in our own sail boat, lined up against Uncle Oliver. We learned an important lesson: never underestimate an old seadog who has circumnavigated the globe solo. In the evenings, we played cards. It was the first time Uncle Oliver had met Edward, and he hadn't seen my brother for a good while. Hearing him talk to the two young men was fun.

"At your age, I'd already been through Sandhurst," he said to my brother, who had just announced that he had finished his law degree.

"You went to Sandhurst?"

"Yup, I was Captain when I came out. But it didn't stop me from turning my attention to other things."

"And would you say that what you do now is your passion?" asked Edward politely.

"I always say, nothing beats being yourself."

That response made Edward blush. "Doesn't seem so easy for me," he replied.

"You have to leave your fears behind, and tell yourself that what you do has worth. And to see you at the helm of a sailboat, I've no doubt it has." That was high praise indeed coming from Uncle Oliver, and Edward knew it. I saw him smile.

At the end of our stay, all three were in fine spirits.

"Your uncle is wonderful. You're like him. Do people always tell you that?" asked Edward.

"Yes, they do."

"You should be proud of that."

"I am!"

By the end of August, I was back in Paris, and the boys had returned to London. I had barely arrived when I decided to rush over to Rue de l'Université. That was where Manuela lived, at her Aunt Isabella's house. I couldn't wait to see my friend and tell her all about my holiday. I climbed the stairs of the sizable Parisian residence and knocked at her bedroom door. I found Manuela flat out on her bed, in tears. Sitting down beside her, I gently asked her why she was crying. She just shook her head. I could see there was no point insisting; she wasn't going to tell me. There was only one solution: take her mind off of it. I began telling her about Dinard, about Charles, Edward, and Uncle Oliver, and then, the funny thing was, I found myself confiding in *her*. I talked about Alicia: our friendship, her terrible death, and the trial. It should have been the other way around! I should have been consoling Manuela, but instead, she generously listened to my stories.

Still, it worked, in a way; she was calmer now. When I'd said all there was to say, she leapt to her feet, full of energy.

"Why not go to your place? We could prepare a little something to eat? You have everything we need, no?"

Well, no, actually. So, having pilfered her aunt's fridge, we set off for the Rue du Dragon loaded with goodies.

# CHAPTER 2

# Photo of Manuela and Me

Manuela sat opposite me, leaning against my huge macramé cushion pushed up against the wall. I mirrored her, sitting cross-legged on my bed. Over her shoulder, I could see the photos Pierre had taken of us that I'd pinned up. We had just finished supper. I could tell, at last, that my friend had something to say.

"I grew up in a big villa just outside Palermo," she began quietly, "protected by my brother and armed guards, who were everywhere. All that seemed natural to me, can you imagine it? I started to ask questions much later, when I was eighteen. My mother looked after me all of the time, trying always to educate me as best she could, you understand? I had a tutor at home who taught my brother and me. And a Frenchman came to give us conversation classes every day. And an English girl taught us…how do you say it? Ah yes, comportment. When I think of it, it is funny, no? Or unusual. A bit oppressive too…."

"Have you only got a brother?"

"One brother, Santino. He is four years older than me. I had another, Fabrizio, whom I never knew. He died from an illness before

I was born; he was two and a half. After me, my mother could not have more children. You know, in our families, it is not normal to have so few. I have many, many uncles and aunts!"

"Like your Aunt Isabella."

"Oh, no, not all my aunts are kind like her. Except for the Abbess Benedetta. It is thanks to her that I got out." She suddenly seemed overwhelmed by her memories. "I don't know if I will be able to tell you everything," she sighed.

I smiled broadly at her, aware that if I didn't tread carefully, we wouldn't get very far. "Try."

"It all started because we used to go on holidays at Easter to Roma, to my Uncle Francesco's house, the brother of my father. Every year, we went to be blessed by the Pope, an Italian tradition. My aunt and my uncle own a big house on the Aventine Hill. Do you know where I mean?"

"Yes, vaguely."

"The Aventine is one of the seven hills of Roma, to the south. In Roman times, it was the popular quarter, and nowadays, it has become the kind of elegant residential place that my family likes. Francesco's house is almost at the top of the hill, on the corner of Strada San Anselmo and Strada Lavernale. It is a residential district, a lot of air, where I feel good always…I am talking and talking, no?"

"No!"

"Three years ago, I am at my aunt Isabella's. I am eighteen. My cousin Emilio is there. He is my brother's best friend, they are the same age, and they adore each other. Emilio is a friend of important artists. When we go to his house, we have fun, we go out; and since I am protected by my brother and my cousin, no one says nothing. Except that my two guardian angels are more interested in looking after other girls than checking on me. That is how I meet Filippo Lippi, a friend of my cousin who spends time in the Via Veneto with the artists and cineastes."

"He's called Filippo Lippi? Like the painter?"

"Yes, incredible, no? His parents are artists, and they could think of no better name for their boy. I suppose they wanted to make him a famous painter…in reality, he became a journalist for *Il Messagero*, the finest newspaper in Roma, where he is in charge of the culture pages. He is very handsome, with incredible eyes, like they are transparent, a bit green, a bit blue, and sometimes brown – it depends on the light. He is ten years older than me. I fell in love with him."

"Do you still see him?"

"You've probably guessed that I don't. I loved him so much…he taught me so many things. It is thanks to him that I at last understood society for what it is. And in particular where I came from. He gave me books to read, asked me to read articles he was writing, to participate in art exhibitions. Thanks to him, I was there when they filmed the scene by the Trevi Fountain in *La Dolce Vita*. I actually had lunch on-set with Mastroianni and all the team."

"You lucky thing! I would love to meet him."

"Before Filippo, I was really naïve. A country girl from the south who had lived in a dangerous world, but a protected world, too. He was born in the capital, at the heart of all that was happening, even if it was Roma and not Milano…I owe him everything, you cannot imagine…." Manuela paused for a while. Her eyes glistened. "We used to meet up in a tiny hotel on the lower side of my quarter. The owner of the hotel was Filippo's friend, and we met there six or seven times during the Easter holidays. During the year, we wrote to each other a little. But I dreamed of him all the time, and I read all the books he recommended in secret, as they were forbidden in my family."

"Did you brother and your cousin figure out what was going on between you?"

"Never. We didn't stay long at the hotel. We were lucky, I suppose. Or rather, we were unlucky."

"Why do you say that?"

"Because the second Easter, I became pregnant. I was nineteen. I realized when I was back home in Palermo. I talked to my mother about it straightaway. She asked me all sorts of questions. Did I love him? His age. His family. The more she asked, the more she grimaced. 'A family of artists, a man ten years older than you, an anarchist journalist? Your papa won't like this,' she said to me. 'He's not married, is he, don't tell me that?'

'Of course not!'

'You say he is Emilio's friend, he is also perhaps your brother's friend. I will ask him.'

'But Mama!'

'I have no choice, my darling.'

Through Santino, and via my mother, I learned the next day that not only was Filippo married, but he had a little daughter. Hearing that, I could not utter a sound. As if I lost my voice. I only had one wish, to hide myself in a hole and die there. When I recovered from the shock, my mother told me that she had arranged everything with Tanta Benedetta. She welcomed me in the abbey. My father did not say a word to me. Even at the moment I had to leave, he refused to see me. I moved to the convent situated near to Cefalu. My aunt Benedetta received me very well."

"Did you stay there long?"

"A bit more than seven months. Until the birth. I lived in a little cell, you know, without anything, really, but I felt safe there. I saw my mother once a week. She would stay two or three hours, give me news, bring me things. She was careful with my father, telling him the truth, but in very small doses, claiming not to know the name of my lover. She made my brother agree to stay silent. That way, Filippo's life was not in immediate danger.

"As for my aunt, every day she asked me if I wanted to walk in the convent gardens. That and reading were all I did. Despite all her duties, she always found time for me. She gave it with all her heart. I profited from that. Under her guidance, I rediscovered the faith I had held as I child. She gave me precise passages to read from the scriptures, she urged me to participate in prayers. In some way, she prepared me for what was going to happen."

"You mean...?"

"When my son was born...Little Roberto. It was six months ago, the 10th of September, 1961." Manuela stopped short. Her eyes filled with tears. "He took eight hours to come," she continued, bravely.

"There was a midwife, Sister Térésina, and my mother. Can you believe it, Kim? I didn't have time to see him, or to hold him in my arms."

"What happened?"

"My mother had organized everything again. She thought that I must not become attached, so he was taken from me as soon as he came out. It was planned that he would be brought up by another family on the other side of Sicilia, but I hadn't known that we would never see each other again…it's like someone had opened me in two, torn out my stomach, emptied my insides. You understand?"

I went to my friend. She fell into my arms. Her sobbing was so painful. I held her, tried to whisper kind words in her ear.

After a long silence, I asked. "So, why Paris? Why Langues O'?"

"To forget. When I arrived in Paris, I understood that they had put me in a golden cage, you know? That I would never survive unless I kept myself very occupied. Mama had taken me out of the convent at night. Once again, all was planned without me. I was exhausted, depressed, it was only three weeks after the birth of Roberto. On my second day in Paris, I met Georges, the cinema critic. It was thanks to Aunt Isabella, who always has guests at her house. Again, I quickly understood that the radio, *Le Masque et la Plume*, would not be enough to distract me from my black thoughts, so I asked myself, 'What is really hard to learn, complicated, different?' The answer came all by itself, when I was walking in the Rue de Lille and I went past Langues O'. I thought that Chinese would probably mobilize me the most."

"If you'd chosen Swahili, we would never have met," I said. And at long last, Manuela smiled a little through her tears.

# CHAPTER 3

# Official Letter from the People's Republic of China

October, 1962.

There were only forty-six students in the second year of Langues O', since only those who passed the first-year exams were invited back. My favorite class was *Civilization of Ancient Imperial China Before the Fall of the Ming Dynasty*, with Madame Vandier-Nicolas. I was in my element, and swamped Manuela with references, books to read, and stories. All the while, we continued to talk Mao and *communisme* à *la chinoise* with our friends at Les Deux Magots.

∽

I continued to tutor Françoise Lestrange. We got on well together. From time to time, I bumped into her father in the Boulevard Saint-Germain. Sometimes, we chatted about what I had learned recently, ideas I had or notions that were bothering me. He told me how Chinese industry was prospering, even in the rural areas – where, under the guidance of "the Great Helmsman," peasants were working in small-scale factories. China was set to become a great industrial nation. His eyes lit up when he spoke. Gradually, I began to feel more confident in his presence. I told him about my dream to go and live in China for a few years.

Shortly before Christmas, I received a letter from my father. It appeared my mother had gotten over my "treachery" during the Cunningham trial and the ensuing silence. "It would be a good idea to come home for Christmas. I'll pay for your flight," he wrote.

Children, I would later realize, carry on in the vain hope that their parents will one day love them as they hope to be loved. My heart leapt at the prospect of us burying the hatchet.

My parents' initial reception was warm. After two pleasant-enough days – being reunited with my brother and at home in Belgrave Square gave me the most pleasure – mother-daughter relations turned decidedly choppy again, specifically on the subject of my new life: my friends, my politics, and the radio show. Sadly, dinners descended into fights.

"First an impassioned defender of justice, and now a Maoist!" pronounced my mother. "What are we going to do with you?"

"I'm not asking you for anything."

"All the same, it's thanks to us you're studying at Langues O', don't forget that," said my father, with a little more moderation.

"But I'm paying for everything else!"

"I should think so, too, considering what it cost us to set you up in Paris," my mother sniped.

"Anyway, I won't be there forever!" I replied.

"Oh, really? Where will you be going?"

"To China."

"Ah, well, we won't stand in your way…."

"Sarah, you can't say that," my father intervened. "Conditions in China are abominable. The reports that land on my desk are extremely bleak."

"We obviously don't have the same sources!" I retorted, flaunting my pristine political opinions.

There was no point talking about it, really; they were always in the right, no matter what. My parents left the table to get on with their evening, and I was left alone with Charles. He had a more practical approach to the issue at hand.

"How will you get there?"

"I don't know."

"You're not going to ask Dad for help, are you?"

"Certainly not. I can manage on my own."

"If I can lend you a hand, I will," he promised.

Back in France, galvanized by the conversation with my family, I sought my teachers' advice.

They tried to put me off, too. "Do you know how many foreigners are living in China at the moment?"

"No, but…."

"Not more than three hundred."

Despite my recently-acquired convictions, I refused to join the Communist Party, as several of my friends had. I didn't want to be a member of any party; I wanted to discover a nation. But I didn't want to go as a tourist (not that China was amenable to such decadent activities anyway). I wanted to live there, not pass through.

"I don't think you would last long as an illegal immigrant," Manuela gently mocked, aware of how the matter was preoccupying me.

All paths seemed lost. Life carried on – until April 1, 1963, when I rang the bell at the Lestrange house and the monsieur himself came to the door.

"Kimberly! The very girl!" He was the only person who called me that, and it always made me laugh. "What would you say to a trip to China?"

"What?" I ran over, tripped on the edge of the carpet, and nearly fell flat on my face.

"Careful! Don't injure yourself. You're needed," he laughed.

"A trip to China? What do you mean?"

I must have looked so stunned that he decided to tell me there and then. "Françoise will just have to wait. Come into my study."

What he explained seemed too good to be true. Apparently, the Chinese government wanted to bring young westerners over to China to help spread the word of the Revolution around the world. They called upon the nation's "trusted friends" to make this happen. Monsieur Lestrange, as an established trading partner, was one of the chosen few. He had been expressly asked to recruit young people in his country.

I couldn't get over it! The government would be ready to put me up, pay me, feed me, and provide the necessary paperwork. "In exchange for what?"

"Ah, well, young lady, now that you're asking...."

"But how can I go without knowing what I'll be doing when I get there?"

"Do you really want to go? Are you really a Maoist?"

"It's my dream." I was careful not to answer his second question, but he knew perfectly well that I wasn't a member of any party and that I wasn't passionate about ideology, even if I was sympathetic to what was happening in China.

"Then go. And don't ask too many questions. Look, you'll be fine. I won't be far away."

When I got home later that evening, I was bouncing up and down with excitement. Manuela was waiting for me outside my door, distraught.

"My father says I can't go back to Italy this summer."

"Why not?"

"Some of the families have been fighting, and people have died. My father has imposed maximum security."

"Really?"

"Yes. Mama told me about it. No one is allowed to leave the villa."

"Gosh. I'm sorry. But I have some unbelievable news that may cheer you up: Monsieur Lestrange has told me about a way of getting to China!"

Quick as a flash, Manuela said, "I'm coming with you!"

Two weeks later, with Manuela's father's blessing, we had our first interview with Monsieur Lestrange's Chinese contacts. But that was just the start…the process soon felt endless. We were always received in a different office by a different Chinese official, each more senior than the last. The hierarchy seemed fiendishly complicated to me, but in fact, it was just a pyramid, albeit a big one.

After a few weeks, we felt as though we had turned into mechanical interviewees. They would ask us about our motivation, our background, our interests. We had fun guessing what the next interviewer would ask. Sibling's favorite color, maybe? And with each and every official, we had to go back to the beginning again. Why? Couldn't they have passed the information on to one another? We were coming up against a Chinese characteristic that I would get to know all too well.

I began to have my doubts. What if Monsieur Lestrange had been fed propaganda from the start? What if they didn't want us in their country after all?

Eventually, we were interviewed by the highest-ranking official in the Chinese Press Bureau in France, who expressed interest in our radio experience. We left the meeting and went straight to Les Deux Magots to buy a glass of wine in honor of our imminent victory. Our friend Pierre, the photographer, could not get over how lucky we were.

"You're going to the country where everything is possible! To the heart of the biggest revolution of all time. I predict we won't see you back here any time soon."

The solemn tone with which he pronounced these words made us cackle like a couple of geese. I looked straight at Manuela, glass in hand.

"Here's hoping! Will you drink to that?"

After a nerve-racking wait, we finally received a typed letter in French, adorned with the Chinese authorities' official stamp: we had been summoned to appear before a committee.

After the usual preliminaries, the chairman asked us, "Do you still want to go?"

"More than ever!" we replied with one voice.

"So be it, and the sooner the better. In two months."

We turned to each other, elated. We would be in China by the end of September.

Just as Uncle Oliver predicted, I came to realize that in the Middle Kingdom, no matter how long preliminaries drag on, once the leaders have given the go-ahead, obstacles fall away. We weren't used to that in the West.

I called my parents, and a member of the household staff answered. My mother and father had gone on holiday. I ran to the Lestranges' house to thank them. Manuela joined us, and we celebrated with a top-notch supper washed down with a distinctively-named Bordeaux: Mouton Rothschild.

∽

Vittorio stands up and stretches. "Leo, how long have you known Marsie?" he asks.

"We met in Hong Kong...."

"Not yet, Leo," I chide. "We have a little ways to go before we get there..."

# CHAPTER 4

# A Sapphire

September, 1963.

I would have loved for Edward to see me off, but London was too far away, and he had to look after his mother. Kate Cunningham was still too fragile to live without help, though she seemed over the worst. She had just been moved from a hospital to a convalescent home. Edward dreamed of living with her permanently, as soon as he had finished his architectural training. Charles had flown off to the United States for an internship with a big law firm. I hadn't asked my parents to see me off, for obvious reasons. As for Uncle Oliver, it was impossible to get a hold of him. "Voyage. Woman. Far away," said Ray, his Indian butler, before asking me a serious of questions about my plans. I was surprised, because I thought Uncle Oliver was already back from Burma. He wouldn't have gone off again without telling me, would he?

That left Isabella, Manuela's beloved aunt, to accompany us to the airport. What to do with the two-hour wait before boarding? While Manuela and her aunt were engrossed in conversation, I went to find a book for the journey. It was a chance to browse in the airport's brand-new shops. I had a spring in my step; the world was at my feet.

The literature section was poorly stocked. I was flipping through a few titles when a little tap on my shoulder made me jump.

"Uncle Oliver!," I yelled.

"My darling. Couldn't very well let you go without saying goodbye, now, could I?"

I wrapped myself up in his arms, and smelled the familiar smell of one of his many aftershaves, all variations of musk and vetiver. I have adored those fragrances my whole life.

"How did you manage it?"

"I have my spies…." So that explained my funny conversation with Ray! And all his "innocent" questions. "It wasn't just him. Your friend Manuela is a peach!"

"Since when do you know her?"

"Since last week when we spoke on the telephone." Across the terminal, I could see both women laughing at me. Manuela waved.

Uncle Oliver and I sat down in the airport's only restaurant.

"Haven't you just gotten back from Burma?"

"You know, I feel at home over there. It's a bit like India."

"Is it?"

"If I hadn't been born in Delhi, perhaps I'd never have become a seasoned hunter of precious stones."

"Weren't you supposed to head off again?"

"I was supposed to, but I wanted to be here with you. I'll miss you."

It was nearly time to say goodbye. There was a distinct tension in the air. Uncle Oliver reached into his pocket, took out a small velvet pouch, and placed it on the table.

"Look what I brought you from Burma," he said. Peeling back the tissue paper, I found a quite magnificent blue stone. "It's a sapphire, fashioned into an oval. It's pure. I wanted you to start a stone collection of your own. This first one is a gift."

"What an amazing color…." I was moved, and a little taken aback.

First call for our flight. We got up. I hugged him and headed off toward customs, without looking back.

Gazing out of the window of the Air France plane, the emotion caught up with me suddenly. My thoughts were a blur: leaving Europe; leaving like this; Alicia, who had so dreamed of going with me; my parents I hadn't said goodbye to…I took Felix out of my handbag. Manuela reached over, took the rabbit's paw, and gave it a kiss. The world seemed less confusing sitting next to a kind friend.

The first stopover was Moscow. The atmosphere was wretched: total mistrust because we were bound for China. You could tell relations between the two nations were frosty. From a European perspective, the coolness between two former "brothers in arms" was baffling. At the airport, the Russian authorities temporarily confiscated our passports, and made us wade through red tape: endless lines, several hours locked in a small room.

The second leg of the journey: Clouds. Sun. Then land. I started to appreciate the distances that separate countries. Looking out the window for hours on end, I saw thousands of miles of steppe under a flawless sun. To refuel, we landed at Irkutsk Airport, a wooden hangar on the furthest edge of the taiga. It seemed so rugged and scruffy. What was I doing so far away? What was waiting for us at the other end of this epic journey?

At last, the airplane began its descent into Peking, as it was known then.

The contrast was striking. From the runway, the little airport seemed spotless compared with the Soviet buildings, though it was tiny for such a big country. We stepped from the cabin and noticed the red carpet. A shiny brass band welcomed us with fanfare and the national anthem. At the foot of the steps, a Chinese official came toward us, bowing his head slightly. He was accompanied by an interpreter. "Well, we don't need *her!*" I thought. When the official started to speak, Manuela and I just looked at each other. We still had a lot to learn.

The gentleman introduced himself as a representative from Radio Peking, the organization we would be working for. He announced this as if it were the most obvious thing in the world. It was news to us! I stood there wondering why on earth they were offering us work there, then realized: Manuela's know-how for all things radiophonic was worth two Chinese visas. I owed her a great deal. I was burning with curiosity, but could see this wasn't the time to ask questions.

Behind the official, there was a little delegation waiting to greet us. Two women and a man. Europeans. Our passports were whisked out of our hands and placed in a secretary's attaché case. The secretary marched off with them. That was a little disconcerting: would we ever see them again? No time to think about it. We were bundled into a state car, the only ones with permission to go on the roads, the interpreter explained. "Otherwise, it's buses or bicycles."

On the way to the hotel, I saw the streets of Peking for the very first time out of the window of the car. Tight crowds of people lined the paths on either side of the large avenues or biked on the asphalt, and hundreds of horse-drawn carts were being driven by rural laborers. Never having traveled outside Europe, I had not been able to visualize the sheer density of the Asian population, even though Uncle Oliver had told me. Our welcoming party was in a second car following behind us. At one point, we had to slow down because of a caravan of Mongolian camels! Anyone would think we were in the desert. They were delivering coal in vast jute sacks, the interpreter explained.

I was sitting comfortably in the back of the car, flanked by Manuela and the man whom we took to be our boss, a little round guy with glasses. The interpreter – she was Chinese, with an odd metallic voice, and strangely ageless appearance– sat in the front. I had to admit I was finding it all pretty intimidating. Luckily, the man was very chatty, though careful to give nothing personal away. It's a precaution virtually all Chinese people adopt, as I found out in due course.

"You will see, the Friendship Hotel is a very agreeable place where you will find everything you could possibly need," he explained. "You will be put up there for the duration of your stay, which we trust will be long and fruitful. It was especially built to accommodate foreign residents in our capital, so you will live among your compatriots and members of other represented nations. Outside of the compound – I was astonished to hear him say that word in English –you can use coupons to buy whatever you require. As can we all. President Mao leaves none of us by the wayside."

I nodded. His speech surprised me.

Silence set in. To break it, I asked: "Is it called the Friendship Hotel because the Russians built it?"

The official stiffened as if I had just pricked him with a pin. He replied enigmatically. The interpreter offered a diplomatic translation: "No, it was the Germans who presided over its construction, but the architect was Chinese. It was entirely conceived by Master Lang Sicheng. He studied in imperialist America, but returned to serve his country. The Party has charged him with modernizing our national architecture."

I had yet to learn that the USSR was as taboo in China, as China was in the USSR.

The car began to slow down. We had arrived. In front of us, on either side of the road, I saw gardens designed to complement the hotel. Baishi Qiao Avenue – the Bridge of White Stones – was one of the wide arteries flowing in and out of the city, lined with leafy trees. The car pulled into the driveway, and stopped in front of a sentry-box with a barrier manned by two uniformed guards.

"You can get in and out by showing this," the interpreter said, handing me a card. "Keep it with you at all times."

"This procedure guarantees your safety," our host added. Our car continued to the main entrance and came to a halt.

The hotel seemed like more of a fortress. A city within a city. I was astonished by the square buildings and pagoda-style roofs, the ornate masonry of the balconies, the colorful ceramic tiles that adorned the walls; and impressed by the beautifully landscaped gardens and ornately carved red wooden doors.

At the reception, our boss (if he *was* our boss) and the interpreter helped us get properly registered. Everyone was bustling about, and a sensation of unfamiliarity overwhelmed me; I had been parachuted into a world where I did not know the social codes. What I had learned at Langues O' now seemed laughably insufficient. Would I be able to adapt? Would I be successful in this mysterious new job?

My musings were cut short by the interpreter's voice.

"A car will come to fetch you at eighteen-hundred hours tomorrow and take you to the Radio Peking facility," the interpreter said.

"Don't you need us before then?"

"You will not be working this evening, due to the time difference. Now, with your permission, I will take my leave. Welcome to China, *Mesdemoiselles.* See you tomorrow." With that, at last, she smiled;

and still, no one had told us what our future work consisted of.

We stayed rooted to the spot, rather awkwardly, with our four large suitcases, at the reception of this strange hotel. Then someone grabbed my arm and began leading me along. I recognized her as a member of the European welcoming party.

"I'll introduce myself again. Hélène Mirande. Shall we?"

My apartment and Manuela's were both located at the rear of the building, on the fifth and highest floor. I climbed the poorly-lit staircase – there were no elevators – and, turning the key I had been issued, entered a quiet and clean space. The window led out onto a stone balcony, exactly like those I had seen from the road. Manuela had the same instinct as me, and was now standing on the next balcony along. We laughed.

My quarters were certainly far more spacious that my studio in the Rue du Dragon. I had a bathroom, a small kitchen, a mini dining room, and a bedroom. The furniture was all wooden and of good quality, and the bed seemed comfortable. There was nothing beyond the bare essentials, but I would soon fix that. I hadn't expected such high standards, and I got really excited by the place, jet lag or not.

However, managing to ignore Hélène Mirande required more energy than I could muster. She swanned about opening cupboards, turning on taps, showing me light switches and sockets, explaining, in a never-ending torrent of words, the disadvantages of buying one's food at the shop attached to the hotel dining room: "It's much cheaper in town." She told me where to rent a bike, where to catch a bus, where to take our clothes to be washed. The sheer volume of words made my head spin. I soon had only one wish: to lie down and rest.

Before long, the neighbors arrived. There followed a half-hour of introductions, chit-chat, and to-ing-and-fro-ing from my apartment to Manuela's. It was like being back at one of the houses in Cheltenham Ladies College. "We're just missing Miss Bonham!" I said to myself as I unpacked under the watchful eye of Hélène.

Despite her fitted, thick cotton dress, pumps, and "I'm-frightfully-busy" air, she was, somehow, washed out, a tapestry left too long in the sun. Her thundering voice and generous proportions made me think of Bianca Castafiore, the exuberant Italian opera singer in one of the *Tintin* albums.

"Tell you what," – she was off again – "why don't we meet tomorrow morning in the hotel restaurant? I'll show you the shops I was telling you about, and then we'll go and see Tiananmen Square. It's being done up for the national holiday. Then we'll go to the Temple of Heaven – it's breathtakingly beautiful, you'll see. As you're only working in the evenings, you'll have plenty of free time."

Finally, praise be, she skipped away with a knowing smile, not even waiting for my response. I was staggered: how did she know what hours we would be working? Apparently, she was better informed about my life than I was. One thing was clear: news traveled fast in this part of the world.

Whoosh. Fatigue and jet lag hit me, and my legs went shaky. Night had fallen. I switched on the bedside lamp, had a quick shower, and without further ado, slipped into bed. I was wearing the Burmese pajamas that Uncle Oliver must have slipped into my suitcase before I left. Another one of his surprises.

I was asleep before my head hit the pillow. No dreams that night.

## CHAPTER 5

# Letter to Charles and Edward

*Peking, November 1ˢᵗ, 1963.*

*First off, I'm so sorry for not writing sooner. You're stuck with a marathon letter now – my punishment and yours!*

*I know you chaps don't share my enthusiasm for the Revolution, but I'm sure you would be impressed by the people here. And astonished at how they smile at us in the street and stare as though they've never seen a foreigner before. Before the Revolution, they could stroll in the area around the Legate's residence, to the east of Tiananmen Square, and meet whole families of Westerners with big blue eyes and white skin. Today, apparently, there are barely three hundred of us "foreign experts" living in the whole country, and perhaps about a hundred in our thousand-year-old city. A lot less now than before the Revolution, I gather.*

*Five or six years ago, the city was walled on all sides, with watchtowers here and there (still standing, I'm happy to report) and surrounded by a trench that was fifty yards wide in places. The real development of Peking started with the building of the Imperial Palace – also known as the Forbidden City, because anyone caught looking up at the walls was supposedly condemned to death. The city was a square with the palace in the center. Nothing changed from the 15th century to 1950. Then President Mao had all the ramparts torn down, built a boulevard right around the city, and expanded Tiananmen Square. Now, more people can assemble there. And that leads me to the Chinese themselves.*

*Sometimes, I get up early and go for a walk. From daybreak, dozens of men and women do* tai chi *in the parks and even in the street: a type of a slow, worshipful dance, unknown to us. Their limbs move, and yet somehow they seem rooted to the ground like trees. Their flowing movements and intense concentration seems to be in sympathy with some inner part of them that is so calm, it's as if nothing could disturb their balletic motion. I gaze at them for ages, until a peacefulness comes over me, too. It helps me start the day.*

*I've discovered a magnificent park at the foot of the Temple of Heaven, where the Chinese love to relax and play* mah-jong – *a game that looks like dominoes to me. It's extraordinary to rub shoulders with all these people outside, who are laughing and chatting together with real good humor. That's certainly one of the most tangible examples of how spectacularly living standards have improved, which I'm always commenting on during my radio program.*

*That's right: I've become an announcer and interpreter for Radio Peking! Every evening at around six, a car comes to fetch Manuela and me from the Friendship Hotel and takes us to the studio, a few miles away. We get home after midnight. We work nights, charged with conveying news of the Revolution's progress to French and English speak-*

ers in Africa, and encouraging them to follow us along our new path. The programs are recorded late in the evening and broadcast at night, which is daytime in Africa. We tell them about the abundant harvests, President Mao's speeches, visits from foreign leaders – Albanians, for example, there are lots of them here. And we talk about the falling-out with the Soviet Union, whose leaders are referred to as "traitors" throughout the communiqué. If I'm honest, I don't entirely buy that.

Before I left, you both told me you wanted to know <u>everything</u>, so here goes. The smell in the street is often atrocious. Firstly, there's the human excrement that needs to be gathered to fertilize soil in the country. It's collected up in gigantic wooden buckets without lids (!) that are piled onto the back of horse-drawn carts and taken out to the farms. Imagine the stink....

Recently, I've identified another smell: the coal used to heat the whole city. The poor use coal dust to heat their stoves, and the acrid odor is everywhere – as well as a thick layer of soot, which you can't see, but you find all over your skin every time you wash.

To top it all off, for the past few days, the very distinctive smell of Peking cabbage has been added to the mix. They arrive by the thousands, and piles of them dominate whole streets and avenues in the city. They're transported by cart, too. People line up to get enough to stockpile at home over the winter.

I've been told that's virtually all they eat, and that each family has more than a hundred pounds' worth in weight. It's not like that for us foreigners – we have much more choice (I've fallen in love with a kind of dumpling made with thin dough, filled with meat or vegetables and served hot), and the restaurants in the city are excellent, and as varied as the country's many provinces. *Actually, I fear the tremendous har-vests I talk about on the radio aren't as substantial as we claim, because the Chinese all seem a bit on the thin side. I've heard it's even worse in the country.*

*When I see the way people live here, I'm torn. Let's just say that every day, I discover new facts that dampen my hopes and my enthusi-astic first impressions. Isn't that always what happens when we become infatuated with something, or someone? No doubt I'll have plenty more to say on that score in my next letter.*

*Let me have your news FAST.*

*Love and kisses,*

*Kim*

*P.S. Edward, how's your mom? And architect training?*

*P.P.S. In case you're wondering about the postmark, I'm entrusting this letter to an English girl who is returning home.*

# CHAPTER 6

# Clipping from the *People's Daily*

After a while, Manuela and I decided to share an apartment. Life was much more fun together.

We got up earlier than usual one Monday morning, and I suggested that we go and wander around the antique-dealers' shops. "I'm sure we'll find some things to make our place a little classier."

"Great idea," Manuela agreed. "You know, in Palermo, I was never allowed to walk the streets or wander around the shops by myself."

"You can make up for it here. 'Dear old Castafiore,'"—as I had taken to calling the operatic Hélène Mirande—"told me where to find the antique dealers. We could go today, if you like."

"But all the shops are run by the state, no?"

"Not these. They claim to be reformed 'capitalists,' but I'm sure they can work miracles."

We went down to have breakfast in the Friendship Hotel's giant dining room: vegetable soup, a bit of rice, and a hundred-year egg garnished with a handful of chives. It went down well with some oolong tea. At about eleven, we got on our bicycles and set off on an impressive ride along Peking's boulevards. Our enthusiasm made for great pedal power.

We arrived in a section of the city that was a mesh of *hutongs* (little streets). Some of them were only just wide enough for a rickshaw to go down. The *hutongs* were lined with grey-brick walls. Behind them were the traditional *sanheyuan* dwellings: we could see the roofs poking over the top. Periodically, we walked past red gates in the gray walls. One had been left open, and we caught a glimpse of a different word: coal briquettes piled high, bikes everywhere, pots of all shapes and sizes, and padlocked letterboxes to one side. We tried to get a glimpse inside the house, but couldn't see past a screen that seemed to be blocking the doorway.

"I've heard about them: it's to ward off evil spirits," I said to Manuela. "Evil forces can't get past the barrier and into people's homes, so they go back where they came from. It's one of the principles of *feng shui* that helps protect a home's positive energy."

We continued on our way. Giving free rein to our curiosity made for much meandering, and soon we had to admit that we were utterly lost. Those *hutongs* snaked this way and that like paths in a forest; we just couldn't get our bearings. The directions provided by the formidable "Castafiore" had long since ceased to be of any use. We stopped to ask directions from two men who were sitting on a doorstep playing chess. Despite the fact that the pair clearly wanted to be helpful, we had trouble understanding them. So on we went, more or less blindly.

Suddenly, we came out onto a wider street. By some considerable good fortune, we had ended up at the right place: there in front of us were shops and stalls selling antiques. We saw a window criss-crossed with tiny panes of glass. Delighted to have made it out of the labyrinth in one piece, and armed with our state coupons and our few *yuans*, we headed inside. The wooden window-frames were a real luxury in a city where most houses still made do with cardboard. An inexpressive *nihao* – *hello* in Chinese – greeted us as we came face to face with a pair of identical twins standing behind the counter. They could have been transported from some distant past, despite their Sun Yat Sen outfits – since renamed "Mao suits" – buttoned up all the way to the top. A dusty sparseness reigned in the shop; it looked as though the half-empty displays hadn't been touched for a hundred years. An ink stone here, blue-and-white vases there. In one corner of the room, a few items of mahogany furniture from who knows what period. On a table, there were scrolls of paper. Somehow, managing to be gentle and authoritative at the same time, Manuela asked if we might have a look at them.

An ancient-looking rice-paper scroll was unrolled for her. On it were etchings of the countryside, decorated with calligraphy. Manuela didn't look particularly interested. She asked to see some others. The twins obliged without saying a word. This game continued for a few minutes. Nothing seemed to hold Manuela's attention for long. I had a feeling the calligraphy was much too recent, and we foreigners were being taken for a ride.

"Come on," I said to her, "let's go somewhere else." She thanked them politely, and we made for the door.

"Wait," said one of the twins.

He seemed to hesitate for a moment, then he beckoned us to follow him, opening a small door hidden behind a curtain. We found ourselves in the back of the shop; perhaps it was the storeroom. We stood in the doorway and marveled at the jumble of items on display, a world away from the sparseness next door. There were heaps of even dustier items of furniture. One of the two dealers – was it the same one as before? – opened up a wardrobe in which a pile of scrolls was wedged between clay and porcelain objects. We were delighted; there was so much to look at!

That day, I left Zhang Brothers with two scrolls, and Manuela left with a 19th-century cloisonné vase under each arm. Owning works of calligraphy made me want to take lessons even more. The interest sparked in Cheltenham was getting keener with every day I spent in China.

Little expeditions into the world of antiques kept us busy for months. We got to know a dozen or so dealers, though we never said more than the few words necessary to make a purchase. Gradually, Manuela and I each assembled quite a collection of Chinese art. We had no clue as to what foreigners were "supposed" to be interested in, because we had known nothing of it before we arrived here. So, quite freely – according to our hearts' desires, you might say – we chose engraved seals, works of calligraphy, and mahogany furniture, some of which dated back to the Ming Dynasty (that's 1368 to 1644, since you ask). Anything and everything that took our fancy. We didn't think for a moment that some of the items we bought would become extremely valuable one day.

Our trips into the *hutongs* and our work weren't quite enough for me. I wanted to really get to know people, to make friends with the Chinese without them feeling the need to be overly polite or to regurgitate a party line. I began to appreciate the hours of obligatory "political education" less and less, in which we had to enthuse about Mao's thinking and say how we would *personally* apply that thinking in the course of the day ahead. Not to mention the official visits – from the President of Albania, for example – during which we had to wave flags in Tiananmen Square. I was shocked to discover, the first time, that we each had a designated place to stand, as indicated by a number painted on the ground.

The longer it went on, the more I realized that the gap between what I said into my microphone and what went on in real life was far wider than I had ever imagined. To the African listeners, I extolled the fabulous harvests that were the pride of the People's Republic of China. I talked about millions of tons of food; I proclaimed the irrefutable progress made in improving rural living standards; I flaunted the glorious steel-production statistics published in the *People's Daily*. At the same time, I saw carts pulled by emaciated horses, with men and women, who were scarcely better off, slumped on the straw. I also started to wonder about the cabbages piled up in the courtyards of the *sanheyuans*: would there be anything else to eat that winter in Peking?

One day, in the spring of 1964, while we were walking around the Lake of the Ten Monasteries, not far from the Forbidden City, Manuela and I asked some Belgian friends what was really going on. They dropped the pretense without much coaxing.

"I wondered when you'd ask," said Gabrielle.

"Do you realize this country has lived through a famine that we knew nothing about?" asked Paul, bleakly.

They had evidence to back this up, revelation after revelation. My image of the glory of socialist China took a hammering. It seemed that the figures for the 1959 harvest were rigged to conform with predictions, and that the tax-in-kind that the government demanded from the farmers in 1960 was nevertheless based upon those figures. That enormous burden, coupled with mediocre harvests the following year, meant that the peasants, unable to spend more time in the fields because they were engaged at the furnaces or the factories, got trapped in the terrible cycle of famine. The Great Leap Forward had already cost millions of lives, our friends explained.

This news really shook us, although we were left wondering how on earth our friends had obtained this information. Much later, I would come across staggering figures: more than eight million people had died of hunger in the province of Sichuan alone.

When summer came around, our *danwei* (work unit) suggested that we see a little of the country. That was fine by us. Perhaps we would meet some Chinese people we could really talk to.

"What would be your preferred destination?" asked Comrade Yu, who was our superior – and, we had recently learned, a rising star in the Party.

"Kim and I would like to go to Tibet," replied Manuela, timidly.

"Very good idea. We will investigate that possibility, and inform you of the outcome."

A few days later, Comrade Engineer Yu examined us over the rims of his spectacles. "We regret to inform that it is not possible to go to Tibet. The train service is extremely poor, and in addition, there were floods this winter, so the roads are in a pitiful state. Some of them are cut off. We would not want anything to happen to you."

"What about Inner Mongolia?" I asked.

After a second refusal just as convoluted as the first, we were summoned to Comrade Yu's office yet again. It was clear from the faces he made that we would never get permission to go to a destination we chose ourselves, particularly an autonomous province.

"What would you say to a visit to the Chinese Venice: Suzhou, the capital of Jiangsu Province?" he asked with a huge smile.

In early August, Manuela and I traveled to the Yang Tse Kiang delta, about sixty miles from Shanghai. Suzhou possessed some of the most beautiful gardens in the country, landscaped in the time of the Ming and Qing dynasties. They were destroyed by the Japanese in 1937, but nearly all had been restored in the fifties – as our very able guide, Mrs. Li, informed us in fluent English. She was given the job of chaperoning us and showing us such sights as the Humble Administrator's Garden. We admired the little stone bridges, mossy paths, clear streams, and strange rocks arranged in shapes that were supposed to represent the universe in miniature. We traveled the canals, visited abandoned temples, and tasted Suzhou meatballs and prawns cooked with tea shoots. Lastly, she took us to the city's famous silk factory. Not once during our stay did we talk to any ordinary Chinese people. Even Mrs. Li remained impervious to our attempts at conversation about personal matters.

Two weeks later, we returned to Peking. We went back to work, but our hearts weren't in it. Something had turned in me, in spite of our pleasant trip to Suzhou. Perhaps I had to face facts: I wasn't made for being a revolutionary. I decided to set about learning calligraphy, instead – at least while Manuela and I decided what to do next.

# CHAPTER 7

# Calligraphy Sample

"You must write a picture, not paint one."
—Zhuang Zi, *The True Painter*, 4<sup>th</sup> century BC

"Painting is a bourgeois art. And yet President Mao clearly stated, in 1952 at Yan'an, that art and literature must be made to serve the Revolution. Would you like to learn to paint? Would that allow you to continue along the path of socialism with serenity?" my superior, Engineer Yu, asked, sitting behind his desk.

I was standing, looking at him as neutrally as I knew how. Hopefully, he wouldn't realize that I was not in the least bit interested in the colorful socialist paintings of Lei Feng, the iconic soldier. He was a revolutionary hero and standard-bearer for altruism who tirelessly helped his fellow citizens. (Rather than replace his own worn-out uniform and waste resources, he would constantly sew it back together.) He had died that very year, and his diary had just been published. His image was everywhere. I waited to see what Comrade Yu was going to propose.

Listening to him trot out his doctrine, I wondered if I should have made the request at all, or if I should have chosen my words more carefully. I had expressed a desire to learn calligraphy, but I had come to see that once the wheels of the state were set in motion, anything could happen.

"We have discussed the matter in our work unit," Yu went on, "and we think that it would indeed be productive for you to perfect your writing, if you intend to become an effective spokesperson for the Revolution. We have found you a teacher. You will start tomorrow. A room will be allocated here at Radio Peking. We hope that he will successfully impart his knowledge to you, and that you will learn to apply it to your own work."

"Thank you, Comrade Yu."

What was said and what was meant were often two different things. I was delighted – I had gotten what I wanted – but I understood that I should have worded my request differently. I should have asked for writing lessons, not calligraphy lessons. There was such a fine line between the two, in any case. The response would have been more straightforward, and the whole process handled more quickly.

The next day, the driver came to get me earlier than usual, and a secretary showed me into a small, unheated room with a large window and a long table and two chairs. In one of them sat the teacher. When I entered the room, he looked right at me without moving, then stood and walked toward me. He seemed tall by Chinese standards, perhaps five foot eleven. He did not have the usual almond-shaped eyes or wonderfully shiny black hair unique to the Chinese. He greeted me with a bow.

"Welcome to our writing lesson, Miss Rochester. My name is Wei. Let us begin."

I was completely disoriented. His looks, and his sheer presence, left me speechless.

"To start with, I would like to give you some guidelines," Wei continued. "Calligraphy is a meeting of the stroke, the breath, and the mind. It reveals an inner truth. You will have to commit your whole self to your work. The simplest of strokes will reveal a great deal about your emotional state, what you are thinking, and how energized your body is. If you want to be a fine calligrapher one day, you must distance yourself from fear, pride, and impatience. This, and much more, will become clear during the course of our lessons." He paused here, and then, in his deep and steady voice said, "Sit down next to me."

I did so without saying a word. My stomach was churning. He gave off such energy.

"Let's see what you can do. I gather you have studied in France. So you know some ideograms, I presume."

He had prepared me a brush, which had been dipped and scraped on the side of the well to remove the excess ink, and he now handed it to me. As I took it, I noticed my hand was trembling. Seeing this, he changed tack, picking up a second brush and preparing it deftly before me.

"Would you like me to write something? The *ma* sign, to begin, is the classic character." He smiled as he spoke. I suppose he wanted to put me at ease by starting off with such a childish exercise; but he must have been aware that I knew how to write the word for *horse*. I had to snap out of my trance.

"*Ma* was one of the first signs I learned, along with *ren*, if memory serves," I said, gripping the brush. My voice was croaky. Bringing my trembling under control, I drew the two shapes on the large sheet of paper, a little too quickly. The two slightly curved sticks of my *ren* – it means *man*, with its sticks looking like legs – appeared next to my *ma*, which was more angular.

The teacher pinged the ball back into my court. "Do you know this one? It is formed from the *ren* radical." He held his brush vertically, and with a combination of passion and stillness, drew a magnificent sign. At its root were four little lines that looked like sideways flames. I was astounded by such precision, balance, and grace. "This character means *remarkable man who stands apart*. We pronounce it *djié*. It applies perfectly to our leader Mao Tse Tung, who carries upon his shoulders the destiny of our proletariat revolution. Long may he live."

This threw me. How could this man, who seemed so sensitive, be concerned with such formality? I suddenly felt as though I were with work colleagues again. I suppose I *was* at work, and in six months, I should have gotten used to such phrases, said in the same solemn tone in which our grandmothers used to say "by the grace of God."

I came back at him: "I also learned the Eight Principles of Yong, but haven't practiced them regularly."

A little calmer this time, I drew the character *eternity*, which includes the eight basic Chinese strokes. With those, you're meant to be able to turn your hand to any new character. I tried to show I was concentrating, and to respect the stroke order and the precise movements that go with each one, as I had been taught.

"Are you aware that this system neglects two important strokes?" my teacher asked.

"I am, but I can't remember which ones." I tried to draw what little I could remember.

"The angle is right, but the break is…let me show you."

I studied his stroke carefully. It looked like an elbow, and I reproduced it, trying to imitate the ease with which he worked. We continued this to-and-fro until, to my surprise, a feeling of well-being came over me.

"There, you are calmer now," my teacher observed.

"How do you know?"

"The stroke is an extension of you. It is your mind in physical form." And then, adopting a more professional tone, Wei added, "You are used to writing as you have been taught, in the regular script. As you grow in confidence, you will develop the cursive script, your own personal handwriting. You will come to realize that you can apply more pressure with your brush. As Li Si said three centuries ago, 'Make your stroke dance like a cloud in the sky, sometimes heavy, sometimes light. This way, you will steep your mind in your activity and arrive at the truth.'"

I didn't understand this strange teacher, who seemed so wise and yet so loyal to the Party, unless he was trying to hoodwink the government apparatchiks and keep them from guessing who he really was. That was a tactic many Chinese people employed, and one that I was learning fast. Nonetheless, I found his behavior disorienting. It didn't help matters that I couldn't stop looking at his magnificent hands.

"And you, Comrade Wei; what kind of calligraphy do you write?"

His response came quickly. "The Grass Style."

I had suspected as much. That kind of calligraphy belongs to the erudite. It looks like wild grass – or a prescription written out by a hasty doctor. To some eyes, it may seem scruffy, but it requires incredible control and sophistication, both to produce it and to read it. This man must have been born into the ranks of the scholarly elite.

I had a good look at him for the first time. There was depth in his eyes, and his lips were sensuous. Then I saw concern flash across his face, as if he had realized that he had unwittingly wandered into enemy territory.

"The calligraphy practiced by our ancestors was a decadent, bourgeois art, proof of a black soul serving imperialist ends. It is an activity that serves absolutely no purpose in our Revolution. However, there is an art form that can show off China's power to the world, and that is what I practice. I am an official painter. President Mao has explicitly asked us to be spokesmen for our new regime, and to expose the force of change that we embody in an eruption of color."

I was amazed by this volte-face. He must have been aware of the inconsistency between what he had just declared and the age-old knowledge he was imparting to me. Did he think someone was listening in? That must be it.

Not wanting to make his position more awkward still, I kept my questions to myself, and concentrated on the rest of the lesson. I was asked to reproduce the *yong* character as accurately as I could. I experienced completely unexpected emotions as I carried out the exercise – one that I had, until now, considered to be fairly mundane. Frustration and irritation slowly gave way to a certain rhythm, an effortlessness. At one point, I experienced a kind of joy; it made me feel alive, in the moment. I sat back to contemplate my work. What had started as lifeless lines had become a well-rounded character, rooted in something. Just then, I heard the calm, deep voice of my teacher, a few inches from my ear.

"If we are too meticulous, the power, the essence, passes us by, it is true. But when we are too rushed, nature passes us by, without us even realizing it is there. It appears you have achieved a middle ground today. We will end here. That is the best way of preserving what you have just learned. Until Wednesday."

His voice made my senses hum. What's more, I understood absolutely everything he said, as if I were suddenly fluent in Mandarin.

As I was leaving, I looked over my shoulder. Comrade Wei was gazing at something I could not see out of the window. What was he thinking about?

I slipped away. In my pocket was the calligraphy sample he had given me.

# CHAPTER 8

# Silk Scroll

One of the Zhang brothers handed me a silk scroll. I unrolled it, just as I had unrolled countless others. A mountainous landscape. Bamboo in the foreground. White on black. The stems and leaves seemed to come off the page, almost leaping out at me. I was dumbfounded; I expected them to start swaying. Not possible, I was informed; they were painted more than a hundred years ago. I bought it on the spot.

It was the first time I had experienced such a strong sensation looking at a calligraphy painting. That was exactly what the artist had been trying to do, I thought: transfer a sense of life from his mind to the page.

Manuela and I left the shop. We stood in the street with our purchases, under the late, still-warm sun of autumn, 1964. It would soon be a year since we had arrived in the city.

"Kim, it is twice that I have spoken to you, and you do not hear me!" Manuela chided. "For the last few days, it feels like I am living with a stranger. What is going on?"

"A letter from my mother," I admitted. "From Paris, where my father has just been posted. Apparently, there was a reception for Jackie Kennedy, who speaks French as though it were her mother tongue. And I even got a full description of her dress, her shoes, and her handbag. And did she once ask for my news? In the only letter she has written in a year? That would be too much to hope."

"And as usual, your mind took you back to those glory years and the glamorous world you left behind. I am sorry to insist, but how did a letter from your mother stop you hearing half of the questions I have asked for a good two weeks? And make you change your outfit three times on Wednesday morning? I am not a fool, you know. Something else is going on."

I didn't have time to answer, because just then, we got on the bus to take us back to the Friendship Hotel. It was packed. Other passengers jostled me to the rear of the bus, while Manuela was stuck at the front. During the bumpy journey, I thought about what my friend had said. How could I tell her what I was going through? In my mind, I played back the events of the past few weeks.

After my first calligraphy lesson, I bought all the equipment I needed to practice. I felt far more ready to face Comrade Wei the following Wednesday. I was pretty sure I had mastered the Eight Principles of Yong, and had diligently copied a line from a classic eighteenth-century Chinese poem that our teachers had given us to read at Langues O': *The Dream of the Red Chamber* by Cao Xueqin. I even decorated our apartment by doing calligraphy on pieces of silk and attaching them to bamboo sticks, like people did with Chairman Mao quotes.

Comrade Wei was waiting for me when I arrived for my second lesson, standing behind one of the chairs. I had to work hard to conceal the emotions that seeing him again brought out in me. As a distraction, I unrolled the scroll on which I had copied out the extract. He looked at it closely, and said, "You chose it, so you must like it. We will reproduce this verse until you really *feel* it." I was disappointed by his remark. He could have told me that I had made a good choice, but part of me expected a reaction like that. To soften his words, perhaps, he added: "It is not like in Europe, where you frown upon copying. In China, it is encouraged. It is the only way to learn."

His attitude was so professional that little by little, my heart stopped racing, and I let myself become absorbed in the calligraphy of the poem. It read like a proverb: *When truth is false, false is true; where there is nothing, there is everything.*

As I was putting the finishing touch on my fourth copy, I over saturated the brush, and made a blotch on the page. I reached out for the little cloth, despite knowing full well the copy was ruined, and I would have to start again. As I did so, Comrade Wei reached out for it, too. Our fingers touched. There was a spark of electricity. My teacher whipped his hand away so quickly that I knew he had felt something, too. He snatched up a new sheet of paper, and I began to copy out the poem again, much too hastily.

We spent the rest of lesson in awkward silence, which turned into a sort of meditation the more I wrote. After an hour and a half and fourteen attempts, my fingers were a bit stiff, but I had done it: I had managed to get a smile out of Comrade Wei.

"You can stop. Error is essential; it is an approximation of truth. You have acquired what you need to make progress."

I could not take my eyes off his face; it was lighting up the room.

For the tenth lesson, Wei brought a little wooden box covered in fabric, and opened it ceremoniously before my eyes: a jade seal engraved with my surname. "Now you can sign off properly."

I turned a deep shade of pink. For once, I didn't have to hide my emotions. After all, how was he to know what I felt for him? I might just have been blushing because of his gift.

"I don't know how to thank you…"

"It is a modest way for a teacher to encourage a talented pupil, nothing more," he murmured. "If I were one of the old teachers, I would have insisted you make it yourself." I looked intently at the seal he had just given me, and at each letter: together, they spelled out "Rochester."

"I tend to forget that in China, you always use your surname in public. The first name is reserved for intimacy, isn't it?"

"That's right."

"My name is Kim," I heard myself say.

"I am Keixing," he whispered, looking horribly uncomfortable.

I don't know why, but his manner made me laugh, and my laughter set him off. That lightened the atmosphere. The two-hour lesson flew by, the first hints of a delightful complicity that made us as light and as playful as birds on the wing.

The next lesson was canceled.

"Comrade Wei has had to attend a political meeting of the highest importance," I was advised by Comrade Yu, in his most official tone. "He will be here next week."

I wondered what that meant. Was it genuine, or just an excuse? Was my teacher worried he had gone too far? After all, I didn't know anything about him. I had obviously failed to cover up my disappointment, and Yu, never slow on the uptake, decided to compound it with one of his favorite observations: "Comrade Rochester, you seem not to appreciate your Mao suit quite so much these days. Do you not have enough of them? If you want some coupons, I can provide them first thing tomorrow morning." His voice made me shudder. I was aware of a veiled threat, but couldn't tell what it was. It was true that since arriving in China, unlike most Westerners, I had taken pride in wearing the uniform of the People's Republic. It made me feel as though I was fitting in. And it meant I didn't waste time wondering what to wear every morning.

Comrade Yu's words stayed with me all day. To appease his urge to reprimand, the next morning, I put on my blue cotton pants and jacket.

The following week, Wei was at our desk, with the Four Treasures of the Study – ink, paper, brush, and water – duly laid out, his Sun Yat Sen suit carefully ironed. He got to his feet the moment I entered the room. I expected to see the usual cheery look in his eyes, but noticed instead the grayish tint of someone who had not slept.

"Hello, Comrade Wei," I said quickly, to put him and myself at ease. He didn't reply. I walked over to him and sat at his side. That way, we couldn't see each other's faces.

"You can call me Wei. Just Wei. I think it is time that I taught you the foundations of all calligraphy work, whether for written script or painting. We got ahead of ourselves by starting with handwriting. It was careless of me."

What was he getting at?

"I would like to revisit some extremely important elements, such as meditation, breath and posture, all of which require attention before doing any calligraphy." He paused momentarily, then said, "Given that we are not in a place of meditation, and that, I imagine, you are not accustomed to the practice, I suggest you stand in front of me."

I did so.

"Relax your arms, close your eyes, and let whatever thoughts you have come freely. Take time to breathe."

I wasn't faring very well, despite the fact that I had already done some meditation with a friend in Paris who had been passionate about Krishnamurti.

In the silence, Wei's presence was stronger still. I could sense him moving about the room, but I couldn't see him because my eyes were closed. Where was he now? I could only picture him. He took up all the space in my mind. I couldn't relax. He must have noticed, because just then, he came and stood right behind me.

"Lay your head on my shoulder, you are too tense. Take the time to focus only on the breath, keeping your eyes closed."

I sensed him right up close to me. His breath on my neck. His gentle voice. Every word caressed me gently. Very softly, he placed his hands on my hips. "Concentrate on your breathing. I want to hear your breath like the breeze in the sails of a boat. Imagine that you are at sea."

After a few minutes, he turned me around, keeping his hands on my hips. Could he feel the tension washing over me?

I opened my eyes, and saw his mouth coming towards mine. I leapt backwards. At precisely that moment, we both heard a noise coming from the corridor. Our room was tucked away from the buzz of activity in the Radio Peking office, but there was no question: someone was coming. I sat down again instantly, as if in the middle of a lesson. He did the same. When the door opened, we must have looked like the very model of diligence.

Comrade Yu appeared at the door, but did not come in.

"Comrade Wei..." he snatched at his words, rather as if he had just raced up two flights of stairs. "You are wanted on the telephone."

Wei left the room, and I was alone to wrestle with my thoughts. They were so contradictory. I had dreamed of that kiss, but at the same time, Wei's political ideas alarmed me. The only person who could help me find a solution was Manuela; that much I knew.

# CHAPTER 9

# A Crumpled Piece
# of Paper

Manuela and I were settled on our beds. It was the middle of the night. We couldn't hear a soul, and not a soul could hear us. Thankfully, the walls were thick, in contrast to the cardboard-like divisions in most Chinese apartments. In any case, we had taken to whispering.

"I'm going to tell you everything, from the beginning," I said.

Manuela had her arms wrapped around her pillow, as if sensing a good story coming. I told her the whole thing, not leaving out a single detail. She listened, punctuating my account with smiles and the odd question. Once I had finished speaking, the real interrogation started.

"He has had an extraordinary life. I could tell that straightaway," I elaborated. "He has a delicate way about him, no trace of the harshness you often come up against here. I would have put money on him being educated abroad."

"Was he?"

"Not completely, actually. He was born in Peking, but went to study medicine in the USSR for seven years. He only got back in 1959, when the Soviet Big Brother had not yet become China's number one enemy."

"So he's a doctor?"

"Yes, but not practicing because the Party decided to make him an official artist. He didn't say why."

"Perhaps he doesn't know. The Party decides, no?"

"I know, but often, people's careers are disrupted because the family is blacklisted."

"Bourgeois, you mean?"

"Yes. I think that may have happened. If he's the son of a scholar."

"The government doesn't stop everyone. Look at Zhou Enlai. He comes from a scholarly family, and he studied in prestigious places, too, and went abroad…oh, I don't know how often, but lots of times, when he was a student and a young revolutionary. To Paris and Marseille…"

"You can't use the state's second most important person as an example. Look, there are countless people who run into trouble because their families don't conform, you know that. Anyway, in Wei's case, things could be a lot worse. He is allowed to work without any problems – they trust him enough to let him teach a foreigner – and he belongs to the artists' union, which pays him a perfectly respectable wage. On top of that, he's allowed to live with his mother in one of those *senheyuans* that we dream of being invited to."

"And what do his parents do?"

"Gosh, did my mother put you up to this?" I asked.

Manuela grinned.

"His father is dead, I think, and his mother is an official translator for the government."

"He must have protection high up. Another reason to be careful."

"When I told him that we buy calligraphy and various things from the Zhang brothers, Wei smiled, and said he knew them. They became friends when he cured one of them – don't ask me which one! Wei still treats people. For free, I gather. And he's studied traditional Chinese herbal medicine."

Silence. I felt my eyes begin to tingle, a sure sign that I was fading fast. I hadn't reckoned with Manuela's tenacity, though; she wanted answers.

"If we're saying your mother sent me, I'd better do the job properly," she joked.

"Go on then, next question…"

"How old is he?"

"I knew you'd get around to that one. About thirty. Well, thirty-two, actually. Do you think that's too old?"

"Not at all. There's twelve years between my uncle and aunt, and they've been happily arguing like cats and dogs for years."

"Well, we're not quite there yet! I have to talk to him about the Revolution, find out where he stands. But how can I, now that I've refused to kiss him? Oh, you'll come up with a plan for me, won't you, Manuela?"

"Well, just remember the story Paul told us. You know, about that Russian who fell in love with a Chinese man, and was caught kissing him. She was deported, and he was sent to a work camp, apparently."

The next day, I arrived at Radio Peking with a spring in my step. I had gotten some solid rest, and felt much calmer after my heart-to-heart with Manuela. That night, I had dreamed of Wei's hands stroking huge sheets of Xuan paper.

Now, the daily office grind was virtually unbearable. And the meetings about education policy were getting longer and more frequent, which didn't help matters. An anthology of Mao Tse Tung's thinking had just been published, called the *Little Red Book*. I made sure I had a copy in my handbag at all times.

That evening, we were called to another meeting an hour before we were due on-air. After forty-five minutes of reading and discussion about the Word of Mao – it reminded me of the Crows of my childhood, and the endless hours spent at Mass – I got up to open a window. It was suffocating in the smoke-filled room, and I needed some air.

Five minutes later, they let us out. As I was leaving the room, I thought I saw Comrade Yu flinch, out of the corner of my eye. But when I turned to look at him, he was glued to his *Little Red Book*, his eyebrows crumpled in concentration.

In the corridor, Manuela whispered in my ear, "I think Comrade Yu is an admirer of yours."

"How do you know?"

"I watched him when you got up to open the window. He looked like he wanted to devour you."

"Oh, that is deeply unpleasant. And if it's true, it won't help my situation with Wei one bit. Yu won't let me out of his sight. He *has* been acting strangely; I thought he was angry at me for something."

"Of course he's angry! He must have realized where your affections lie."

"I don't see how...."

Then I remembered the day he had commented about my clothes. We had reached the studio door. Manuela went in ahead of me and took her place at the microphone. And then, seconds before we went live: "Eyes like a frog, body like a bear, and behaves like an eel. Comrade Yu is quite a catch, no?" she sniggered.

It was as cold as ever in the little classroom on Wednesday. When I saw Wei in his blue suit lined with raw cotton, preparing the ink by gently rubbing a soot stick on the wet ink stone, I felt myself melt. There was an incredible force building up inside me, and it made me tremble.

Wei had not said a word since I entered the room. Perhaps he was put out by my slightly brutal reaction at the previous lesson. Suddenly aware of the silence, I walked over to the table and took up my usual position. I breathed slowly and started to empty my head of thoughts, as he had taught me. After a while, I realized that our previous silent understanding had been broken.

I opened my eyes and saw that Wei had moved away from me. He was standing bolt upright in the corner of the room with his arms folded. It was the first time that I had seen him adopt such a defensive position. He was looking at me vacantly; it was very unlike him. The bags under his eyes were unmistakable.

I felt awful, but I didn't dare say anything. Instead, I sat down, picked up a brush, dipped it in the ink, and started to inscribe with a heavy heart, copying the poem by Niu Xiji – who wrote around 900 BC, during the Five Dynasties – that Wei had written out on the sheet in front of me.

*In the pale sky, shine*
*The stars, rare and small.*
*The falling moon lights up her face,*
*I see dawn in the sparkle of her eyes,*
*The dawn of separation.*

When I got to the last line, I looked up at Wei, questioningly.

"I am going to ask Comrade Yu to find you another calligraphy teacher," he informed me.

A gulf opened up. "Why?"

"The Party has asked me to undertake a fresco for our capital's central station. Unfortunately, I no longer have the time."

I was winded; I could hardly speak. "Won't I see you anymore?"

"No. It won't be possible. I'll have too much work to do."

I put down my brush. There was no point carrying on like this; I might as well finish things then and there. I didn't want him to see me in a mess. I picked up my belongings and made for the door.

"Goodbye, Wei," I said as I passed him.

He grabbed my arms, stopping me in my tracks. I looked up at his face. There was such sadness there. He pulled me towards him and murmured: "You are driving me mad! I dream about you day and night. I can't concentrate on my work. You are the most beautiful woman I have ever met. But I am Chinese."

He gently pushed me away, then slipped a piece of paper into my hand.

Outside, I unfolded it, and read: *You have to leave me alone. Please.*

I was stunned. It was in English. Could Wei have asked someone to write it for him? Impossible. Too dangerous.

I went back home, utterly shaken.

# CHAPTER 10

# Fur-lined Glove

"Go on! I have a surprise for you." Manuela let go of my hand and pushed me into the dark, familiar back room of Zhang Bros. She quietly shut the door behind me. I stayed still for a few seconds while I got my bearings: the little window in the roof, the only source of light; the piles of dusty furniture; the back door leading out onto the street, its cracked sign letting in a few shafts of sunlight.

Wei was only just visible in the half-light, but his presence was strong and imposing. My heartbeat rocketed. He came toward me. I could feel his warm breath on my forehead.

"You have a true friend. And resourceful, too," he said.

"You speak English? How?"

"Are you cold?"

"I haven't eaten much these past two weeks."

"There was nothing I could do. I had to think things over and speak to my mother. Fate often defies us, and events can take turns we little expect."

A huge door to the unknown was opening in front of me.

"And your English?" I repeated.

"My mother taught it to me. I cannot tell you everything yet," he began quietly. "Certain things are too dangerous. But you should know this: my father was a scholar who passed the Imperial Examination very young, at the age of twenty. The year was 1900. You have doubtless heard how difficult that exam was, how it took some people years to prepare for it, how it was a prerequisite for all of the Empire's civil servants."

"I learned that at Langues O', yes."

"My father, Wei Xuantong, was named a *shujishi* – a doctor of literature and calligraphy – and then he took charge of the Imperial Palace's calligraphy collections, teaching that discipline, too. He married a woman whom he adored, but she died in childbirth. Crippled by grief, he swore he would never remarry, but fate decreed otherwise. His best friend, Li Fucheng, a fellow calligrapher, had a daughter whom my father watched grow up. By the time the young Li Shaoqin turned eighteen, he was madly in love with her. They married, and I was born not long after: in 1932, when my father was fifty-two."

Wei paused for breath and invited me to sit next to him on a table top, which he first wiped with his glove. We huddled close to one another, like two children in a tent swapping secrets before they fall asleep. I laid my head on his shoulder, and he wrapped an arm around me.

"In those days, the Empress was long since dead, and the Empire with her," he began again. "The Republic of 1912 ran into all sorts of trouble, especially given the games the Western powers were playing. My father continued to care for the imperial calligraphy collections as best he could, as they passed from one leader to another. Chang Kai-Shek took a particular interest in them. When the government fled in the face of the Japanese advances of '37 and took refuge in Chongqing, in the province of Szechuan, we followed on behind with the most important items."

"So you managed to escape the Japanese air raids on Chongqing. I've heard they were bloodier than many of the Second World War campaigns?"

"Yes, we survived thanks to my parents' love of nature. My father had chosen a beautiful house in the mountains, far away from the city, in an area that mercifully escaped the bombs. I have marvelous memories of that place, despite our reasons for being there."

"How old were you?"

"I lived there between the ages of six and fourteen. During that time, I was able to make the most of my father's teaching. Every morning, we did *tai chi* to wake ourselves up, looking out at the mist gradually rising up and covering the mountains. You cannot imagine how those sights are etched in my memory, and how they sustain me to this day. Then my mother would bring us breakfast and prepare our ink, brushes, and paper. She spoke fluent English, and refused to speak Mandarin with me. She was a Buddhist and my father was a Neo-Confucian. They were worlds apart, but united in their love of nature and calligraphy."

"Why did your mother insist on speaking to you in English?"

"I'll come to that."

I let him speak, swearing not to interrupt anymore.

"My days were nearly all the same in that strange world. Death was ever-present, in the form of the awe-inspiring planes overhead that set my imagination whirring. After my morning calligraphy exercises, we would go for a walk, and my father would tell me all about the hidden properties of plants, as his father had taught him. I inherited my love of medicine from these two men, and from my mother, whom I helped during her afternoon calls to treat the wounded. Once, we had a visit from a man – who today occupies a very senior position – and his wife, both of whom got on well with my parents. I learned a great deal, and my character underwent a profound change, thanks to that period of exile. It brought the three of us together. Before Chongqing, I was impetuous, furious sometimes, a wild sapling. My father's teaching of Confucianism and calligraphy served as a support; tied to it, that sapling could grow tall and straight and true."

I couldn't help but smile at this. Imagery from the world of nature is prevalent in China, but it was ingrained in Wei. Now I knew why. I knew, too, that I had been wrong about him.

"I wanted the war to keep us in that place forever," he sighed, "unlike the majority of citizens, who suffered or even perished because of it. In August, 1945, we returned to Peking. Now, for some months, my father's *qi* – his vital energy – had been weakening considerably. No one could tell what he was suffering from. He was about to turn sixty-six, and had many long years ahead of him, judging from our forebears. My grandfather was still in good health. But not so his son: two months after our return to the capital, he died of lymphoma, a known illness, but a rare one. I saw the life sucked out of him, and I saw him suffer. I did not know how to relieve his pain. In the end, we managed to find him some opium. He drifted away on a cloud, if I can put it like that...."

Another silence. Then, quite suddenly, I felt Wei's hand in mine. It was warm and reassuring. I had to make a real effort to concentrate on what he was saying.

"A short while before sinking into an opium haze, my father asked my mother to send me to England, and, through her friend who worked at the embassy, see to it that I had somewhere to stay there. But I refused to leave; I wanted to assist my father until the very end. I don't regret staying in the slightest, for those final moments with him defined me."

He started to stroke my hand. His tactics were working like a charm; quivers ran over my whole body. He stroked my arm, then his fingers gently caressed my neck.

"In the end, I went to boarding school in Edinburgh for four years. My mother made me come home just before my seventeenth birthday, a month before Mao proclaimed the birth of the People's Republic of China in Tiananmen Square in early September, 1949. I was there. The enthusiasm of that day outdid everything I had ever experienced. We witnessed a new dawn for our beloved nation, which had languished in the shadow of foreign powers for so long. I thought Mao was our liberator – even if many of my parents' friends had fled. I was even thankful that death had carried my father off, so he could not see part of his cherished calligraphy collection removed to Taiwan by Chang Kai-Shek – where it remains. For my mother, who had been partly educated in Japan and always moved in revolutionary circles, communism stood out as the only means of ordering a country that had been left behind and was suffering. She had long since shared our house with families of peasants who came to the city, who held her in high esteem. She translated works for the government, too. All in all, those were memorable days. I followed my mother's lead when it came to relieving suffering and ill health around us. The rest, I have told you…."

Wei gently turned my head to face his. His fingers drew the outline of my mouth, and then his sensuous silk lips touched mine. We kissed. Such intense softness that it was almost violent…my body traveled to places I didn't even know existed. I wanted to melt inside his embrace, so we would never have to part. I wanted there to be no beyond, no time, no China. Just the two of us.

A few moments later, Manuela knocked at the door to warn us it was time to leave. I hadn't even heard her. Nor did I remember saying goodbye to Wei. Now, Manuela took me by the hand and I followed her, zombie-like, holding Wei's glove tight. Luckily, our lessons had never been officially canceled, so we could pick them up again the following Wednesday.

It was only much later that evening, when I found that same glove in my coat pocket, that it hit me. There was no turning back. I was utterly in love with that man; but I could not ignore the terrible position that love put us in.

# CHAPTER 11

# The *Little Red Book*

"I promise you it will work!" said Manuela.

"You must be joking! With Yu following my every move all day long, how are we going to manage?"

"That proves that he's looking for a companion, a special friend. And that, under his cockroach exterior, he is susceptible to the charms of nice Western girls, no?"

"What are you going to do?"

"Leave it to me. Do you want to be alone with Wei for the whole of your lesson, without being disturbed?"

Manuela knew the answer to that. Besides, her plan seemed well thought through.

The previous week, when Yu had asked me how my lessons with Wei were progressing, I thought I could detect veiled hatred beneath the usual Party talk. In his prying eyes, I noticed a spark of violence glinting through his spectacles. How would he react if he knew what was really going on between Wei and me? I couldn't imagine. Another man mentally transgressing his country's famous moral code and thinking of women as…goodness knows what. By then, I was all too aware of the pervasive hypocrisy and fear.

At five the next evening, I went to Radio Peking, wrapped up in my warm coat, my heart racing. As usual, the place was a hive of activity. Secretaries were typing endless communiqués, policy meetings were taking place on nearly every floor, and messengers were coming and going carrying fat envelopes. As I made my way up the stairs and silently along the corridor to our little room, the noises became more muffled, and the passers-by fewer and fewer. How lucky we were to have that room. And how ironic that Comrade Yu couldn't have chosen a better love nest for me if he'd tried...save for the complete lack of central heating.

At the door, I got my breath back. What if Wei wasn't there? What if he had gotten cold feet? What if someone had stopped him from coming?

I turned the handle and found him smiling straight back at me, looking happier than I had ever seen him before. I shut the door quietly and raced to his arms. He wrapped me up in them, then lifted my chin and kissed me softly on the tip of my lips. I shut my eyes, overwhelmed by sensation.

The atmosphere was so utterly different from that of our last lesson. The sadness that had gripped me then was no more than a distant memory. In its place was hot desire – in stark contrast to the room temperature. I hadn't even noticed our alibi carefully spread out on the table: the Four Treasures of The Study, neatly arranged, and a few sheets of calligraphy already written out, just in case someone should knock at the door.

Wei removed my coat. We were both crazy with excitement, and a bit tense, too, maybe.

Wei seemed to come to his senses. He grabbed the chair and wedged it against the door.

"Don't you think it's dangerous?" I asked. I didn't know what frightened me more: being discovered, or being left to the mercy of our desire.

"Manuela is with Yu. I have every confidence in her powers of seduction," he said, sounding self-assured and faintly amused.

Where was the serious fellow who had taught me art for the past few months?

We held each other tightly. He assailed me with kisses, some soft, others wild: on the cheeks, lips, eyes, neck. He took off his shirt and lay down on my thick coat.

"Come and lie beside me," he said.

I did as I was told.

Then he stopped moving. Our faces were just a few inches apart. "I want to look at you. I want to hold this sight and keep it deep inside me forever." We moved closer together again. I no longer tried to suppress the tremors that overwhelmed me as his hands roamed all over my body – and soon, my hands were all over his back.

Time stood still. I closed my eyes, then heard him whisper into my ear: "The first lesson of Taoism is self-control."

I opened my eyes, surprised and annoyed.

Wei burst out laughing. "You're a real wild child, aren't you? We can't possibly go any further. If we were caught, it would be too terrible for both of us. I promise you, I will work something out, so that we can see each other in a safe place. Trust me."

∼

"Lucky that your grandmother is stopping the story there, otherwise I would have to ask you to cover your ears," says Leo disapprovingly as he enters the study.

Kenya and Vittorio throw each other a look of complicity.

"Is that why you chose that precise moment to come in with tea and biscuits, Leo?" I ask.

We all crack up laughing. Leo knows I'm going to keep telling the story, though. A story told in love. My grandchildren may be young for some of the details, but they are mature enough to know how important this part of my life is to me. And I want them to know how beautiful it was, too, in the midst of all the danger.

∼

Meanwhile, in Yu's cramped office, Manuela was crossing and un-crossing her shapely legs – let it never be forgotten that my friend put her body on the line to help me. The head of our work unit could not take his mole-like eyes off her. He was almost drooling. They were having quite a heart-to-heart.

"And if you want to leave your country, what do you do?" he asked.

"Pardon?" Manuela leaned in closer toward the Comrade Engineer. She pretended not to understand Yu's question, and he repeated it. "Oh, well, it's simple: we show our passport at customs, and we leave," she replied with a smile.

"You're lying to me. It's impossible for a citizen to have a passport in his possession."

"But I swear to you, Comrade Yu!" Then, inspired, she adopted the tone of a true confidante. "For example, my sister, last year, went to Greece for a well-earned holiday. She works a lot, which women in Italy don't always have the opportunity to do. She is a doctor. A pediatrician. She married a general in the air force, and he is often away. They met in Athens, and then went sailing around the Cyclades. Do you know the Cyclades, Comrade?"

Yu was not expecting such a flurry of words. For once, he let his curiosity get the better of him, and risked a personal observation: "I did not know you had a sister. You have never mentioned your relatives."

Manuela kept her composure, and continued to invent a whole new life story. "Rosalita, my sister, is the product of my father's first marriage, to a woman who died, may her soul rest in peace. I love Rosalita. She is intelligent and has lovely blonde hair. She is extremely charitable. She does everything she can to help her neighbors."

"Somewhat like Soldier Lei Fenh," said Yu, relieved to be back on familiar ground.

"Exactly, Comrade. And, just like him, she keeps a diary. I only hope that she has as long a life as our hero."

"You said 'our.'"

"I did," said Manuela, subtly glancing at her watch and then back to Yu to make sure he was swallowing all this. "It's because I feel so Chinese," she carried on, blinking slowly at him. The Comrade Engineer was squirming in his chair.

"In a week, I am invited to the Friendship Hotel for a meeting with the manager. Afterwards, I might have lunch in the restaurant. Do you...do you often eat there?" he ventured.

Manuela did not know what to say to this. Thankfully, time was up. She made for the door, excusing herself with talk of getting back to work. Yu remained behind his desk, momentarily stunned. He wondered for a second what he had done to deserve a visit from this beautiful foreigner; he couldn't remember what she had said to him when she first came through the door. Never mind. This woman had taken a shine to him, that much was certain; he had felt it.

Just before Manuela left the room, Comrade Yu's strident voice called after her. "I would like you to have my *Little Red Book*." Then he added: "Um...in future reports, I order you not to leave out details about your private life. It does your reputation as an Advanced Worker no good at all."

Manuela pocketed the book and promised not to let him down. He looked pleased to be back in charge. Manuela did nothing to disabuse him, and even asked him to sign his book for her.

After recounting her hour spent with "the cockroach," Manuela threw me Comrade Yu's *Little Red Book*. "Here, a souvenir! He has even signed it. You should have heard how patronizing he was. I said goodbye, and he said: 'We will see each other soon, don't worry.'"

"I can't thank you enough."

"Do you want a tea?" Manuela did not like to be thanked. And yet I knew full well that the little scene she had just played out can't have been her idea of fun, given Yu's character. I appreciated her not asking me a single question about what happened with Wei. She had come and knocked discreetly on the door three times. When I opened it, she just smiled.

I was lost in the memory of that "lesson," so I didn't hear Manuela's next question. She tried again: "And what's going to happen next?"

"He's got a plan!"

# CHAPTER 12

# Jade Stone

Escaping from the Friendship Hotel incognito and getting to the Nanluogu *hutongs* in the Dongcheng district was not, in itself, too difficult an undertaking. I could have taken advantage of the late-winter weather to wrap myself up in some thick clothes, albeit at the risk of being discovered because of my height or my eyes. However, getting into a *sanheyuan* without being seen was nearly impossible.

Unless you had accomplices.

For several years now, Wei had cared for the people of his neighborhood for free. When he wasn't busy painting, he took time to relieve their ailments. Sometimes, he had no choice but to lock himself away completely to honor the commissions made by the Ministry of National Defense, or some such state body, for a painting or fresco. But most of the time, he could not resist following his vocation.

Among the people whose lives he saved, no one was closer to his heart than Liu, a young peddler from Hunan Province who had once been stricken with pneumonia, and whose mother Wei had also treated. Liu owned a cart that he used mainly to transport coal dust, which was considerably cheaper that actual coal. He filled voluminous jute sacks, and unloaded these in local coal stores. Once the coal dust was stowed, women used it to make the famous coal briquettes that were piled up in every home. To do so, they simply poured the coal dust into a mold. They would then pack the briquettes tightly into the stoves. In winter, there was a great deal of to-ing and fro-ing around the coal stores, so no one paid the least bit of notice to a cart pulling up in the courtyard of a *sanheyuan* toward the end of the afternoon, any more than they were interested in the sacks themselves. The fact that one of them was particularly heavy that day – so heavy, in fact, that young Liu almost buckled under the weight – was a detail quite lost on the numerous residents going about their business.

As for me, I was covered in bruises after my jolty journey across the city. I breathed with some difficulty through a hollowed-out bamboo stem, which protruded at the sack's knot so as to remain invisible. My heart was in my mouth, partly because of the severe discomfort, partly because of the questions running through my head: how was I going to get into Wei's apartment? How was Wei's mother going to react to me? I couldn't be sure that "everything would go off just fine," despite Wei's repeated assurances to that effect.

After what felt like an eternity, I sensed we had arrived. Liu gently lowered the sack containing his frozen, aching load to the wooden floor. At last, I was let out. When I poked my head out of the top of the sack, I saw a gloomy cubbyhole. Liu left to check the lay of the land. Before he did so, I went to thank him; but he whipped his hand up to his mouth, and I understood that I was to shut up at once.

I waited, hidden behind the door. From where I stood, I could hear all of the noises of the household. A crack in the wood allowed me to see out without anybody seeing me. The combination of acute excitement and watchfulness put me in such a state that I hadn't stopped to think about what was happening to me. My dream was coming true: I had been invited inside a *sanheyuan*. Except, before meeting Wei, I would never have imagined the circumstances of my visit being quite like this.

Wei's father had inherited the house from his uncle, who had carried out considerable renovations. In particular, he had furnished the courtyard with a small, round garden bordered by stones, in the center of which he had planted a now hundred-year-old pomegranate tree. From Lake Taihu, south of Yang Tse, he brought a special type of stone that is said to represent the world in miniature, and of which the Chinese are extremely fond. He also had a basement dug out. What was he frightened of in those days, I wonder?

His vision for the place was shattered by Wei's mother's habit of putting up several families in her own home, long before the local committee enforced such a practice. It now looked more like a bric-a-brac shop than the carefully landscaped garden her husband's uncle had conceived. As well as clotheslines, someone had set up a communal washtub for laundry and two stoves for cooking, thereby freeing up more valuable space inside.

As a result, Wei and his mother had two small rooms to themselves, and used the communal kitchen. Wei had explained as much the last time we saw each other. His occupation as a painter demanded that the whole of the north wing be set up as a studio, and he had also found space there for a 19th-century wooden bath-tub. Wei himself insisted on having a cold shower once a week, like the rest of his compatriots. "That's what Scottish boarding school does for you!" he said.

A noise suddenly made me jump. I snapped out of my reverie and spun around to see someone coming up through a trapdoor in the floor, which I had failed to notice. A hand beckoned me down. I felt my way in the dark, letting myself be guided by a woman I took to be Wei's mother. Entering a softly-lit room, after having negoti-ated a flight of wooden stairs and a second trapdoor, I saw just how beautiful she was. I could not hazard a guess at her age. She spoke to me in English.

"Welcome to our home, Kim Rochester," she said, gently bowing her head.

Li Shoaqin was dressed in a Sun Yat Sen suit, quite a light one for the time of year. Her face was soft and attractive, and looked back at me with curiosity and benevolence. Her eyes, fascinatingly intense, betrayed a formidably strong spirit. Not a woman to cross.

She beckoned me into the room and toward a chair. I was in an artist's studio, and saw before me pots of paint, brushes, half-com-pleted canvasses, rolls of paper, a bed, a stove, the old-fashioned bathtub, and a table, upon which were laid out some delicious-smell-ing dishes.

Wei was waiting for me by the stove; he was radiant. He brought over a kettle for the tea, laughing at the sight of me covered in coal dust, and sat down. When the tea had steeped, he served me a cup. I noticed he hadn't gotten properly close to me yet. Was that out of respect for his mother?

She had prepared a simple meal of fried rice, three different cabbage dishes, duck, and hundred-year eggs. She used the bones and skin of the duck to make a delicious clear soup as a starter. The food instantly made me feel more relaxed.

The curtains were drawn, and everything seemed quiet outside. The neighbors must all have gone indoors. There was only the muffled sound of life carrying on in the next room. Even though Wei had predicted as much, I was surprised by how well I was received, and the perfect English they both spoke. It was certainly a change from the traditional Chinese welcome, which was somewhat frosty at the best of times, and even frostier given the fear and risk of denunciation that pervaded.

As if he had read my mind, Wei spoke – quietly, so that I had to lean in to hear it all.

"I'll tell you why we speak English. It is the nationality of my father."

I gasped. "What? I thought he was a Chinese scholar!"

"My adoptive father was. The man who married my mother when she was pregnant with me, the man to whom we owe so much. But my real father, Peter, was an English explorer and ethnologist. He came to China to observe the people of Inner Mongolia. He was only twenty when his ship docked at Shanghai. On the way, he stopped at Peking, and that was as far as he got."

"Why?"

"Via a Belgian friend, who was working on the building of the railroads, my biological father met Li Fucheng, the man who would become my grandfather. Li revealed the art of calligraphy to him. My father asked Li to be his teacher, and he accepted. My father began to come here every day – to this very room – to learn calligraphy. He would arrive early in the morning, eat his lunch here, and leave in the late afternoon. For a year. Then his visits became less frequent, because he was helping his Belgian friend with his business. Nevertheless, he had time enough to meet my mother and fall in love."

Wei looked to the lady herself, as if inviting her to take up the story. She began, her voice measured: "My mother – Wei's grandmother – was one of several women who were sent to Japan to be educated at a time when our country's progressive elite despaired for the Empire. There was a well-respected school in Tokyo called Shimoda Utako. My mother was well-versed in the Chinese classics and the teachings of Confucius, and had, as a result, won favor with the administration of the Empress Dowager Cixi. Provided one had the money to get there, going to study in Tokyo was well thought of. Young women from good Chinese families were, in theory, taught how to be model wives and mothers. In reality, it often opened their eyes to the world and brought them into contact with new languages – Mother spoke impeccable Japanese, as well as English – and made them realize just how much China yearned for new blood and new ideas."

Li Shaoqin paused. I was hanging on her every word. How elegant her English was. Wei poured me another cup of tea, and I

brought it straight to my lips. I had a feeling there were more surprises in store.

"I wanted to explain, my dear Kim," she continued, "how this
remarkable woman, who died on my fifth birthday, brought me up,
how she never bound my feet at a time when all aristocratic daughters had to submit to that shameful custom. I should add that my
father married my mother *and* her ideas. He believed in modernity, too. So you can see why he gave Peter his blessing to court me.
When Peter asked for my hand in marriage, my father was pleased;
he had never remarried himself, but lived instead with the memory
his wife. I was the one who ruined everything...."

Another pause. Wei's mother seemed lost in her thoughts. I
glanced at her son, and noticed that he was frozen in a kind of uneasy anticipation.

"For you to understand what I did," Li Shaoqin went on, "you
have to know what was going on here in 1930, just before Wei was
born. China no longer belonged to the Chinese. Foreigners con-
trolled everything, and Chang Kai Shek's government was next to
useless. Young, educated people, of whom I was one, were torn between the desire for modernity, for liberty – copying the Western
model – and the desire to build a brand-new country of our own
from scratch. I was so in love with Peter, and I wanted so much to
be free from the restrictions that ruled our lives, that I gave in to
his desire. I gave myself to him two days before he left for England;
a leap of faith, you might say. I was only eighteen, impulsive and
intense by nature.

"Once Peter had left for England, to tell his parents that he was going to bring back a Chinese bride, I realized that I was pregnant. It was a massive shock. Everything collapsed around me. There was no question of my marrying Peter now: how could I meet his family without heaping shame on him? It was impossible. I decided it would be better to abandon the marriage straightaway, or rather, simply never reply to his letters, cut him off, and quickly find a Chinese man to marry. I cried all night, and then I went to my father and admitted everything to him. That good, intelligent, respected man could not deny me; he loved me beyond all measure. The same afternoon, he invited his oldest friend, a fellow widower, to the house, and asked him to marry me. What he could not have known was that, for several years, Wei Xuantong had harbored an affection for me that went beyond that of a family friend. My father made him a happy man, without knowing it. As for me, not once did I ever regret being married to this man. He always treated me lovingly, and brought up Wei in a manner that few fathers could have done."

Li Shaoqin held out her cup to Wei, and he refilled it. I was dumbstruck by this story. Wei's mother seemed worn out by her confession.

"Would you like some fruit?" Wei asked. He took out a knife and sliced some kumquats in two. I, meanwhile, had found my voice again.

"And what became of Peter?"

"We don't know to this day," he replied. "In 1931, before leaving China, he had already envisaged that it might be impossible to return. He left assets for my mother – in quite a peculiar form – so

Myriam Ullens

she could fund the voyage herself, if need be. We learned what little we know from the letters he wrote to my mother from England. He began by trying to convince his family to accept his bride-to-be. They did not want to know. It didn't help that he was gravely ill by the time got home; he had contracted jaundice, which kept him in bed for several months. During the illness, he wrote to my mother a lot. Of course, she never replied. And then she sent him a letter announcing her marriage to Wei Xuantong. After that, we never heard from my biological father. The Chinese businessman who acted as my guardian when I went to study in Scotland had never heard of him. I did not try to seek him out myself."

"What was his full name?" I asked.

"Peter Seymour."

"Doesn't ring any bells." I had hoped I might have heard of him. You never know…but still, I now understood a good deal more than I had. In particular, I understood why Wei had put aside his patriotism to pursue me; it had surely only ever been a façade designed for self-preservation.

Li Shaoqin stood up abruptly. She looked exhausted. "I will leave you."

She walked with little measured steps towards a small door that I hadn't even noticed. Before reaching it, she turned to look at me with those intense eyes. "I am very happy to meet you, Kim. Look after my son. He deserves it. And you," she said, turning to Wei, "look after her. We have a saying: what is beautiful is fragile. I want to leave you this." She took off the pendant she was wearing and placed it on a table. "It will bring you luck. May you both live long."

194

And with that, she was gone, noiselessly closing the door behind her.

Her son got up, picked up the pendant, and came over to me. He gently placed it around my neck and fastened it. It held a jade stone. I felt it against my skin: smooth and still warm. I still wear it every day.

Without saying a word, Wei picked up the large kettle from the stove. He took me by the hand, leading me toward the bath. In the gentle glow of candlelight, I had not noticed that it was already full of warm water.

# CHAPTER 13

# Coal Dust in an Envelope

It was pouring outside. We could hear the murmur of the raindrops at they streamed down the glazed tiles. There was very little heating in the room; in other circumstances, I might have felt cold. For months, I had dreamed of this moment.

We approached the large oval bathtub made of wooden staves hooped with metal bands. It was sitting on the tiled floor in a corner by the bed.

"Don't move," whispered Wei. He proceeded to peel my clothes off delicately. "Close your eyes," he said, with more authority.

I did as I was told. As each item of clothing was removed, a volley of soft kisses set me quivering.

Soon I stood naked. Wei picked me up in his strong arms and lowered me into the bath. I began to tremble with cold, with joy. With anticipation. Sitting in the warm water, I gathered from the rustle of clothes that Wei was undressing. And then he was next to me. I looked. I don't think I will ever forget how his eyes glistened in the half-light: gentle, brimming with love.

Wei took the soap and turned it over in his hands for some time. "Stand up."

I couldn't have resisted him had I wanted to. He laid his hands on my shoulder, and so began a ballet of caresses. I savored each sensation, each stroke. My shoulders, my arms, my hands. I let myself go, enthralled by the slow, circular motions. Then he lightly touched my breasts, my stomach. I felt an unknown force building up inside me. He no longer needed to tell me to close my eyes; the lids glided downwards of their own. His movements were so delicate that all self-consciousness, all tension melted away. Soon, I was covered in lather, and felt as light as a soap bubble. I heard him move – perhaps he was reaching for the kettle on the stove next to the bed. Yes, I was right. A cascade of warm water flooded over my head and down my body. It was so good.

Wei helped me out of the bath, wrapped me in a towel, and lay me down on the bed. Then he lay down next to me. For a few moments, we just looked at each other by the glow of the little oil lamp. Then Wei leaned toward me and slipped three little words into my ear that echoed like some strange, overwhelming signal: "Cloud and rain."

If I wasn't so Chinese by then, I would never have understood this allusion. But all the tales, all classical narrative, all veiled references have it thus: cloud and rain are metaphors for physical love in the Middle Kingdom.

I let myself go in the arms of Wei. Throughout that long night, we did not sleep a wink.

Far too soon, day crept between the cracks in the curtains. At the touch of his soft, warm hand, I realized that I was going have to drag myself out of the torpor that had washed over me only a few moments earlier. The realization that we had spent a whole night together made my heart swell. Wei looked at me tenderly. I could tell I was not the only one filled with that sense of joy.

A little knock at the door brought us back to reality. Wei's mother was warning us of Liu's imminent arrival; and his cart, the only safe means of transportation.

Eventually, I swung my feet over the edge of the bed. As they touched the ground, the prospect of leaving suddenly seemed unbearable, and a lump formed in my throat. *Not enough sleep, too many emotions,* I thought to myself, trying to ignore a dreadful foreboding. I quickly put on my clothes. Outside, the rain had stopped, but day had not yet dawned. I finished dressing, putting on my coat and noticing Felix's head poking out of the pocket. He had certainly accompanied me on plenty of adventures.

Wei could tell I was anxious. He hugged me.

"We won't always me able to see each other here, but we'll find other ways," he said gently.

Then he opened the trapdoor and disappeared down it, before reaching up again to take my hand and guide me down, too. Having walked the length of the dark corridor, we found ourselves in the cubbyhole. Happily, Liu was not yet there. We threw ourselves into a tight, passionate embrace, as though we might never see each other again. When at last we let each other go, breathless, we noticed that

Liu was standing there with us in the dark, terribly embarrassed. How long had he been there? Unsurprisingly, we hadn't heard him come in.

Before climbing into my jute sack, I said quickly, "See you Wednesday!" Then an idea struck me. I took Felix out of my pocket, and gave him to my lover. "I'm leaving you a little piece of me; look after him. You can give him back before I go home," I said.

"Never!" He smiled. "We're friends for life, your Felix and I."

As uncomfortable and long as the journey back was, it seemed only to last a matter of minutes to me, so absorbed was I in the memory of our night together: what we said, as well as what we did. I felt more alive than I had ever thought possible. As if everything was in my power....

Mind you, I was still stuck in a stuffy sack, and having trouble stifling my coughs. When we reached the Friendship Hotel, I overheard the exchange between Liu and the guard. The latter was incredulous: if a coal delivery was due, he would have known about it. His tone turned threatening. For a minute I feared he was going to start searching through the sacks, but in the end, he let us pass, worn down by Liu, who spoke as loudly as he could and brandished an "official" paper forged by Wei.

I wound up in another dusty cubbyhole, considerably larger than that of the *sanheyuan*. I left quickly, though not before warmly thanking Liu. I was in a hurry to find Manuela and tell her everything.

The sun was still coming up over Peking. It wasn't a bad day; the rain had cut through the mist, and the air felt warmer.

I bounded up the stairs in our block. On the landing outside our apartment, I froze. Something was wrong. I strained to hear the voices coming from inside. Who could it be? With my ear planted against the door, I made out the disagreeable tones of Comrade Yu.

"Tell me where your friend is," he insisted, "or I will ask the police to look for her. Perhaps they will find her in a place near the Forbidden City, in a certain Chinese house. Do not underestimate how dangerous that would be."

My blood turned to ice. I pushed open the door. Manuela's unusually high-pitched voice hit me – "Ah! You see, Comrade Yu, she *is* here!" – and in an instant, I discovered a talent for acting.

"Comrade Yu," I said, mustering the broadest smile I could manage, "how lovely to see you!"

Judging from the look Manuela gave me, I had said the right thing. The mole-like Yu looked more a snarling wolf now, getting ready to devour a helpless lamb.

"I was just explaining to our friend here how you love to get some fresh air first thing in the morning," she said.

I was playacting without a script. Thankfully, Manuela was there to prompt.

My line: "Ah, yes, nothing more glorious, Comrade, than taking a stroll among all those *tai chi* practitioners while one admires the sunrise. And look what I took to read," I said, waving the *Little Red Book*, which had been stuck at the bottom of my coat pocket for a week. I wondered if I had gone a little too far there. Apparently not: Yu walked towards me with a look of genuine satisfaction.

"Comrade Rochester, I am happy to see that your revolutionary fervor has not waned. And Comrade Barzini, please accept my apologies for my insistent questioning. One can never be too careful. I was worried, you see."

We resisted the temptation to ask why. To our great relief, he made straight for the door at which I was still standing. He got so close that his putrid breath hit me full in the face. I took an involuntary step backward. As I did so, Yu's eyes fixed on my face, and reaching out with his small, pudgy finger, he wiped a smudge of coal dust from my cheek. Dread washed over me. He took his leave with a brief nod of the head, and disappeared down the corridor.

Manuela and I looked at each other but didn't dare speak; we strained our ears to hear his footsteps fade away. When at last there was silence, we both let out a colossal sigh of relief.

"What if he checks with the guard?" Manuela wanted to know.

"He won't," I replied, confident we had gotten away with it.

"Go and have a shower – you look like a miner!"

I looked in the mirror, and my confidence quickly gave way to anxiety. I was sure that Comrade Yu had guessed the whole story. How could I warn Wei?

Well, nothing could be done there and then. As I got ready to take my shower, I decided to collect some of the coal dust in an envelope. A souvenir of that magical first night.

～

As I speak these words, I feel flat. Remembering how I met Wei fills my heart with sadness.

Vittorio guesses as much. "Let's get the boats out for a mini regatta," he suggests.

Kenya moans, because she thinks we were just getting to the good part, like a soap opera you can't tear yourself away from. But she agrees to come, too.

I need to empty my mind after all the effort of recalling my life's twists and turns.

And it works: As the wind whips our faces, I tell myself: It's pretty good to be alive, after all.

# CHAPTER 14

# Dream Stone

The following Wednesday, I dressed in white, knowing how much Wei liked that color. I didn't care about Yu and his acerbic remarks.

I had not stopped thinking about Wei for a second, or hearing his words reverberate in my mind. The prospect of spending two whole hours together made me giddy; I virtually skipped to work and waved at the guard before climbing the stairs. Soon I was heading down the corridor on "our" floor, to "our" classroom. I burst through the door.

Comrade Yu was sitting bolt upright, his Sun Yet Sen suit – and he himself, for that matter – more starched than ever, the corners of his mouth raised in a little enigmatic smile.

"You seem disappointed to see me, Comrade Rochester," he said. "I have some bad news, I'm afraid. Your friend will not be coming."

I noticed his use of "your friend," not "Comrade Wei" as form dictated. I waited for his next words, unable to speak. "From now on, I will replace him and take your lesson on Wednesdays. The Party has instructed me to do so." It was then that I noticed the usual materials, laid out with Spartan precision: the ink, brush, water, paper. But ordinary paper, dull, nothing like the gorgeous traditional rice paper from the Anhui Province that Wei always provided. "We will begin the lesson where I presume Comrade Wei left off; that is to say, the constituents of the word *aï*. Take off your coat, and sit down next to me."

Had he said those last words with a sort of unctuousness, or was that my imagination? I was incapable of taking in anything. Thoughts were crashing through my mind. What had happened, exactly? Why wasn't Wei there? How would I contact him? How could I find out what was going on? The worst of it was, I could not ask Yu a single question without running the risk of being accused of having a relationship with a Chinese citizen.

Yu held out a brush. "You know how to write the *aï* character, don't you, Comrade Rochester?"

"Is that a joke?"

"Not at all! It is lesson number fifty-six in the official calligraphy handbook."

I contained my rage, and set about drawing the ideogram for *love*.

"Good. Now, I am going to ask you to break it down into its four radicals."

Not missing a beat, and almost violently, I drew the characters *water*, *friend*, and *eye*.

"There's one missing," said Yu, moving closer to me than was necessary. I distanced myself by a few inches, my brain paralyzed with fear. "Well? Don't you know it?"

This time, I knew I hadn't imagined it. He was too close, and his voice was threatening now. He snatched the brush from my hand and scribbled the word *heart*. He threw the brush down onto the table so it bounced up into my face. "Do you think I don't know about your little game with Comrade Wei?" He got closer still, almost touching me now. "I will break him. He will be sent to a correction camp, and you…I will have you expelled from this country if you don't do exactly as I say."

I was trembling with fear, plunged back into the vivid memory of that vile night by the pool with Alicia's father. I thought Yu was going to throw himself on me…

Just then, the door flew open.

"Kim, I need you to do some translation!" sang Manuela, displaying not a hint of surprise at what she saw.

Engineer Yu immediately stood up, adjusted his spectacles, and began to flick imaginary dust from his suit.

"Well, I suppose we shall continue the lesson next Wednesday."

His stiff, courteous tone was sickening. Manuela's arrival had, mercifully, snapped me out of my stupor. We walked away briskly, leaving the cockroach to stew in his own juice.

"Manuela, you just saved my life. How did you manage that?"

"By chance, I was passing Yu's office, and noticed he wasn't there. I went in and asked his secretary where he was – don't ask me why I did that, I don't know myself. When she told me that he was your teacher now, I knew that you needed me. Why was he so angry?"

At that moment, I knew something terrible had happened to Wei. And it was highly likely that Yu was behind it. I felt powerless, with no idea what to do, what to say.

Manuela broke the silence. "Tell me what's going on."

I recounted what had happened in the classroom.

"Of course, Yu didn't tell you anything…and Liu, could you contact him?" she asked.

"No, not Liu, not Wei…"

"It is an awful thing I am going to say, but I think you can do nothing except wait, no?"

Waiting. The one thing I hated doing. A sickening anxiety came over me, and didn't lift all evening. I could barely concentrate on my work. I prayed I wouldn't meet Yu in the corridor. Manuela did her best to soothe me with kind words, but it was no good. I was a bundle of nerves.

After two weeks, I couldn't take it anymore. There was still no news at all. Just one bit of luck: my calligraphy lesson with Comrade Yu had been canceled – no one said why.

Spring was in full swing in the capital. Young girls in blue suits and black pigtails played with hula hoops and danced Revolution-inspired farandoles and sang songs such as "The Orient Is Red." As the sun rose higher and higher over the grey *sanheyuan* roofs and the colored tiles of the palace, everyone seemed to be coming back to life after the winter. Not me. I was wasting away.

"You're not eating," Manuela said.

"I'm not hungry."

"Your clothes will look all baggy, and Wei won't recognize you when he comes back."

"You think he's going to just show up, do you?"

"If you want, I'll go and find his mother," Manuela offered.

"We've talked about that, it's too dangerous. You gave it your best shot last week by trying to grill Yu, and it didn't get us anywhere."

A few weeks after that – I had gotten up late, I remember – I found Manuela in the kitchen, beaming from ear to ear and holding a letter. For a second, naively, I thought it might be news from Wei – but no. Her mother had written to her. She looked as though she might burst.

"He held him in his arms! He loves him, he wants me to go home!"

"What are you talking about?"

"My father! I knew it, I was sure. He couldn't resist my boy forever!" she whooped. "It's thanks to my mother. She gave my son to our Sicilian nanny, and then she simply told my father she just couldn't keep traveling every week, and that from now on, Roberto would live in the family house. My father did not dare refuse – deep down, he must have known she was right. And my brother, Santino, he was always on my side anyway. The days went by, with Roberto's laughter and chattering filling the house. My father could not stay disinterested for long. One morning, in his study with one of his advisors, he forgot to shut the door. Roberto slipped in without making a sound, apparently. When the meeting was finished, my father found the little boy asleep on the carpet behind an armchair. He picked him up, and that was it – he cracked! And at that very moment, my mother walked in and discovered her husband – *il Padrone* – weeping, my boy asleep in his arms. 'Tell her to come home. This child needs his mother, I need my daughter. I miss her too much,' he said to my mother."

Manuela didn't speak for a bit. And then: "I'm going to see Roberto again! Oh, Kim, it's wonderful...." Her eyes were sparkling with emotion. She took my hand and squeezed it tight.

Of course, I was delighted for Manuela, despite my initial disappointment. It meant she would return to Palermo.

"Look what I put on your plate," she said. "A letter from *your* mother. She has written, too!"

I sat down beside her and opened my mother's letter, in which she told me about her new life in Paris. There was nothing special in it, but somehow, it did me good.

"At least I know where my parents are."

"Let's go out," said Manuela. "Let's go for a walk. Perhaps a bit of fresh air will help us think of how to find Wei."

As we were about to leave the building, we heard a muffled voice.

"Comrade Rochester! Comrade Barzini!"

At first, we couldn't tell where it was coming from. We walked toward the boiler room, and our hissed names became clearer. We opened the door. Liu was wedged in a corner of the coal store. He looked terror-stricken.

"Comrade Rochester! Comrade Wei has had to flee. He wanted me to let you know as soon as I got back." Liu looked exhausted, starving. He smelled terrible, too. His clothes – and he – couldn't have been washed for weeks. I was beside myself, petrified. I couldn't speak. Manuela stepped in.

"Let's go and get you something to eat, and then we can talk."

Liu shook his whole body. "No! Impossible. If anyone sees me with you, I am in a lot of trouble. I don't know how I am going to explain my absence as it is."

Manuela didn't persist. "Well, wait here then. I'll see what I can do."

The young man seemed to prefer this plan. He calmed down slightly, and breathed out slowly. Manuela checked that the coast was clear, and slipped out.

At last, I found the strength to speak. "What happened, Liu?"

"Someone denounced Wei. For his relationship with you. Luckily, he has lots of friends, and they warned him in time. He had to leave straightaway. I went with him on the journey for as long as I could, but…." Liu jumped when he heard the door open: Manuela with a thermos of tea and filled bread rolls.

"It's all I could find."

Liu pounced on the food, barely stopping to chew. When he finished, he fell to the floor and began to cry.

"I should never have left him! But I had to come back to look after my mother. She is helpless without me."

The torrent of tears just kept coming. I tried to get more explanations from him. All I could gather was that Wei had left for Hong Kong. I shuddered. It was a hazardous journey; fugitives were regularly caught and thrown into camps. What's more, I knew that without his dependable friend, and that friend's dependable cart of coal sacks, Wei was on his own. I tried to figure it out: it had been two weeks since Liu had left him to return to Peking. Where would Wei be now?

Before slipping away, Liu handed me a little parcel. Inside was a sheet of paper wrapped around a little dream stone covered in a swirl of abstract patterns. I had often seen Wei holding this in the palm of his hand and staring at it thoughtfully. He said it was his lucky charm. I smoothed out the paper feverishly. *Rendezvous in Europe*, he had scribbled. Hope.

Liu left, worn out, asking us to stay in the boiler room briefly so we wouldn't be seen together. We stayed hidden while Liu's cart wove its way off from the Friendship Hotel.

The foreboding I had felt on the morning I left Wei made sense now. I had been right. But what could I have done? And what could I do now?

CHAPTER 15

# Chinese Medal
# of Honor

I tossed and turned all night, but in the morning, my mind was made up.

"I understand," Manuela said, when, for the fourth time at least, I told her I was determined to leave the country. "But the difficult thing is to find a good excuse for getting out, no?"

I watched her, knowing full well that when she got that serious look, a good idea wasn't far away. She leapt out of her seat. "Follow me! Paul and Gabrielle will know, for sure."

We went down a floor and knocked on our Belgian friends' door. They answered it in their dressing gowns, and led us straight to a gargantuan breakfast sourced from two continents: fried rice, dim sum stuffed with red beans, fresh mangoes, and biscuits and chocolates straight from Belgium. They invited us to join them, apparently only too pleased to have some help eating it all up.

"You'll be surprised to hear," Paul announced, "that we're thinking of leaving for Europe."

Manuela and I looked at each other.

"We want to go home, too," I said.

Paul got up to open the window. The cool morning air and the thousand sounds of the city spilled into the room. He started to explain how and why they intended to leave China behind.

"I think the situation here is going to get more and more difficult, and life could get tough."

"What do you mean?" asked Manuela.

"From what Mao Tse Tung has been saying in his speeches, and what we can see bubbling up in the streets, I'm pretty sure that he is going to shore up his domestic authority one way or another. He has the means to do so, no question about that." I loved it when Paul talked about the political situation; he certainly knew his stuff. "Mao is turning to the youth of the country, the only group strong enough to push aside the heavyweights who are criticizing him and preventing him from getting his own way – such as the mayor of Peking. If he manages it, God only knows what he could do. And God only knows what the young would be prepared to do in the name of ideology. Our work is frightening enough as it is. I imagine it's the same story at Radio Peking, isn't it?"

I confirmed that it wasn't only "expert engineers" like Paul; we too were assailed with endless policy meetings and denunciations. Of course, I didn't need to look far for an example.

"My calligraphy teacher has just been denounced for having an affair with a Western girl."

Paul smiled gently at me. How much did he know?

"I heard that," Paul said. I held my breath. "A man named Yu, himself an engineer – and head of the section, too – denounced a teacher. They opened an inquiry, but then it was shut down. Yu got all sorts of hassle from the Party. I've no idea who was behind it. There are obviously power struggles at the highest level. It shows what dangerous times these are."

We hadn't seen Comrade Yu for six days, it was true. I assumed he was away visiting a different Province, as he did from time to time.

"What happened to him?"

"I gather from the President of the Association of Engineers that Yu was posted to Sichuan at the start of the week."

I couldn't hide my relief.

"You look a bit flustered, Kim," he said.

Pulling myself together, I replied, "No, I was just thinking; that explains why Comrade Yu hasn't been in the office. To be honest, I'm pleased to be rid of him. He's a four-eyed lecher who took delight in ogling me whenever I had the misfortune to be in the same room with him."

"You should choose your conquests more carefully, Kim," said Gabrielle, raising an eyebrow.

"Especially since it would appear your teacher has run for the hills." Paul looked me straight in the eye.

"We became close…." I tried to make my voice sound as neutral as possible, but it was no good; it had started to tremble. I wasn't sure I could keep it together much longer.

"I see," said Paul. "Then it really is time you returned to Europe." I thought of Wei's mother, and felt a stab of anxiety. If the state police could find no trace of Wei, they were bound to go for Li Shaoqin. No more doublespeak.

"Paul, do you know if they've been hassling Wei's mother? Would you have access to that kind of information?"

"Look, I am in contact with someone who is very well-informed," he replied. "You won't believe this. Apparently, Wei's mother works for Prime Minister Zhou Enlai – there's a family connection, or so my contact says. I would be amazed if anything happens to her."

I was half-reassured. I had learned two things. First, Paul had squeezed information from his "contact" for my benefit. Second, I was the one who was misinformed. Wei hadn't told me everything – or I hadn't read the signs. It sounded like he had influence high up in the system, in which case, perhaps there was a chance he *could* make it to Hong Kong, provided there wasn't a political upheaval.

Now I felt nothing but gratitude to Paul.

Gabrielle served us more tea. Then Paul fetched his pipe and tobacco. He sunk back into the armchair, clearly pleased he had been able to pass the information on to me without having to invent some pretext that would have made everybody feel awkward.

Manuela leapt in with a question of her own. "How did you inform the Party that you plan to go home?"

"You can't imagine what a minefield it was," Gabrielle replied. "At first, we simply asked permission to leave, and that led to endless discussions with Bao Lin, the Party man who deals with us.

Eventually, we understood that he just needed an acceptable reason, so that he wouldn't lose face. You know how important that is to the Chinese. In the end, Paul had a brilliant idea." And she beamed at her husband, inviting him to take up the story.

"I don't know about brilliant, but expedient, I hope. And I'm sure it might give you one or two ideas. We asked if we could spread the word of the Revolution in our homeland. Basically, we said we had seen for ourselves what is happening here, how well the Chinese system works, and so on. We suggested we would be more usefully engaged converting our Belgian engineer friends at home than hanging on here, particularly since – and this is just good luck, I admit – the project we were working on is in the monitoring and maintenance phase."

"We can! We can tell them that, too!" Manuela enthused. "And we're journalists – our word is important back home, no?"

By the time we left our friends, we had a plan of attack. Manuela and I spent the rest of the day trying to imagine what Wei's journey was like, and second-guessing how our new head of section might respond to our request. We could only speculate, since we didn't even know who had gotten the job yet. Around and around in circles we went.

"I just hope he's understanding," Manuela said.


Six weeks later, an official limousine drove us to the People's Assembly – the parliament – which was adjacent to Tiananmen Square. Four other foreigners, Manuela, and I were escorted with great pomp into one of the reception rooms, where various important characters were waiting for us. I instantly recognized Zhou Enlai himself. I was flabbergasted. Did his being there have something to do with Wei? I told myself to stop letting my imagination run riot.

Young soldiers led us in single file to Zhou Enlai, and we lined up before him. He briefly thanked us for our contribution to the country's greatness, and presented us with our "reward" in the name of the People's Republic of China. Then his assistants pinned the gold medal of honor onto our outfits. I actually felt quite moved, despite everything.

A bit later, Comrade Xue Zhong, our new political representative, gave us the official send-off.

"In the name of the Party and the working committee at Radio Peking, I thank Comrade Rochester and Comrade Barzini for their loyalty to the Party, and their continued good work over the course of these past two years; work that has allowed the thoughts of our venerable president Mao Tse Tung to be broadcast to Africa's Francophone and Anglophone working masses. Today, we pay homage to the courage they are displaying in returning to take on the capitalist forces in their respective countries, to their willingness to carry their stone to the communist edifice. Let their strength be a shining example, for it is pushing back the frontier of the People's Revolution and furthering the dictatorship of the proletariat throughout the world."

If that's what it took, so be it! We were all one big family, after all. So as not to seem too overjoyed, I only let out half a smile, but it could have lit up my whole face. We had done it! I savored the memory of the agonizing six-weeks' wait.

After sitting patiently through discussions and never-ending Chinese finessing on the theme of the propagation of the Revolution around the globe, we received the endorsement of our working committee as well as that of the high-ranking officials present, who, one by one, gave their assent. Eventually, we established that we would be leaving on September 23, 1965: I by train to Hong Kong, where Uncle Oliver would be waiting for me, and Manuela by plane from Peking to Palermo.

"Once the dam is burst, the water flows plentifully," Comrade Xue Zhong had remarked a few days prior to our trip to parliament. Yu's replacement was quite brilliant: an affable, rotund fellow equipped with an infectious enthusiasm for the rise of the proletariat class, whose endless qualities he praised to the skies.

What's more, he indicated that we would be allowed to take back all the items we had bought in China. Trunks would be provided, and the freight taken care of. The People's Republic was paying for our journey back, of course, just as they had paid for the outbound fare.

"And you can stop off *en route*, if you so wish. You just need to specify your stopover destination," said the representative from our local committee who had come to find us in the offices of Radio Peking.

I whisked off a telegram to Uncle Oliver, and planned for a stopover in Canton before reaching Hong Kong. All of my plans were immediately approved by the Chinese authorities.

And that was it! The whole thing done and dusted. Except that beneath it all lurked my fears for Wei. Still no news. But that wasn't a reason not to say my goodbyes. While I was busying myself with paperwork, parcels, trunks, suitcases, and the distribution of our surplus items to various people, I thought of a way of contacting Liu.

I followed him from the lockup where he kept his cart. Then I walked alongside him for a few paces, and pretended to bump into him by mistake. What would have looked like the briefest of polite exchanges between strangers in the street actually served two purposes: I slipped him a letter to Wei's mother – I couldn't visit and risk exposing her – and he gabbled the following: "Wei not returned. Mother sad but coping."

Before long, it was time for one of the hardest goodbyes. In the lobby of the hotel, the red carpet had been rolled out in our honor. Two cars were waiting for us: one to drop Manuela at the airport, and one to take me to the station for a train to Canton.

Manuela was standing by my side in a long beige overcoat. I had opted for my Sun Yat Sen suit, perhaps for old time's sake, perhaps in homage to what had been, after all, my adoptive country for two years. We hugged and hugged and hugged.

"Next time we see each other, it will be at my house!" announced Manuela proudly, smiling hard so she wouldn't cry. I was having trouble myself. Paul and Gabrielle had left China two days before, in the same circumstances as us. They planned to stop over in India. We promised the four of us would meet up in Europe.

Manuela turned and waved before getting into the car, which sped away. I sat in the back of mine. Leaving this country was harder than I had thought it would be. In the pit of my stomach was a sense of dread I knew all too well. How would we all fare – the Radio Peking crowd, the foreigners from the Friendship Hotel, my Chinese friends – in the turbulent times ahead?

~

"Tell us, Marsie, did you see them again?" Kenya asks.

"Some, but most of my Chinese friends disappeared. It was very difficult to know where people were who had gone into hiding – and others weren't that lucky, and were sent to camps. Besides, for years, all my thoughts were of Wei…."

# CHAPTER 16

# Pearl Necklace

The trip to Hong Kong was epic. An official put me on a train bound for the Lo Wu Bridge, which crossed the river Sham Chun at Shenzen: the only permitted point of entry from the People's Republic of China into the British enclave of Hong Kong. The air was sticky. As the train rumbled on, the trees by the tracks became fewer and fewer until we reached the bridge. There, I caught sight of a white shed adorned with huge letters: LO WU STATION. My heart rate went up a notch. This was the end of the road. In a few moments, I would leave China behind and be reunited with Uncle Oliver.

In front of us stood the solitary frontier post with its red star. And beyond it, nothing but the wooden bridge separating the "two Chinas." I was struggling to carry my suitcases, they were so full. More endless formalities. I was surprised to see my passport, in the hands of the customs officials, covered in stamps: I had not had it in my possession for such a long time. Eventually, I was free to cross. Just a hundred yards of no man's land to go. My chest suddenly tightened. I couldn't take another step. I shut my eyes. I tried, one last time, to take in this country that I might never set foot in again. I was transfixed by the image of Wei's eyes, their spark. Where was he? How would I find him again? Was he still alive? My head buzzed with questions.

I walked on. The solitary sound of my footsteps resounded on the wooden planks. I was in limbo, between the past and the present, struggling to keep a grip on reality. Then something brought me back. A familiar shape in the distance, by the checkpoint. The shape loomed into view and became…Uncle Oliver.

I fell into his arms. What joy! After a long embrace, Uncle Oliver held me at arm's length and seemed to study my face meticulously. He was quite moved.

"A child left me and a woman returns. Should I still call you 'my treasure' anymore, I wonder?"

How soothing his voice was.

A chauffeur from the Hotel Peninsular, Hong Kong's finest, held open the doors of a black Rolls Royce. Uncle Oliver sat beside me in the back, and, as was usually the case when emotions were getting the better of him, talked up a blue streak. I gathered we were both invited to the Governor of Hong Kong's residence that evening, and that Uncle Oliver had arranged for me to wear a dress made by Betty Charnuis, the Duchess of Windsor's favorite couturier.

The conversation plunged me into a world I had almost forgotten, a world that seemed alien to me. It was quite a shock. I was agog at the narrow streets lined with tall buildings, the bright signs, the cleanliness, the British policemen in their beige summer uniforms with truncheons stowed in little holsters on their belts, the red and white taxis zipping around, the private cars, the dark green and red double-decker buses, the people in "normal" clothes calmly going about their business. Everything seemed odd and strangely colorful.

After a few minutes, Uncle Oliver noticed I was disoriented. He stopped talking, smiled, and squeezed my hand.

We soon arrived in the immense hotel lobby where we were met by an armada of porters. When I got up to my magnificent suite, I went to the window and gazed out at Kowloon Bay: the port, the merchant ships, the giant ocean liners and the wooden junks crammed with whole families. I sank into a soft armchair, and my thoughts turned to Wei yet again. How I missed him.

Over a cup of tea, I plucked up the courage to raise the subject. We were settled in one of the hotel's sitting rooms, on a comfy leather sofa.

"I need your advice, Uncle Oliver"

I told him all about Wei…well, not quite all. I drew a veil over the small matter of our relationship.

"Well, if your friend speaks English without an accent, I should think he would have gone to the British Embassy. I'll talk to the governor this evening."

Uncle Oliver asked no direct questions when I spoke about a "friend" fleeing the communist regime. If he suspected Wei was more than that, he didn't let on.

"I say, all this chatting!" he exclaimed. "We nearly forgot your fitting with Betty. I think you should be the belle of the ball tonight, my gal."

We headed back upstairs for my appointment. When the couturier left the room after the fitting, I looked in the mirror and couldn't believe my eyes: I was decked out in a long, blue chiffon dress and high-heeled shoes. It had been such a long time since I had dressed up, I hardly recognized myself. Part of me wasn't sure I wanted to be that young woman staring back at me, but then again, I had to admit I did feel light on my feet, and pampered, too. Uncle Oliver had given me a beautiful pearl necklace that I wore with pride.

As I descended the staircase that led to the lobby, a look of wonder spread over my uncle's face.

"Gosh, I can see I'm going to get some envious looks tonight! Very proud to have you on my arm." And with that, he gave me a peck on the cheek.

At six o'clock on the dot, we climbed into the car to be driven to Government House on Upper Albert Road. The building proudly overlooked Victoria Peak, one of Hong Kong's mountains. On the grounds was a rather odd-looking pagoda. House Guards from the British Army stood at attention at the door. Several cars were lining up to discharge their passengers.

"Looks like an official celebration," I said to my uncle.

"Heavens, no! Just a cozy little gathering. I can tell you've come over from the other side!"

At last, it was our turn to climb the flight of stairs lined with Chinese staff holding flaming torches. From the reception rooms, we were led out into the extensive gardens, celebrated for their magnificent azaleas. It was hot and humid.

"They're in full bloom in April. You'll have to come back then," joked the Governor as Uncle Oliver introduced us.

He bowed and kissed my hand. I was a little put off by the eyes that glinted slyly behind tortoise-shell-rimmed spectacles, and the flabby mouth adorned with a pencil-thin mustache. About a hundred guests were gathered together, evenly scattered over the lawn and terrace, where a buffet was laid out. Uncle Oliver kept nudging me and pointing out the men looking my way. I felt uncomfortable; all the more so because I noticed some of the women shooting daggers in my direction. It took me back to those parties my mother had thrown at the embassy.

Scanning the room, my eyes fell on a female guest who looked rather tipsy. I noticed how she snatched a glass from the silver tray proffered by a Chinese waiter. She knocked back half the contents, and then, to my astonishment, tipped the other half over the waiter's head.

"Ugh! Disgusting! How dare you serve me that?" she screamed. "I told you I wanted a gin fizz, not a vodka!"

I walked over. The hysterical woman was hurling abuse at the young waiter, who remained stoic. Perhaps he didn't speak much English.

"She would like a glass of gin fizz," I said in Mandarin, hoping to rescue the situation. But the woman would not let it lie, despite the obvious distress it was causing the waiter, who had vodka dripping off his nose. She continued to insult him, calling him a pig and other rude names. As obviously drunk as she was, something told me she was going to get away with her behavior. By now, the whole place was silent. Everyone was waiting to see how the governor would react. He broke off his conversation, and with a click of his fingers – a gesture that was somehow authoritative and off-hand at the same time – ordered the Chinese waiter back to the kitchen. Then he took the head waiter to one side and demanded the man be fired.

I was shocked. What little appeal this party had held in the first place had now disappeared completely.

"Let's go," I said to my uncle.

"I know a restaurant you'll like. Come with me," he replied without batting an eyelid. He never ceased to amaze me. I was itching to give that woman a piece of my mind, but we opted for discretion, and agreed to slip away without saying goodbye – à *l'anglaise*, as the French call it   rather appropriately, in this case. Before we left, I wanted to try and help the Chinese waiter. I had an idea, but hadn't dared mention it to Uncle Oliver.

〜

"It was Leo, wasn't it?" cries Kenya.

"Was it, Marsie?" Vittorio asks. "Is that where you met?"

I smile.

〜

A short while later, we were looking out over Hong Kong from the restaurant of the Carlton Hotel in Victoria Heights. And what a view of the bay it was: certainly one of the most beautiful in existence.

We were sitting opposite one another at a table by the window, and making quick work of Cantonese duck followed by crab fried in garlic. A bottle of Haut Brion 1947 washed it all down. My uncle had not lost his touch.

At last, we were really together again, talking and laughing as if we had never been apart. I told him everything: Radio Peking, my Belgian friends, The Friendship Hotel, Manuela, our trip to south China, my new-found calligraphy skills. What *didn't* I bring up? Well, certain matters of the heart. I had said enough on that score already with the reference to my "calligrapher friend." Nor did I want to spoil this wonderful moment by bringing up the "bastard child" business. Now was not the time. He looked at me with just the same tenderness and fondness as when I was a girl, but I noticed a glimmer of concern in his eyes. Maybe he was wondering just how I could have grown up so quickly.

"You remember, I'm sure," he said, "that I promised you a present when you came home. Well, it's waiting for you in Brittany, where I'm spending a lot more time these days. By myself, I might add; Ray has retired. I'm quite valet-less. Not easy, replacing him…but anyway, as your parents are in Paris now, you can very well come sailing with me on weekends. On your very own…catamaran!"

I stood up to give him a kiss, but promptly sat back down, now doubly determined to mention my idea.

"Did you just say you're looking for a new valet?"

He looked a bit taken aback by my sudden change of tack. "Uh, yes, of course I am, since mine has run off!"

"Well, I've got someone in mind. You recall how upset that poor waiter was, the one who got fired. I took his address before we left. There would be two distinct advantages for you: first, someone to look after you in the manner to which you have become accustomed, and second, seeing me in Brittany whenever I can get there, since I'll need to practice my Mandarin!"

"So the catamaran was not enough, huh?" he guffawed. Then, more seriously, "Kim, I have a sneaking suspicion you're sad to leave China behind."

As ever, Uncle Oliver was spot-on. He asked for the bill. As we left the restaurant, I took his arm and found the right words to say *thank you*. And not just for the boat.

The next two weeks were taken up with our various efforts to find Wei. I escorted my uncle everywhere. He seemed extremely eager to help. We took advantage of our administrative comings and goings to procure a passport and visa for his new valet, Luo Feng.

Eventually, we had to face facts: there was no sign of Wei anywhere. Not at the British embassy or the American one. It seemed likely he would have requested a passport, given his British heritage. Then again, I thought, couldn't he have procured one under a false name? Still, there wasn't anyone on any list who corresponded with the physical description I gave. It appeared he had, quite simply, disappeared.

During the daytime, when I was with my uncle, everything was fine. But at night, all alone in my sumptuous suite, I was incredibly sad.

Finding Luo was something to be thankful for. This young man, with full lips and pleasant, round features, seemed very mature for twenty. When he found out that Uncle Oliver had offered to take him on, he wept with joy. One afternoon, he sat down with me in one of the hotel's sitting-rooms, and told me a bit about himself.

He was born in 1945 in Shanghai, into one of the lower-middle-class families who managed to make a decent living on the fringes of the foreign concerns. Their background was in cotton weaving, but when foreign competition, coupled with the war with the Japanese, rendered trade impossible, Luo's family made the decision to go into the restaurant business.

So Luo Feng spent his early days surrounded by pots and pans, delicious smells, and shouts from the kitchen staff. When he was eleven, the Great Leap Forward and the famine that followed made the restaurant the object of envy and greed. The state police turned up one night in April, 1959, claiming that the family was anti-revolutionary and on the payroll of capitalists. The police led everyone away, allowing the local Communist Party committee to get their hands on goods they had long since coveted.

Luo Feng and his big sister, Luo-xi, stayed hidden all the while, as their mother had instructed. She must have had a hunch about what would befall her family: she made her daughter sleep with a small quantity of gold sewn into her nightdress, and told her over and over again how to get away, if need be. That foresight saved her children. Luo Feng, aged eleven, and his sister, aged seventeen, somehow managed to get over to Hong Kong: they were among the thousands of refugees who crossed at the famous Lo Wu Bridge.

The two children arrived in the peninsula at the start of 1960. Having no relatives in the area, they were put up by the local pastor, Sheung Wan, who gave them jobs preparing and serving meals at church functions. However, six months into her new life, Luoxi died from dysentery she had contracted during the treacherous journey. Luo found himself all alone. A short while later, the butler of the then-governor, Sir Robert Brown Black, spotted him at one of the pastor's functions. He offered him a position among the household staff, where he was well received and flew up the ranks despite his youth. By the age of eighteen, he was a trusted member of staff, and often served at the high table; but in April 1964, a new governor was appointed and the atmosphere changed completely. That culminated in the gin-fizz incident.

As Luo told his story, he smiled at me with real affection. He told me how happy he was to be leaving China. He thanked me, and promised he would never let us down. I got the impression that he wanted to leave behind the past and start a brand-new life. I was touched by that. Did part of *me* want to turn the page, too? Then Luo said he wanted to change his name. I had heard of this tradition: At any point in their lives, Chinese people might take a new first name in response to certain important events.

"Have you ever thought about calling yourself Leo? It's similar, but brand-new at the same time. And in English, it's an astrological sign that stands for courage and pride. Just right for you!"

"Henceforth, please consider it my name," he replied rather grandly.

Two days later, all Leo's paperwork finally came through from the British embassy. Then, one week before we were due to leave, we found out that Uncle Oliver's mother had become very ill. We decided to take two different flights: Uncle Oliver and Leo would go to London, and I would go to Paris to meet up with my parents.

# PART THREE

# 1965-1969

# CHAPTER 1

# Menu from Chez Ladurée

Kenya jumps off the sofa and runs to the kitchen to give Leo a hug.

"Now we all know your story! What good luck that you crossed paths with Marsie, otherwise we'd never have been spoiled by you. And we'd never have tasted your famous biscuits," Kenya says as she grabs for one.

"I am the lucky one for meeting your grandmother, as you know very well…"

I can't help but feel a glimmer of pride to think that Uncle Oliver and I changed his life for the better. At a time when I was feeling so helpless and full of so much pain, it helped to be able to do something good for someone else. Though now, of course, Leo has returned the favor in spades--and then some.

~

October, 1965.

Evening in Paris Orly – the modern airport *par excellence*. State-of-the-art escalators. French customs. The arrivals lounge. I was jumping up and down with excitement. But no; instead of a familiar face, I saw a sign with my name written on it. And behind it, a chauffeur standing as stiff as a member of the Horse Guards. What a welcoming committee…I should have known.

The car glided through the cold October night to the British Embassy in Rue du Faubourg Saint-Honoré, just around the corner from the Elysée Palace. I was met by the Head of Protocol, Lawrence Hutchinson. Looking rather solemn and somewhat apologetic, he explained that my parents were at a reception at the American Embassy, that they were sorry not to be here to greet me, and that they proposed meeting at eight-thirty the following morning for breakfast. Then he showed me up to my quarters, and at last, I was alone. The bedroom's high ceiling was decorated with a gold frieze. Light from the comforting fire blazed in the fireplace, which a 19th-century mirror reflected back into the room. The floor was carpeted, unlike the highly polished floorboards elsewhere, and by the window, my supper had been laid out on a mahogany coffee table: cold meats, mustard, a salad, and some fruit. The room was certainly nice and warm; the same couldn't be said for the welcome.

On my bedspread was a letter from Manuela, which my mother had taken the trouble to open, of course. Well, it had been a long journey, and I wouldn't have been much company anyway. I decided to see things like that. The truth was, I felt sad and out of place, but devouring my cold supper and my friend's letter lifted my spirits up a little.

At last, some good news! Life with her son was a real shock at first, she wrote. He didn't recognize her, and refused to let her pick him up. But he gradually got used to her, and exactly one month after her return to Palermo, little Roberto called Manuela "Mama" for the first time. She wept with joy. Ever since, she had spent all her time with him, and was over the moon. The atmosphere at home was superb, the tone having been set by a massive welcoming party. Manuela could never have imagined, when she left Italy as a shamed daughter, that two years later, she would find a united family all clamoring for her return; her brother had thrown the party in her honor. She signed off by begging me to come and join her, saying that everyone had heard all about me and was eager to meet me. She wrote of our plans to finish our studies in London and recalled our Chinese adventures.

Her letter delighted me. I went to sleep picturing her bright smile.

The next morning, I met my parents for breakfast in the marble-floored dining room. The contrast with the reunion described by Manuela was pronounced. My mother greeted me with her usual coldness.

"Here she is! Our angry little communist!"

Was that a way of letting me know just how badly my trip to China had gone over in the extremely insular world of western diplomacy? She stopped short of calling me a dangerous traitor, but with every look – or rather, every time she sized me up – she seemed more inclined to let loose on me.

"You don't imagine for a moment that I can show you off in Paris dressed like a pauper? Think of our reputation."

"Hello, *Maman*, it's lovely to see you, too!" I said, approaching the table.

So why *had* I chosen to wear my Sun Yat Sen suit that morning? Of course, I hadn't imagined her reaction would be that violent. I hadn't imagined anything. I did it because I wanted to. Because I felt comfortable in those clothes; they reminded me of my recent past, and took some of the shock out of my present. Apparently, I had forgotten where I was and who I was up against.

"You know, *Maman,* in China, everyone dresses the same, and it doesn't kill them!" I stopped my anger in its tracks and sat down beside my parents.

"Well, my girl, you had better get used to things, and quickly. This is a civilized country. From now on, I expect you to come down to breakfast dressed properly; otherwise, you can eat with the staff. I didn't bring you up in *haute couture* for you to throw it back in my face like this."

My father seemed to be cowering behind his newspaper. "Hello, Kim," he said. I went around to his side of the table and gave him a kiss. My mother was back to her own newspaper by now, and she barely looked up to say, "I suppose you found the letter from your new friend on your bed." Then she fixed her eyes on me. "Don't think she's ever setting foot in this house. A single mother and her bastard son. I hope you choose your friends more carefully in the future."

Enough was enough. Brimming with anger, I spun around and marched over to her. My father's newspaper fell to his lap. I'm sure he thought we were going to come to blows. Sarah's jaw dropped; perhaps it occurred to her for the first time that she was up against an equal adversary. I opened my mouth, but before the torrent of words could come crashing out, the door of the dining room flew open, and a whirlwind whipped through the room. Edward and Charles hugged me, kissed me, picked me up, and hustled me out of there. It was fairly obvious that they had guessed what was going on. We left my parents to it. Breathing steadily and telling myself to stay calm, I climbed up the stairs to Charles's room, assailed by noisy questions on both sides.

"Kim, it's so good to have you back!" Charles bellowed, his face lit up with joy. "If Mom and Dad had given us more warning, we would have been here yesterday."

"We could have gone out dancing," Edward added, beaming.

"Uncle Oliver had to go back to London for an emergency, and that meant I'm a week early; but don't worry, guys, I had the warmest of welcomes."

Charles rolled his eyes. "*Maman* jumped down your throat, I suppose. She is abominable at the moment. No one can do anything right. Come on, I'll take you somewhere crazy for the breakfast of your life! Chez Ladurée is right around the corner."

Being back after all that time, all those miles, at the junction of the Rue Faubourg Saint-Honoré and the Rue Royale, in that Second Empire patisserie infused with delicious-smelling croissants and chocolate: now *that* did me no end of good. I felt I was home at last. Particularly because my brother and my dear friend, who had both grown up so beautifully in their different ways, were sitting beside me. They were messing around, pretending to sign their autographs for me on the Chez Ladurée menu, trying to outdo one another with a series of extravagant signatures. In the end, they presented the menu to me as a present.

They were both full of tales to tell: Charles had finished his law degree and was apprenticing at a big firm of solicitors in London, and Edward was in his last year of architecture at Saint Martin's School of Art. I was thrilled to pick up where I had left off with the pair of them. I thought I would die laughing when Charles told me how, one spring morning, *Maman* had walked into her bedroom in London and screamed her head off upon discovering ten young men, in various states of undress, sleeping off the alcohol they had poured down their throats the night before.

"All great friends," my brother went on, "and *Maman* had them thrown out, of course. They're a little left-wing, as our parents would say. I just know you'll love them. Obviously, they're *personae non gratae*, so we'll see them when Mother and Father aren't around."

Edward had set himself up in Little Wittenham in Oxfordshire, on the little estate his mother had inherited from her grandparents. I knew he had been planning to do that for a while.

"It's huge. There are three buildings that need renovating, a little cottage, some land, and magnificent trees," he enthused.

"Sort of a dream come true for an architect."

"Exactly. As soon as you're back in England, I'm taking you to see it."

Despite the wonderful breakfast with my two "brothers," I decided to leave the embassy first thing the next morning. I had planned to go looking for my friends, find Pierre at Les Deux Magots, and have a few laughs with the old gang; but, truth be told, I was feeling very confused, and more and more fearful that I would never see Wei again. I wanted to jump on a plane and go back to China. I was furious with my mother, and upset by my father's attitude toward her. If I stayed in Paris, I was going to explode.

What I needed was a place to think, a place to pull myself together. A quick telephone call to Miss Bonham did the trick: she said she would be delighted to see me, and would get a room ready.

~

"Trust me, Kim. If you feel that the man you love is still alive, act accordingly," Miss Bonham said.

"Meaning?"

"Live! Go forward, build something. If he is meant to join you, he will."

Marvelous Miss Bonham. She hadn't aged a bit; nor had her temperament changed one iota. And she had certainly stayed true to her word. She had promised to help me see things clearly if I ever got lost. I left Cheltenham with a newfound serenity. Thanks to that peerless woman, who had not judged me for one second, I resolved to grab life by the reins again. While I waited for Wei, I would get back to studying.

There was another thing I learned during that visit, when I saw the bedrooms, the classrooms, the pool: Alicia might well be a friend from my past, but she would always be a large part of my life. Because those we love, who have died, stay with us forever. In a phrase we utter, an attitude we adopt, sometimes not even consciously, they come back into our lives and give us a little nod of encouragement.

In London, at our home in Belgrave Square, thankfully devoid of my parents, I found Charles and Edward. They were getting the place ready for a party, as promised.

At that time in the sixties, it was good form in student circles to declare oneself a Maoist. When our guests learned where I had come from and what I had been doing, they bombarded me with questions. As we drank glasses of beer, smoked Dunhills, and ate delicious English sandwiches – how I'd missed those – I heard some pretty senseless views expressed.

There were four of Charles's friends who were either starting their law careers or in their final year at Oxford; two of Edward's from Saint Martin's; and three girls who seemed very "with it." They all seemed to have an opinion about China and what was happening there, although none of them had been. I was confronted with their preconceived ideas about the miracle of Maoism, about the ends justifying the means – in other words, it doesn't matter how many thousands of people are locked up, so long as the masses prosper – and about the Great Helmsman's scintillating personality. It was like being back in the policy meetings at Radio Peking.

In any case, no one seemed to understand anything I said, or even admit that reality might differ from their version of things. I began to get angry, and wondered if I would be better off turning in early, when a friend of Charles's suddenly stood up for me. He hadn't joined in any of the conversations so far, just looked on with a wry smile.

"None of you people, as far as I'm aware, have ever set foot in China, have you? In fact, who here would have the courage to go?" Charles's friend said.

Edward's friends responded in a chorus of "Three cheers for China!"

It had to be said that, what with the beer consumed, the standard of political debate had slipped a little. I offered my "savior" a glass of ginger beer. We left the others to their speechifying, and sat down in the kitchen. The young man, Badji, studied law with Charles, and was also paving the way for a career in that field. There was a real passion in his eyes as he described his life and his ambitions.

"It's a very nice name. 'Badji.' Where's it from?" I asked.

"Somewhere far, far away. Can't you tell?" he said with a little chuckle.

As he didn't seem inclined to expand on this, I didn't insist.


The evening came to an end. We returned to the sitting room where the other guests were starting to say their goodbyes. Soon, Badji left, too. We had promised to get together again.

It was very late, but Edward, Charles, and I slumped on the sofa for a little while before going to bed.

"I wish Manuela had been with us this evening; it would have reminded me of those nights out in Paris," said Charles wistfully.

"Well, I tell you what. She's invited us to Palermo, to her father's place. She was very insistent that we three should go."

And with that, our Christmas holidays were sorted out. I was dying to see my pal again, and to finally meet little Roberto.

# CHAPTER 2

# Gold Bracelet

On December 17, 1965, at five-thirty in the evening, we arrived at Boccadifalco Airport near the city of Palermo, laden with presents for Manuela and her family. We stepped onto the runway and, without any formalities, without saying a word, in fact, two men swiftly ushered us toward three cars: one empty, reserved for us and them, and the other two occupied by more men in suits. Charles raised an eyebrow, clearly impressed. Edward was at a loss for words, for once. Manuela had warned me that she wouldn't be there to greet us, but I hadn't expected a welcome committee worthy of a Hollywood film. From the look of them, and the bulges in their jackets, it wasn't hard to surmise that they were heavily armed.

With our two guardian angels sitting in the front, we spoke in hushed tones.

"What's all this about?" whispered Edward.

"Perfectly sensible precautions," Charles replied knowingly. "You may or may not recall that a couple of years ago, seven police officers were killed by a car bomb. It sparked a war against organized crime."

"Sorry, I had other things on my mind at the time," said Edward flatly, gazing out of the window at the road flashing by.

We sped away from the town in a southwesterly direction. We went through the little village of Croce Verde without stopping until, at the end of a long drive, we came to a vast house with an enclosed courtyard: *la casa greca*. It was guarded like a small military fort. Once we were safely inside Don Filippo Barzini's property, an armed guard came to open the car doors for us. The other two cars were being parked elsewhere.

On the steps of the huge nineteenth-century house, Manuela appeared, her little boy clutching her hand. She and I hugged each other tightly, then I knelt down to Roberto, who was looking at me earnestly with his big black eyes under long lashes. I planted a kiss on each of his round red cheeks.

"He's adorable," I said.

Manuela beamed at me. Charles could not take his eyes off her. When it was his turn to greet her, I could see he wanted to hug Manuela, too, but opted for a more formal kiss on both cheeks. Manuela was having none of that: she threw her slender arms around his neck, making it very clear she was in a completely different state of mind from the last time they had seen each other.

Finally, we were greeted by our hostess, Manuela's mother, while various members of the household staff carried our bags away. In a colorful fusion of French and Italian, she welcomed us, and we introduced ourselves.

"Welcome! We'll eat at eight o'clock. Meanwhile, I'll let my daughter show you our home. I'm sure you are impatient to catch up with one another. Come with me, Roberto," she said sternly, "it's time for your bath."

We were shown up to our enormous bedrooms, which were just as Manuela had described them. I was delighted to be reunited with some of our Chinese furniture, which had reached Europe several weeks after us. Manuela and I couldn't stop chattering. The boys, meanwhile, were unpacking in their bedroom at the other end of the corridor.

There was something different about her, I thought. She was more sparkly. And more beautiful, if that were possible!

"Where's your brother?" I asked. "I thought I was going to meet the famous Santino at last."

"He has gone to Roma. He said I should send his greetings. He will be back for the Christmas celebrations."

At suppertime, I was given pride of place next to Don Filippo Barzini. This massive figure of a man, with thick black hair and giant hands, made quite an impression. He exuded power and certainty, but I had imagined him as less attentive than he turned out to be; less flexible, more primitive, perhaps. He struck me as an upright man, someone who defended the honor of his clan and the values of his family, while at the same time keeping an eye on the future and new ways of thinking. He had piercing eyes that seemed to read my face, giving the distinct impression that he knew me better than I knew myself. He, too, managed to make himself understood with a hodgepodge of Italian and French, and plenty of gestures.

When I caught him staring at my brother, who himself was staring at Manuela and overcome with admiration, I could not gauge his reaction at all.

After a few days, I ceased to notice the armed guards and guard dogs around the place. It seemed perfectly natural to be escorted everywhere we went. We were invited to dances and parties almost every evening. At one of Manuela's friends' houses, we saw a projection of a film that had won a Palme d'Or at the Cannes film festival the previous year: *Il Gattopardo – The Leopard* – directed by the Milanese count Luchino Visconti, starring Alain Delon and Claudia Cardinale. We were admiring the ballroom scene when Manuela's friend said it had been filmed right there, in her house in Palermo! We spent the rest of the evening trying to spot places we recognized from the film, and miming the action.

During that wonderful stay, I learned to put my anxieties aside. I had to, if I was going to make the most of the hikes the four of us took together in the Sicilian countryside, our trip to Mount Etna, and our strolls through the streets of Palermo. Our bodyguards were never far away, and we were armed ourselves – with all manner of snacks prepared by the woman we now all called *la Mama*. Two weeks of tasting *la dolce vita* didn't seem nearly long enough, particularly considering how much fun Edward and I were having witnessing the dazzling romance between Charles and Manuela. Every scene that played out was more intriguing than the last. One day, we noticed they were holding hands. The next, we caught them kissing behind a hedge. On the third, they disappeared completely for two hours, and neither we nor the increasingly vexed body guards could find them anywhere. They claimed they had gone to buy a bracelet for *la Mama*, and had to wait for ages for the assistant to run and fetch it. Do you think we believed them, despite the shiny pink wrapping paper? Put it this way: under the tall Christmas tree decked with Murano glass baubles, there were all manner of presents, but no sign of a shiny pink one.

I met Santino, at long last. He was just as I had imagined him: the spitting image of his father, only younger. He arrived on Christmas morning, weighed down with presents for Roberto, who seemed to adore him. Santino only stayed for a few hours before racing back to Rome, where he had more business affairs to see to, apparently.

The day before our departure, *la Mama* organized a farewell supper. At the end of the meal, the men retired to the sitting room to smoke their cigars, and the women stayed in the dining room drinking *tisanes*. That was the tradition in such families, and no exception was to be made on our account. Through the glass doors, we saw Don Filippo and Charles cross the room and head toward the study, looking positively conspiratorial. At this, a very nervous-looking Manuela got up and left the room. Half an hour later, Don Filippo and Charles came back. *Il Padrone* was solemn. My brother had broken out in a sweat, but seemed to be smiling victoriously. The two men stopped in front of us.

"Call your daughter," Don Filippo ordered his wife.

Manuela must have been just behind the door, because she virtually fell through it.

"Yes, Papa?"

"I understand you love this man."

"Yes, Papa."

"You can have the wedding in late spring. You have my consent… and my blessing!" At last, he smiled broadly.

Manuela threw herself into her father's arms, and smothered him with thank-yous. *La Mama* wiped away a tear. I hugged Manuela and congratulated my brother. Edward launched into a discussion about the ideal date for the wedding.

Once we had all recovered ourselves, more or less, *la Mama* offered us all a glass of Marsala and cookies straight from the oven that Pia, the cook, had made. We all sat down, together this time, to raise our glasses to happy times. *La Mama* sat slightly apart, in her favorite armchair by the fire. She smiled as the tears rolled down her cheeks.

"Mama, don't cry! You should be happy for me," said Manuela quietly.

"It's just that you're going to leave us again…."

"I know, Mama, but we can visit each other whenever we like, you know."

Edward chose this moment to interject.

"I have a proposal to make, too. To all of you," he clarified, but seemed to be looking straight at me.

He cleared his throat.

"As you know, I have decided to live in Little Wittenham – it's a property in the South of England that my mother has inherited. There are outhouses that need restoring, because they're old and in poor condition. I would be delighted if a young couple, dear to my heart, took the job on…and lived there with their son, of course."

Manuela and Charles stared at each other, bowled over. Then, still looking intently into each other's eyes, they nodded and smiled.

"We accept! Joyfully!" Charles announced, taking his fiancée by the hand. "I have to say, we didn't see that one coming, fella!"

Nor had I. But there was more.

"And for Kim," Edward carried on, "at the far end of the grounds, there's a superb little cottage. I know you'd love living there, once we've fixed it up. So? Are you in?"

"Edward, you are amazing. Of course I'm in! Nothing would give me more pleasure than to live close to all of you."

Edward was particularly keen to impress upon us that Little Wittenham was down the road from London, but nonetheless counted as the countryside; he told us so fourteen times, at least. He just knew how happy we would all be there, and insisted we go and look as soon as we got home. Why not next weekend? It was a date.

By now, it was late. Manuela's parents had gone to bed. The four of us stayed up. Charles and Manuela handed me the notorious shiny pink present. I opened it: a delicate gold bracelet on a red velvet cushion.

"Thank you for making us so happy!" Manuela said.

"So, it *was* true!" I laughed. I explained to them that Edward and I had been convinced they had plucked the bracelet story out of the air, because they had better things to do. The couple blushed.

We laughed and talked far into the night. We were all at a sort of turning point in our lives. Adolescence was behind us, and so was our innocence, to a degree. Charles had a job, but wanted to make partner as soon as possible; Edward was about to launch his career and set up his home; Manuela wanted to be a student again, and specialize in Chinese antiques. And as for me...what was I going to do?

As they all reeled off possibilities, ambitions, and new avenues to explore in the world of work, I retreated into my thoughts. These thoughts took me out of the room, whisking me over thousands of miles and back through time to Peking and the day Wei and I had said goodbye. I saw the clandestine meeting with Liu, and the note he had given me: *rendezvous in Europe.* My hand jumped to my jacket pocket. The note was still there, wrapped around the dream stone and safely stowed away in a silk pouch. Daydreams of being reunited with Wei were all well and good, but they quickly evaporated when I came back to the real world. Manuela could see clearly that I was suddenly sad.

"When Wei gets to England, you must invite us all to supper at your cottage," she whispered in my ear.

Yet again, she had read my mind. I responded with a little smile; then, determined to chase away the blues, I proposed one last toast to the happy couple.

I look at my grandson, who seems moved by what he's just heard. And I catch him sneaking a glance at his cell phone. Does he have a girl of his own? After all, he's just the right age for first love...

CHAPTER 3

# Navy Blue Scarf

What a contrast between the warmth of the Barzinis' farewells and the arctic greeting we received in Paris. The same sign held up by another chauffeur I didn't recognize. What a shame Max had moved on…and my parents, who knew to expect us, were not free until the following morning. Again. They had left a note. The lights were off in the apartments at Rue du Faubourg Saint-Honoré. We packed our remaining things – we were leaving for London the next morning – and met up in the kitchen for a snack.

Over some rather scrumptious pudding we found in the fridge, I took the plunge: "How are you going to tell them about the wedding?"

"Easy," Charles replied. "I'm twenty-six, I've graduated, and I've got every right to marry whomever I like."

"I don't want to be a wet blanket, but have you met our mother?"

"Listen, that's why we're here. I'm not saying it will be *Maman*'s dream match, but I am so in love with Manuela that I think she'll accept her. Through gritted teeth, perhaps, but she'll accept her. Don't forget, my relationship with Sarah has never been quite as fraught as yours."

The next morning, I was awakened by a noise downstairs. I jumped out of bed, half-opened my bedroom door, and instantly heard my mother's shrill voice, taut with tension:

"I tell you again, it is out of the question! An unmarried mother? The unwanted child of some Mafioso, to boot? You're out of your mind!"

I couldn't make out my brother's reply, but I could tell from his tone of voice that he was giving as good as he got.

"Well, fine. If that's the way it is, you can get out!" she yelled. "You won't set foot in this house, or in Belgrave Square, ever again."

This time, I heard Charles's words all right; he was bounding up the stairs toward my bedroom. "You can think what you like, I'm marrying her anyway! I really couldn't give a damn whether you approve or not." He arrived at my door and burst in. "If she thinks she can run my life, she's got another thing coming! I'm getting my stuff together and going to Edward's. I hope he can put me up in London for a little while. *Maman* will change her tune when she sees I'm happy."

*You don't know her*, I wanted to say, but he was already out the door. I washed up and threw on some clothes, then went down to the dining room. Breakfast had already been cleared away, and there was no sign of anybody. I hunted around for a cup of tea.

I was just on my way back upstairs with a steaming cup of English Breakfast when I heard my father's voice. "Kim, is that you?"

"Yes."

"Come into your mother's study."

My turn, I thought to myself.

I could feel the tension in the air when I entered the room. My mother was sitting in an armchair at her Louis XVI desk. She looked furious. My father was standing bolt upright at her side, a hand resting on his wife's shoulder: not a good sign.

"Can you tell us who this belongs to, exactly?" he said quietly, picking up a knapsack and depositing it on the desk with a certain solemnity. I approached the desk and opened the bag. I was stunned to recognize the navy blue scarf that Wei used to wear in the cold. My blood froze.

"Where did you find it?"

"We're asking the questions, thank you," my mother said dryly. All the same, my father launched into an explanation of some sort. I didn't hear him, because I had just found a bundle of letters addressed to me. They were written in Chinese. My God…I was so absorbed by what I was reading that when my mother slammed her palm down onto her desk, it made me jump.

"Listen to your father when he is talking to you! The Chinese authorities have been here to see us. They knew where to look, of course. The individual who penned the letters was obliging enough to write your name on the envelopes along with – more useful still – your address in London." She interrupted her ironic diatribe to look me up and down. "Are you aware that you are putting us at risk with your nonsense? This man is considered extremely dangerous. You are getting your family into trouble. You really can be very stupid sometimes, Kim. Are you listening?"

I lifted my eyes from the pages, and replied as neutrally as I could. I knew I had to tread carefully.

"He's my calligraphy teacher. No one can stop him from writing me letters, can they? Anyway, it's only an account of his travels, that's all. He's just telling me what he's up to."

"He tried to leave China because he was wanted by the authorities. He was considered a traitor. Anyway, he won't be causing us any more embarrassment: he died somewhere between Shenzen and Hong Kong. A fisherman found him, along with his bag, in the river something-or-other, the one which acts as the border."

I had heard enough. To my parents' astonishment, I snatched the bag and ran out of the study. I bounded up the stairs three at a time, got to my room, grabbed the few things I had unpacked, slammed my suitcase shut, and headed straight back down the stairs. My head was spinning. The friends' weekend at Little Wittenham would have to wait for another time. I had to leave urgently, escape, get my thoughts straight. I had to speak to Leo.

On the train to Dinard, I settled into a compartment all to myself. I had just had time to call from a phone booth to announce my arrival on the 15:37. Little by little, I calmed down. At long last, I got out Wei's letters, and laid them out on the little table in front of me. I recognized his beautiful wild-grass handwriting, so refined, and in such contrast to the coarse paper, the cheapest you could find in China. My heart rate leapt again. This time, it wasn't surprise, but anxious curiosity. It was as if I had glimpsed someone in the street I knew was supposed to be thousands of miles away.

There were nine letters in all, of various lengths. I devoured them, both disappointed that he didn't once mention our love, and grateful that he had thought of the consequences of his missives being intercepted. He described the people he had met, but was careful not to reveal names, conversations, or surroundings. Everything and everyone he came across were set down in words, a tableau of China south of Peking. Though never explicitly, he hinted at his moods, his moments of sorrow and hope; and, I noticed above all else, he signed off each letter with the Chinese ideogram *ren – man –* a nod to the early calligraphy lessons he gave me. It brought tears to my eyes. I squeezed the bag tightly to my chest.

All morning, one thought had been zipping around my brain, sowing confusion. How was it that the letters were still intact? I mean, if the bag really had been recovered from the water, then they should be illegible, or at least partly so. That certainly was not the case. It could be that Wei had protected them with a plastic bag, but I could find no trace of one. None of the other items smelled of mud or seemed to have been damaged by the water. There was his knife, the navy blue scarf, a toothbrush, a map – also intact – and ration coupons from all over China. Was it possible he had meant to fake his own death?

Leo was waiting for me at the station. He carefully took my suitcase and showed me to Uncle Oliver's car. For the first time since that morning, I perked up a little. Uncle Oliver was due back the next day; he had gone to London for the week. We reached Dinard and then Mansfield Manor, tucked away in its pocket of greenery.

Leo had made a fire in my room, and it was soon roaring. I threw myself onto the bed. My brain was whirring. What was it all about? Were my parents telling the truth? I was missing a piece of the puzzle, I was sure of that. I couldn't stop running over the same questions in my mind, in a loop, unable to think of anything else. Leo made *dim sum* for supper, my favorite. But I hardly touched it.

"This isn't like you at all. What's going on?" he asked.

When Uncle Oliver got home around midday the next day, I must have looked like death warmed over. He was in fine form, mind you; bursting with energy, his eyes sparkling. He reminded me that the present he had promised me was waiting patiently in the boathouse for its new owner. I changed and followed him out.

It was a beautiful day—still and sunny, exceptionally so for a winter's day. On the way, I inhaled the sea air that seemed to caress my skin.

When Uncle Oliver opened the boathouse doors to reveal my magnificent present, I was taken aback. A little catamaran, the latest model. What a gem. Sleep-deprived or not, I had to try her out. Before I knew it, we were sailing. The wind picked up. Uncle Oliver was at the helm; I was put in charge of unfurling the sail. In a few seconds, we were tacking back and forth. It did me good to be totally absorbed in a physical action.

"When we get in, we'll do a bit of shopping. How long since you've seen the Maraîchers?" asked my uncle.

"I don't know. A couple of years, at least."

"They'll be delighted to see you."

The name Maraîcher always made me smile. It means *vegetable gardener* in French, so it was thoroughly appropriate for a family of greengrocers, who, over the generations, had branched out into other groceries, and fish, too. I used to love going into their shop when I was a little girl. They would give me delicious things to taste. It was quite a reunion, celebrated with plenty of goodies: toast and pâté, seafood, white wine, and so on. So many questions, stories, and gasps of delight.

All of a sudden, my head began to spin. I made my apologies and went back to the car. On the way home, I was violently sick. Back at Mansfield Manor, I hurried to bed. I was in terrible shape. Leo tried to nurse me for two days, without much luck. I didn't eat anything; nor could I sleep. I was utterly worn out. Uncle Oliver was very worried. He called the new local doctor, one Paul Le Kern, who was young, but by all accounts, brilliant.

Sometime in the late afternoon of the third day, my bedroom door opened, and the young doctor came in. He seemed rather un-sophisticated, and looked at me with wide eyes. He took my pulse, examined me from head to toe, and decided to take a blood sample in case I had contracted jaundice in Asia. He was odd, this Paul Le Kern fellow. He prescribed various pills and tiptoed out of the room.

A few moments later, I heard the front door shut. I decided to get up and talk to my uncle. Perhaps he would know what to do. I was dizzy, and took the stairs one step at a time. When I reached the kitchen door, I stopped. Leo and Uncle Oliver were in mid-conversation, and neither man had heard me.

"I know she witnessed a row...an unpleasant argument, you know...between her brother and her mother. That must have brought on the insomnia. She's a sensitive thing," Uncle Oliver confided to Leo. Through the crack of the door I saw Leo nod his head, but he clearly wasn't convinced.

"You speak with her," replied Leo enigmatically.

"Is it something serious? Tell me that, at least."

"Yes. Serious."

"Has she spoken to you about this?"

"Yes."

"Why won't she tell me?"

"She thinks you don't say to her everything you need say."

I had heard enough. I opened the kitchen door and stood before my uncle. "What are you keeping from me? I think I deserve to know."

Uncle Oliver was certainly surprised to see me, but he didn't take long to react.

"Go and have a shower, and we'll meet for supper in an hour. You're right, we need to talk."

CHAPTER 4

# Dog's Collar

Night had fallen. From my window, I had watched the sun slowly disappearing until it was swallowed up by the sea. The January air was cold, but it was warm in the house, with a crackling fire in the dining room.

Ever since I had begun to wonder about the nature of my connection to Uncle Oliver, I had been on edge as to what I might discover. What astonished me was that he saw at once what I wanted to know, though I'd never questioned him directly on the subject.

"Your mother and I met at Oxford, at a dinner. She was a second-year English undergraduate," he began.

"Was this before my father?"

"No, they were already engaged."

He and I were seated at the table, facing one another. The dining room was lit by candles, which gave it a cozy glow. Leo had made us a nice, simple supper, and decanted a bottle of wine. The aroma of truffles scented the air.

"Your mother was a ravishing French woman, well-educated and completely fluent in English. She charmed everyone. Miss Tyler: that's what she called herself. And she turned heads from her very first day at Oxford, I can tell you. That was two years before I met her. Her adoptive father had been a don at Magdalen College there, but had recently died, leaving her alone in the little family house."

259

"Her adoptive father? I thought she was French through and through?"

"Her real family was. But she'd fallen out with them and come to stay with Mr. Tyler, who had been her English teacher in France when she was a girl. Around the time I met her, his death was really getting to Sarah –not that she ever let on. Everybody wanted to be introduced to her, you know. Lisa and I were a young married couple, and our Beatrix had just been born. My wife was close to your father, Gordon Rochester's, family – just one of those quirks of fate – and one day, he invited us to his birthday party. When I saw your mother for the first time, she was dancing in the arms of the young officer from Sandhurst: Gordon, before his accident. I wasn't attracted to her at first. She was just another figure twirling around the dance floor…if a shade more elegant than the others. A few dances later, Gordon and Sarah came over to the buffet. She asked me to pass her a napkin, I recall. I did so, and our eyes met. I had never seen different-colored eyes before, and it caught me by surprise. I didn't have time to conceal my amazement. She smiled. That was how we struck up a conversation. I quickly realized she was cultivated and funny as well as beautiful."

"Funny?"

"Let's say she had a taste for extreme irony. There was always a ring of young people around her."

"I can't believe that," I said. Oliver stopped momentarily, lost in thought. He was describing someone I didn't recognize and that someone was my own mother. "Go on."

"I couldn't sleep that night. Sarah had bewitched me. I found some pretext to arrange a meeting with her at the Eagle and Child Inn, near where she lived. After that, we saw each other often. Any old excuse would do: a record to lend, a book to borrow, a play to go and see…until the day came when things went further."

"What about your wife?"

"Lisa knew the score when we married. We had a pact, you might say. She turned a blind eye to my philandering, provided I remained married and 'bore my responsibilities,' as she put it. It suited me perfectly."

"But I can't imagine it suited my mother very much."

"Exactly. At first, she wasn't aware of the situation. Well, I hadn't been terribly clear about the arrangement with my wife. Not long after we met, I took your mother to Italy. We had a magical time in Portofino, in a little hotel perched on the side of a mountain. *Il Splendido*, it was called. I'll never forget it. We stayed there a week. Every morning when we woke up, it felt like we were still dreaming…

"When we got back to England, the damage had been done: we were deeply in love. Sarah wanted us to live together; she tried to convince me several times. But it was complicated. And not just from my point of view; from hers, too. After all, she was engaged to your father, and yet…it was impossible for us to leave one another. It was a clear conflict between love and duty – like something out of one of Corneille's tragedies. Our discussions went around in circles and descended into arguments from time to time, despite our love for each other. Then, of course, Gordon had his parachute accident."

"I thought he had his accident before he met *Maman*."

"That's what your parents told you. The truth is very different: Sarah wanted to leave Gordon before the accident had even happened. She had announced as much to me, hoping to make me give in. We talked all night long. I couldn't go through with it. The following morning, we found out about your father's accident. Sarah made a choice, and kept to it: she went to the hospital to look after Gordon. She did the decent thing, staying at his side throughout the ordeal. I didn't see her again until your brother was born, in February, 1939. At least, not in private.

"At the time, we were all living in London, in Belgravia. War had not yet broken out, though we knew it was in the cards. The atmosphere post-Munich was electric in the political circles we moved in. When we next saw each other, your mother and I, your brother had just been born, and my Beatrice was just a bit older."

"And you succumbed, didn't you?" I couldn't help but say it. I was fascinated and impatient to know the outcome, and felt sure it was going to concern me.

"We couldn't help ourselves. The attraction was too strong."

"Where did you meet?"

"We went to the Connaught. I was good friends with Betty, the barmaid there. She was a real local treasure, heart of gold. I did her the odd favor, and she let us slip up to the first floor, to a gorgeous bedroom...seemed like paradise to us. We carried on like that throughout the start of the war. Then you arrived. Your mother dreamed of having another boy. She was hugely disappointed when she gave birth to a little girl. Little by little, her personality changed. I discovered a whole new side of her. The funny, energetic young woman I had known became cynical and aggressive. I couldn't make her happy. Getting divorced from our respective spouses was out of the question; we would have been social outcasts. And was it what we really wanted...?"

"Did you really have the courage, you mean? When did the relationship end?"

"When I had the nerve to take you out of that damn boarding school. Your mother never forgave me for doing that without consulting her. She was probably jealous, seeing how devoted I was to you, seeing the unconditional love that I had and still have for you."

Neither of us spoke. We simply stared at each other. Then I took up again, my voice charged with emotion.

"So in the end, you destroyed everything, and no one was happy." I paused; my next question would hit home. "Am I your daughter?"

"Yes, you are."

I gasped. Then, what I'd kept to myself all those years exploded. I leapt to my feet and began to stomp around the room.

"Why have you waited so long to tell me? For years, I wondered if I was mad, deluding myself that you might be my father. You and *Maman*, you've lied to me, hurt me. I was eaten up with sorrow, with doubt...you've been horribly selfish, both of you. You were so ashamed of me, you dumped me at a boarding school! I am so much like you! What would have happened if Gordon had refused to let me take his name? Would you have left me in the doorway of a church?" I wanted to hurt him now. "He's the only one who's been genuine in all of this. He loved her so much that he accepted it all. The affront, the humiliation, the deceit. He brought me up as if I were his daughter, he soothed me when I was ill, he looked after me. And you just got all the good parts! A few holidays here and there, and you couldn't be bothered with all the rest…."

I know you might be thinking that wasn't very fair to Oliver, that he was always there for me during the really hard times. But at that moment, I didn't care.

Leo brought in a dessert he had lovingly created: a huge Black Forest cake, dripping with cream. The two men shared a sheepish look. But I wasn't finished. I marched up to Oliver, who hadn't moved a muscle the whole time.

"If I asked you to legally recognize me as your daughter, would you do it?" Tears were streaming down my cheeks.

"No. Legally, it's not possible."

I couldn't take any more. I seized the cake and flung it against the wall, then bolted up to the first floor, my whole body trembling. I leaned up against the giant mahogany wardrobe in my room and tried to catch my breath.

When my mind eventually calmed, I could hear the muffled voices of Oliver and Leo in the dining room below. Oliver's cigar smoke wafted up the stairs: a sure sign that my "begetter" was thinking hard.

The sun shone brightly the next morning. For half an hour, Oliver and I walked in silence, our eyes glued to the ground.

"I am so sorry," said Oliver finally. "I know you have suffered in all this. Don't judge me too harshly. We don't always do what we want to do in this life, you'll learn that. Sometimes our education and our contradictions get in the way. I often wanted to tell you, but...I just couldn't. I was a coward."

I didn't say a word, waiting to see what would come next.

"When I bought Mansfield Manor," Oliver went on, "I talked to my lawyer about the possibility of recognizing you as my daughter. I would have had to adopt you, but I needed Gordon's consent, and that was out of the question. It would have wrecked his diplomatic career. I have lived with that choice for the rest of my life. It stopped me from having you as a daughter, stopped you from carrying my name – and I wanted that so, so much. Especially as little Beatrice was taken from me so young. My real mistake was not telling you the truth sooner, and letting you grow up with a lie. One thing I *could* do was put the house in your name. Mansfield Manor belongs to you. You can throw me out if you don't want to see me anymore. But you need to know this: you are the most precious person in the world to me, even if I haven't always known how to express it. I love you, Kim."

I stopped walking. So did Oliver. His big arms closed around me, and we both wept. The salt air and his aftershave combined in a strong but comforting scent I will never forget.

As Oliver broke away from our embrace, his gaze fell upon my neck and the jade stone that Wei's mother had given me. I had taken the habit of wearing it when I felt the need for warmth.

"Why don't you tell me all about this jewel?"

I didn't need to be asked twice. In truth, I was longing to tell him. It was like a dam breaking. I let the words pour out of me, and the whole story cascaded from my lips: about Wei, the relentless aggression from Sarah, her argument with Charles. My doubts, my fears, and my suffering. And above all, my hope of seeing Wei again, despite all the portents suggesting I never would.

"I should have paid more attention," he said and took my hand. We started to walk again, among the seaweed left behind by the receding tide. "Leo and I will take this on, I give you my word. We'll find out what's happened to this Wei of yours if we have to move heaven and earth." We had reached the boathouse by now. "Reminds me, I need to fetch a hammer. Broken gate up at the house. Come in with me, will you?" said Oliver with a note of excitement in his voice – not over a hammer, surely….

Waiting for me inside was a six-week-old Labrador, busily tugging at one of the ropes of my catamaran. My childhood dream had come true! I picked up the puppy and held him against my chest. He licked me clumsily. Oliver looked on, leaning against a wall out of the way, while I got to know the little fellow.

"I don't know how to thank you," I said.

"He's a French dog, so you'd better find a name starting with a C. That's how they do it over here; different letter every year. *C'est l'année des C*, don't you know?" He held out a superb dog collar. Together, we decided to name him Caïus. Then we went outside to finish our walk on the beach. I could not believe that so much had happened in just one day.

For a good week or so, I wallowed in the happiness that Oliver
and Leo brought me, then I decided to get back to London, leaving my new four-legged friend in their care for the time being.
The search for Wei began in earnest. After a month of patient
research and requests for information from all over the place,
the pair received confirmation of what we already suspected: the
bag had been recovered by a fisherman, but the body was never
found. Still, as the weeks and months passed, my slim hopes got
slimmer still.

# CHAPTER 5

# Wedding Invitation

May, 1966.

Manuela shone in her blue satin empire-waist dress with a tulle veil, and a three-yard train carried by several young bridesmaids. She seemed to glide over the marble and porphyry-encrusted floor toward the altar on the arm of her father. Don Filippo Barzini was dressed in a formal frock suit and immaculate white shirt. A quick glance at the congregation, sitting attentively in the pews of Palermo Cathedral, showed that everyone was hypnotized by my friend's beauty.

There were aunts and uncles, cousins and second cousins, and every other relative under the sun sitting amongst Sicilians from all walks of life: the well-off and the not-so-well-off. All of them were indebted to Don Filippo for something or other. The bodyguards were also in attendance, dressed in their Sunday best, their jackets bulging, as usual.

The English guests were very much in the minority. Edward and Charles had invited some of their friends, whom I hardly knew. Oliver and I brought Leo along, and he sat up straight in a black suit that was slightly too big for him. No question of my parents or their relatives coming; in fact, they only learned of the wedding a few days before. So as not to upset them, and with Manuela's consent, my brother had told his in-laws that Sarah was unwell, and could not make the journey to Sicily. There would be time enough for a more honest appraisal at a later date. The Barzinis were eagerly letting it be known that their daughter was marrying an ambassador's son, which was perfectly true, in any case. Luckily, Manuela's father insisted on covering all conceivable costs.

In the cathedral choir, children were arranged in a semi-circle under the strict eye of the choirmaster. Above them, light streamed in through the window of the dome.

That very morning, in the family villa I had gotten to know so well, I caught Manuela's eye – and we shared a look not just of friendship, but of certainty. Our lives were now intertwined for evermore.

"My brother is someone with a big heart, someone thoroughly honorable. I know that all he wants in life is to make you as happy as can be, and…." I couldn't finish my sentence. We fell into each other's arms and held on tightly for what felt like minutes.

"You know what is going to be hard for me?" Manuela asked. "Not crying when I say 'I do.' It would be a shame to ruin the make-up you've done so nicely."

I was sitting with Oliver in the cathedral, trying desperately to log the day's events into my memory for all time. My best friend and my brother both said their vows before the bishop, pledging to have and to hold, in sickness and in health.

It was a gorgeous day in early June, and the sun was up. Outside the cathedral, the crowd showered the newlyweds with rose petals, then wandered down the Via Bonello and onto the Piazza. Meanwhile, the happy couple was being helped into a black Rolls Royce by Don Filippo's chauffeur. The car pulled away, boxed in by two other cars containing the usual contingent of bodyguards, *il Padrone*, *la Mama*, and Santino, Manuela's brother, who had taken time off from his activities in Rome for once. Oliver and I followed close behind.

We arrived at the reception. Cars streamed into the large court-yard, gravel crunching under their weight. Security guards checked the presents at the main entrance. An expansive tent had been erect-ed in the walled garden, just by the swimming pool. A lavish buffet, decorated with huge bouquets, awaited the guests. Musicians played traditional Sicilian pieces while we sipped cocktails, and, later on, ten jazz musicians arrived to liven up the party.

At one point, I found Charles in the garden, champagne glass in hand – Manuela must have been circulating. He was different, sud-denly: could he have grown up in a few hours? His voice was more assured, and he seemed taller, somehow.

"It's the best day of my life. I would never have met Manuela without you. Thank you," he said.

"You're welcome! Thank you for giving me the sister-in-law of my dreams."

Later on that evening, after the fireworks, Oliver noticed I was preoccupied. "Don't be sad, Treasure. You'll find your Wei soon…."

"I hope so, with all my heart. I'm sure you'd take to him straightaway."

When the celebrations had run their course, Manuela and Charles climbed aboard a large sailing boat that belonged to one of her uncles. They planned to idle around the Mediterranean for a month. Once I'd seen them off, I packed my suitcase – making sure I didn't crumple the wedding invitation, I wanted to keep that – and jumped on the first flight to London. Since October, I had been studying at the London School of Economics and Political Science. I didn't have much choice: my parents had prescribed the LSE, and frankly, I didn't know what else to do with myself.

# CHAPTER 6

# A Fishing Knife

Edward's property was in Little Wittenham, in Oxfordshire, about fifty miles west of London.

Three months before the wedding, we had spent a weekend there together, to get to know the place. Breathtaking grounds encompassing hundred-year-old trees and broad meadows: it was clearly a place steeped in history and splendor. A fine part of the world in which to live.

Edward was eager to make us fall in love with the place. He played the role of guide perfectly, and saved the best till last. After our rapturous praise of the grounds and gorgeous rhododendron beds that went right down to the banks of the Thames, he made us walk down a driveway leading to the main property. We came to a 19th-century red brick house and two large cottages. It was obvious that several families could live there without getting in each other's way. The price to pay was also clear for all to see: sweat and toil. The electrical wiring, plumbing, and plastering all needed redoing, not to mention the obligatory coat of paint. We immediately got stuck in noisy discussions about who would live where and what needed doing, everyone chipping in with their two cents. Soon, it was getting dark. We decided to continue the guided tour the next morning at dawn; we knew it would be worth struggling out of bed at that hour to see nature waking up, too.

At five in the morning, suitably outfitted with hiking gear and flashlights, we set off, eager to discover the surrounding area. We tramped across meadows, disturbing dozing sheep. As the sun came up, its rays caught the dew. We walked in silence, at a gentle pace, with the feeling that we might stumble upon something precious and extraordinary at any moment. And that's precisely what happened. We came to a clearing where a doe and her fawn were grazing peacefully. Edward gestured to us to crouch down quietly, and we took in the magical sight. A light mist rose from the ground. But the animals must have smelled us: they bolted. Just then, through the mist as if out of nowhere – a delightful little cottage appeared. The sight of it moved me, so much so that tears filled my eyes. I knew, somehow, I would find peace there.

How could I fail to fall in love with such a romantic little dwelling hidden away in the woods? It was a simple two-story, two-bedroom house with a huge chimney. I could just imagine myself writing in my journal there (I had managed to keep one since returning from Peking).

Edward was particularly enthusiastic. "It's all yours. You'll have your work cut out! No, of course, we can do it together, when we get some time off."

"Don't you worry, I'll be happy with candlelight for the time being, and the outside water pump will suit me fine."

Charles and Manuela wandered around the cottage hand in hand. My brother suggested we open the picnic hamper we had prepared the night before. We started a fire in the grate and tucked into breakfast, chatting about this and that.

"When will your mother come and live with us?" I asked Edward.

"She'd love that. But I'd rather wait until we've fixed the place up," Edward replied. Kate was settled in Oxford, not far away. She had decided to go into a convalescent home after her discharge from the clinic two years previously. London was out of the question, and she had sold the place in the south of France: too many bad memories.

Before long, we started work on the place, with some help from a local builder; we didn't have enough time to take on the whole job ourselves. Saturday after Saturday, we took the train from Paddington to Didcot, the nearest train station. A gamekeeper met us at the station in an old minibus. Over those few months, I realized two things: first, Edward was not wrong when he said Little Wittenham wasn't far from London; second, I was a hundred times happier fixing up old houses than I was learning about economics.

By the time I got back to London after the wedding, at the beginning of June 1966, my motivation for studying was at rock bottom. I was still living in my old bedroom in Belgrave Square, on the second floor of the family home. As my studies weren't too onerous, I went out in the evenings to my favorite nightspots: mainly jazz clubs. I had developed a taste for jazz when I lived in Paris. I was so excited at the prospect of my brother and sister-in-law settling into Little Wittenham. I knew we would spend a fair amount of time there, not just weekends. We promised to work for the whole summer once they got back from their honeymoon.

One evening, some friends and I went to Ronnie Scott's, my favorite Soho club. We sat at a table and ordered a few drinks while we waited for the main attraction: the American saxophonist Stan Getz. The emcee had already begun to announce the evening's line-up when we noticed a group of young people come in. They took the table next to ours. I recognized Badji, Charles and Edward's friend whom I had met just after I got back from China, and waved at him.

Badji came and sat next to me at the end of the concert, and we struck up a conversation. At one point, he launched into an impression of Stan Getz himself. Everyone guffawed with laughter: it was spot-on.

"Looks like you've been practicing your whole life!" I said to him.

"You're not far off. I've been pretending to play the sax for ten years."

I hadn't had so much fun in a long time. Spilling out of the club late that night, we decided to see each other again.

Over the next few months, we blitzed the jazz clubs and dance halls. Badji loved going out, and I felt it was high time I let my hair down, as though staying out all night was a way of fitting back into the world where I thought I belonged, far from China and my lost love. I discovered a group from Liverpool called the Beatles. I couldn't stop talking about them, which made Badji laugh.

"Anyone would think you'd only just noticed them!"

"I have been in China, don't forget."

"Well, in that case, my little Chinese friend, allow me take you on a journey through the most violent musical revolution since the days of Stravinsky."

One afternoon, when I was working at my desk without much conviction, I heard a car beep in the street. I poked my head out the window, mildly curious. There was Badji, standing by a little green Austin car that belonged to his mother, waving and beaming from ear to ear. I ran downstairs.

"I'm taking you to Wembley!" he announced.

That very evening, we saw the Beatles at Wembley Arena. The place was so packed, we were worried we'd lose each other. Badji held me tightly against him. The concert was practically inaudible because of the fans' screaming – mainly delirious women and girls – but I had a wonderful time nonetheless. I pressed up against Badji, caught up in the swell of madness around us. Driving back to Belgravia in the middle of the night, we chatted about the evening.

"I like it when you let yourself go," said Badji.

"What do you mean by that?"

"You sometimes seem a bit reserved."

I smiled.

He went on: "Being free is also about letting yourself have feelings, and showing them."

He looked over at me, and didn't push it further. I got out of the car and we said goodnight.

I found him at my door at eight o'clock the next morning.

"Feel like going for a jog in Hyde Park?"

"I thought you were a night owl."

"That's right, jogging is perfect for getting rid of all the smoke you inhale the night before. Can I tempt you, or are you frightened I'll leave you in the dust?"

What with the concerts, jogs, jazz, and candlelit dinners, not to mention the tennis and dancing (he was excellent at both), I barely noticed the months tick by.

Then there was the day he invited me to meet his family, for his maternal great-grandfather's 90th birthday. At six o'clock one evening in July, 1966, I turned up at a large apartment in Soho where Badji's parents lived. I now realized why he talked about "being free" so much. Children, adults, the young, and the not-so-young all jostled about busily. There were uncles, aunts, nephews, and nieces: some black, some white, and some *café au lait*, as the Paris crowd would say. Their faces were all open and friendly.

The explanation for this astonishing variety lay with the great-grandfather himself, an ancient-looking Kenyan covered in wrinkles and sitting upright on a chair in the middle of the dimly-lit room. He had an almost magical aura. Badji took me over to him and introduced me.

Later, back amongst the family brouhaha, I caught Badji admiring me.

At suppertime, about twenty adults sat together around a long table. There were at least as many children eating in the room next door. I had never seen such an entertaining crowd. We chatted, drank, and laughed, digging into vast communal dishes that everyone loudly proclaimed to be "delicious!" What a contrast to our stuffy English upbringing.

Eventually, the time came to celebrate the great-grandfather's birthday. Having eaten in his own room with his sons, he was carried into the middle of ours on his chair. No candles. No cake. Instead, one by one, we all received his blessing. When my turn came, I felt a sense of calm wash over me. He laid his hands on my head. Then I heard a murmur. I leaned toward him, straining to hear.

"The past is the past," he said, mischievously. I looked up and met his gaze, dumbfounded. How could he have known?

At the end of the evening, Badji drove me back to Belgrave Square. As we neared the end of the journey, I said: "Thanks for inviting me to this wonderful celebration. I love your family. And your great-grandpa, what an amazing man."

"You weren't shocked?"

At first, I wondered what he meant, then realized Badji was referring to the color of his skin. "Of course not!"

"I thought long and hard before inviting you."

"Why?"

"I was frightened it might make us less close."

"What nonsense!"

Neither of us spoke.

"Then again, if you were frightened, it means you doubted me. So, learn to trust me!" I said.

When we pulled up outside the house, he stopped the engine and turned to face me. Slowly, he leaned forward and stroked my cheek. He brought his lips to mine. Just then, Maria, our cook, happened to walk out onto the front porch. I got out of the car and blew Badji a kiss. He smiled and started the engine. How could I have failed to realize that he was falling in love with me? From the porch, I watched his little car disappear around the corner.

And what about me? Could I love Badji? For the time being, I had no such feelings; he was more of a brother. I still thought about Wei all the time. My pain and longing may have faded somewhat, but I was far from over him. All the same, I had heard his great-grandpa's message loud and clear. And Badji was there in the flesh, with his seductiveness, his laughter, and his exquisite saxophone-playing....

Eventually, my brother and Manuela got back to London after their three-month voyage. They were tanned and happy, and it did me a world of good to see them again. Little Roberto had stayed behind in Palermo with his grandparents, but his mum had already found him a playgroup near their new home, which was virtually finished. We decided to tackle Edward's house next.

That was the start of an intense period of work, combined with mirth, late nights, and endless chats. We organized our workplace quickly, and in good spirits. We all slept on mattresses on the floor of the building site itself. Miss Eleanor, a vivacious and efficient young woman who lived in the next village, shopped for us and made our meals. I found a workshop less than a mile away, where an experienced carpenter provided all the materials and advice we could want. We were constantly covered in layers of plaster or paint, depending upon the stage we were at. Everyone got involved.

When I wasn't conscientiously whitewashing walls, I set about organizing the work efforts. I realized that I loved doing that. And for relaxation, I attempted a little trout fishing in the stream that ran along the west side of our land before emptying into the Thames. That way, I made the most of the outdoors, and tried my hand at a skill Oliver had shown me when I was a girl. Often, Charles came with me. He loved fishing, too.

As far as my studies went, my first year at LSE had finally come to an end. To this day, I have no idea how I passed the end-of-year exams.

Around then, Badji decided to come and join us. He showed up like Father Christmas one evening, bringing board games, his sax, and his *joie de vivre*. Over time, I noticed that he wasn't a natural laborer. On the other hand, he knew how to keep up the troops' morale, and we spent many a lively evening around the fire, sprawled on our mattresses playing Monopoly, backgammon – or, his specialty, poker. We would listen to him play jazz standards, or hits by Frank Sinatra, Harry Belafonte, and especially the Beatles.

As the days went by, I let him hold my hand and get close to me, but never let him kiss me. Sometimes, I thought of what his great-grandfather had said to me; sometimes, I let my mind flood with images of Wei. Of course, Edward had noticed what Badji was up to, and gave me the occasional knowing look. As for Manuela, well, she fell for his saxophone-playing.

One night toward the end of August – we had finished supper, and were still covered in plaster from head to toe – Badji got down on one knee.

"Kim, I am crazy about you. Will you marry me?"

Everyone burst into spontaneous applause. Badji took full advantage of the distraction and kissed me on the lips. I was surprised, but let myself get caught up in the intoxicating affection on display. Although I didn't say yes…or no.

We sat in a semicircle by the fire, and the conversation turned more solemn.

"As of September, I will be an attorney with Morgan & Tyers. I received confirmation today," my suitor proudly announced.

My brother stole his thunder somewhat: "In that case, we'll be working together!" It transpired that Charles had swung the job for him in the firm where he was well-established himself.

Edward piped up: "Why don't you and Badji set up in the house opposite? That would be fantastic, we'd be all together. Charles, Manuela, and Roberto here, my mother and me next door, and you two in the third house, when it's ready."

"Until then, we could move into your cottage, Kim," said Badji.

"No, that's *my* place, *my* paradise!"

Badji was taken aback by my fierce riposte. I didn't really understand it myself; it was as if someone was speaking through me.

Just then, Edward intervened by thrusting a glass of champagne into our hands to celebrate. Charles said, "You can use the cottage for thinking in peace, a long way away from bores like us!"

Edward looked at me intently as he handed me my glass. "I want to make you an offer too, Kim. How would you feel about working with me? I've decided to set up my own business renovating houses. I thought of you when I first had the idea, but now that I've had the chance to see how good you are, I'm sold. Would you like to be my business partner?"

This time, I replied with an enthusiastic "Yes!" The idea certainly appealed a great deal, though I was well aware I had a lot to learn, and would have to work hard.

I knocked back the champagne, feeling trapped—and a little drunk, too. I was twenty-five years old, and two men had just told me they needed me, each in his own way. I was fine with the job offer, but the declaration of love was a very different prospect.

Early the next morning, I decided to go fishing and do some thinking. I took a bag with all my fishing gear, my rod, my waders, and the flies I had carefully fashioned. It was time to hit the river. Before long, Charles came to join me; he knew where to look. He was in his waders, too; the water was over our thighs.

I had just cast off, and was watching the fly glinting in the sunlight, when I heard him say: "I'm happy for you, he's a really decent guy. You should say yes. I've been friends with him for four years, and we've had some good times together. If you ask me, he's generous, funny, a hard worker – though perhaps home improvement is not his strongest suit. But from time to time, he can be temperamental, blow a gasket, even. Basically, he can be an angel one minute and a bit of a monster the next." My brother stopped talking and studied my facial expression. "I suppose you're going to say yes?"

"I am. I've known him for more than a year. We make a good team. I feel happy with him, and it's high time I moved on. I can't forget Wei completely just yet, but I'll get there. Trust me, I'll nurture his angelic side, and send the monster packing."

Just then, a trout bit. I yanked on the rod too abruptly, and lost my balance in the strong current. The pull was leading me downstream.

"Let go of the rod!" shouted my brother.

"Not a chance!" I wasn't going to give up on that fish. I held on to my rod with one hand and struggled to get a fishing knife out of my pocket with the other. I was going to have to pierce the waders if I didn't want to drown. Soon, I felt the cold water seep into the space around my legs, and I decided to let myself be carried along until I reached calmer waters. Charles, meanwhile, was running along the riverbank, a lot more worked up than I was.

The river broadened out and became shallower. Soaked through, I clambered to my feet. I looked at the trout, still struggling on the end of my line, and laughed. Charles was out of breath by the time he made it over to help me unhook him. What a catch! Between three and four pounds, at a guess. My brother got his camera out. Once the whole ceremony was complete, we let the fish go, as always.

On the walk home, my brother asked, "How are you going to tell *Maman*?"

~

Recalling the fishing adventure so many years ago makes me want to go swimming right now. The water around Mansfield Manor is cold at this time of year, but it will do me a world of good.

"I don't think I really want to hear more about Grandfather , even though I'm intrigued to know what you saw in him."

"You know, Vittorio, people change, for better or worse. You have to give them a chance to make things right one day. You mustn't hold it against him…." I said. But it is a sign to me that maybe Vittorio and Kenya and I all need another little break, a few hours to live in the present. And I want some time to myself. The rush of cold water, the pull of it, the sense of release and the way you can't help but be in the moment when you're struggling to keep moving against the bracing current—that's what I long for.

The kids go about their business: writing emails to friends, doing a little homework, watching television. Mozart, as usual, keeps me company as I leave the house. Looking out to sea, I don't notice that Leo is watching over me from the first-floor window. What happened the other day frightened him. He doesn't trust me….

# CHAPTER 7

# A Second Dried Rose

There was nothing going on at the end of August, 1966, in the Rue du Faubourg Saint-Honoré. Paris was still deserted because of the summer holidays. My parents had been back for a week. They didn't bat an eyelid when I announced my impending visit, and can't have had a clue why I wanted to see them.

It was going to be tricky. After five days of spending every morning with them, I still found some pretext or other to put off the conversation about the wedding. Once I had said yes to Badji, I knew I would have to lay the ground before introducing him to my parents. That's why I was there by myself.

Everyone was up to speed now except them. Oliver seemed surprised when I told him, but said he was happy for me. He even suggested that the reception take place at "my" house in Brittany. Badji's family was over the moon. Everyone at Little Wittenham was busy getting our new home ready. It was time to be brave.

I was standing bolt upright, facing my mother's little desk, staring straight ahead. Sarah was sitting on the other side of the desk, and Gordon was standing to one side of his wife with his hand on her shoulder: they were waiting. It was a familiar scene, and not one that filled me with delight. I dove in, though I knew perfectly well the water was going to be freezing.

"I want to let you know that I am going to live with Charles and Manuela at Little Wittenham, and that I am going to be married next year. In the spring."

My mother jolted in her seat. "Married to whom?"

"I don't think we've been introduced…." my father said.

"What does he do? Will he be able to support you?"

I answered this question straightaway. Easier that way.

"He studied law with Charles, and he has just started work at Morgan & Tyers."

Instantly, and for the first time in ages, my mother really smiled. "That's marvelous! Why haven't you introduced us to this boy?"

I didn't have time to reply. She was on her feet and pirouetting around the study like an excitable honeybee. She promptly began to hatch all sorts of ambitious plans. "I know exactly what we'll do: we'll have an enormous party. First, we need to celebrate your engagement, and then, for the wedding itself, we'll have a celebration in France, and another one in London. It's wonderful! When can we meet his parents?"

"Whenever you like, *Maman*."

"I can see it all: the best caterers, the fanciest florists, and oh, if your engagement ring isn't pretty enough, I'll give you my grandmother's!"

I had never seen her euphoric before. She was gabbing away: a heroine in a fairy story, sparkling with happiness. Then, suddenly, she stopped and grabbed me by the shoulders. "We'll have a hundred guests! Give me a kiss, my darling...ah, now tell me, what's his name?"

The lump in my throat seemed impossible to swallow It was the first time she had called me anything other than Kim, and now she had a brutal disappointment coming. My stomach was tied in knots, but I had to finish what I'd started. I took a deep breath.

"Badji Smith."

"I beg your pardon?" My mother looked stunned; her smile was rigid. "Could you say his name again?" Oh, how her tone of voice had changed.

"Badji Smith."

My father stepped in. "What nationality is he?"

"English," I said.

"And his parents?"

"English, too."

"And his grandparents?"

"English, too. His great-grandfather is Kenyan. And he's wonderful!"

My mother collapsed into an armchair. "My daughter is crazy. First she wants to marry a Chinaman, and now she's found herself a black."

"Who told you I was in love with Wei?"

She looked thrown by my question, but only for a second or so. As usual, she picked herself up pretty quickly. Her joy had turned to anger.

"Who do you think I am? Don't you think I knew what was going on in China between you and him? I read his letters."

My mind was whirring. Impossible. Wei had written to me in Chinese; she wouldn't have understood a word. She was keeping something from me; her response to my question had been too caustic, even for her. What was behind it?

My father, well aware that the atmosphere had turned highly combustible, muttered something about a meeting and exited the room, leaving us face to face.

"Don't think for one second that we would let you marry a black man!" she said.

Another deep breath. "*Maman*, he's as white as you or me. Look, isn't it time we called a truce? Let's stop fighting all the time. Let's be friends. We can organize the wedding together, be happy together. It can be a special time for us both; that's what I've dreamed of."

"You're forgetting I'm your mother, not your friend. You're confusing me with that Italian tart your brother married, the one with a Mafioso for a father. My children are insane!" Hearing her insult my best friend and sister-in-law was unbearable, but I was trying to keep calm. "And now you want to bring a negro home!"

I couldn't contain myself anymore. "I won't let you insult my friend or the man I'm going to marry! What gives you the right to judge other people like that when you yourself had a lover for years? I'm living proof! Setting a moral example, were you?"

The slap reverberated around the room, and nearly knocked my head off.

"Get out of this house! The day you marry a black man, I will declare both of my children dead – dead to me, in any case."

"*Maman*! You can't say things like that, and anyway, he's not black."

"Your children could be; it's the same thing."

I looked her straight in the eye with all the self-assurance I had left. "You will have demolished everything around you. Can't you leave your past behind, for once, and break out of your shell? It's stopping you from being happy!" I knew I was running out of arguments. And I could see she was standing firm; nothing I could say would make her change her mind.

"I will send all your belongings on to England, or to Oliver's. You're not to set foot here or in Belgrave Square ever again." With that, she left the room, slamming the door behind her. I was all by myself. And miserable.

Before packing up my things and going for good, I decided I needed some breathing space. I left the embassy and hailed a taxi, asking the driver to take me to the gardens of the Château de Bagatelle in the 16th arrondissement. I loved that place, just as I had loved the Summer Palace in Peking. Smelling the roses calmed me down.

As I walked among the flowers, my mother's words about Wei kept ringing in my ears. Could she have hazarded a lie to get at the truth?

I stayed there a good while, making the most of the serenity of the place. In the end, it completely won me over. Night had fallen. I wandered off in search of a taxi. It was time to go home, and back to Badji in England.

∾

"I knew your mother was harsh," declares Vittorio, "but from what my father said, I could barely believe it."

"One is often more demanding with one's children," I told him. "It's hard to accept that they live life as they see fit. We think we know what's best for them, and all we do is make them defensive. It takes time to realize everything we have in common."

"Yeah, it's like Mum," Kenya adds. "She always wants me to be girly, but I like jeans and sneakers. I hope she understands me one day.!"

We smile at each other. And I marvel a little to think that what I just said to Kenya is, in a way, a defense of my own mother. Despite her years of cruelness and how she denied me the love I craved, she was never able to get me to stop being empathetic, never able to stop me from making efforts to understand and to forgive. It heartens me to think of that.

∾

Dinard: May, 1967.

My wedding at Mansfield Manor was certainly not the high-society event my mother had hoped for. There were about a hundred guests who were all very dear to me, mostly from England, but also Italy, France, and Belgium. There was Badji's family (minus his great-grandfather), Manuela's family, the Lestranges from Paris, Miss Bonham, Paul and Gabrielle (our Belgian friends from China), Oliver, Leo, of course, Charles and Manuela, Edward (who came with his mother, Kate, and a friend), and Margaret Black, my nanny for all those years.

Friends from Brittany were also invited: the Maraîchers and Doctor Paul Le Kern. He looked admiringly at me, which I wrongly attributed to the magnificent dress I was wearing, which Oliver had had made for me by a young Parisian designer by the name of Yves Saint-Laurent.

The little chapel I had always adored was covered in roses, my favorite flowers. Oliver accompanied me through the doors on his arm. I felt like a young queen, despite my parents' absence. Perhaps it was better that way. I stood tall, proud to be walking down the aisle with that charming, radiant man: my real father.

I took my place beside Badji, and tried to concentrate on the service.

Back at Mansfield Manor, a gorgeous reception was waiting for us: *petits fours* and a huge cake with buttercream frosting made by Leo – not to be thrown around the place, this time!

While the guests were eating, Oliver and I slipped out into the garden. He certainly didn't beat around the bush. "Out of interest, why have you married Badji? Out of love? Out of defiance?"

I had been expecting him to ask. I rested my head on his shoulder as we ambled along. "No, I'm happy. He's funny. Kind. I think he'll make a good father."

"It's not the most romantic appraisal. I'm not hearing grand declarations of love…Kim, a partnership wears you down with time. It takes lots of love, lots of imagination for a couple to survive."

"I'm sure I can make it work."

"You've got a strong character, you know; you need to learn how to compromise, add some water to your wine, as they say 'round here."

"That's not how you taught me. I don't like watered-down wine." Neither of us spoke for a bit. Then I added, "Married life is off to a flying start, I must say!"

Oliver smiled at last. "Well, give me a good crop of grandchildren. I'm looking forward to seeing them grow up in this house. I had a nice chat with Leo. Offered to give him a decent allowance and send him home to China, but he's not having any of it. He can't imagine life without us. We're family to him now. When you have kids, he wants to come to London and work for you."

"Oliver, you know, I can't take on Leo. Later, perhaps."

"I've made provision for you and him. You'll see when I'm not around anymore."

I gave him a hug. "We'll talk about that in forty years!"

We were surprised to bump into Leo and my old nanny around the corner, deep in conversation.

"Perhaps Leo won't be *allowed* to go back to China," said Oliver with a wink.

It was late, and the mildest of evenings. Far off, we could see the lights of Saint-Malo and what looked like the famous ramparts. Some of the guests had already left. Others were lingering, chatting and laughing in little groups. Oliver went up to bed. Badji came to find me, and we sat together on a little bench at the back of the house. Time for a breather before getting back to the party. Our intimate moment was soon interrupted by the arrival of my brother and Manuela. She sat down beside us on the grass. He smiled knowingly at her. As soon as he opened his mouth to speak, I guessed what was coming.

"Manuela and I would like to tell you something…"

She leapt up and went to join my brother., saying the rest for him: "We're going to have a baby." They were so sweet, entwined like that, flushed with excitement.

"What wonderful news!" I said, hugging them both. "Well, you know what this means? We'd better get a move on with the building work at Little Wittenham."

# CHAPTER 8

# Two Plastic Identity Bracelets

Their baby, Michael Rochester, turned out to be quite a little gurgler. He was such an easy, accommodating baby that anyone would think he had been made-to-order. Or could it have been the influence of an attentive big brother? Roberto used all of his seven and a half years of experience in the world to tend to Michael, dropping everything if his *fratello piccolo* showed the slightest sign of distress.

By now, the houses were all fixed up, and our little community was fully operational. Kate became a universal grandmother, apt to spoil us rotten. She had, at last, rediscovered a taste for life: her ordeal and long illness were now behind her. She often looked after the baby, especially since Manuela had decided to open a shop selling Chinese antiques.

Badji and my brother were barely around anymore; their workload was staggering. Mind you, Edward and I weren't much better off. We certainly didn't drag our feet when it came to finding new properties to work on. In those days, the mews in Kensington, Chelsea, and Westminster weren't fashionable, and it was possible to buy them up with the help of a mortgage – in our case, a considerable one. Our "portfolio," as Charles called it, consisted of ten of them.

Some of these former stables, which once housed the equipage of the adjoining wealthy households, had become a place to dump unwanted objects, but most were just modest dwellings – until we got our hands on them. I spent days stripping and hanging wallpaper, painting, and so on. My hands never seemed to tire of the work, but they looked less and less like a respectable young lady's hands, and more and more like a mason's. Badji was forever pointing this out to me.

In March, 1968, just when I was starting to believe I wouldn't be able to have a baby, I got pregnant. I was overcome with joy, and everyone was full of congratulations. Manuela was delighted – "Michael will have someone to play with!" – and Oliver was in seventh heaven.

I wrote to my parents straightaway. I told myself that this letter would go unanswered, just like all the others, but I couldn't help but write anyway; I just had to let them know. Sure enough, no reply was forthcoming.

Then, three months later, in Doctor Meacham's surgery…

"Are you sure?" I asked.

"Well, unless my stethoscope or my ears are deceiving me, I can hear two heartbeats, not one."

At Little Wittenham that evening, I convened a council of war.

"How are we going to cope with four kids? Your two and my one were going to be tricky enough," I pointed out.

"What are you worrying for?" asked Manuela calmly. "We'll manage, won't we, Charles?"

And that was when Charles had the bright idea of asking my old nanny Margaret Black to come and live with us.

"I expect she'd be eager to keep herself busy."

"Sounds like typical Rochester luck," Badji added, to taunt me, I suppose. I had noticed that he was making fun of people a lot more these days. He had let himself go a little, too, as if it was all too much for him.

The following Friday, he got home late, well after suppertime. He'd stayed behind to see an important client, apparently. I'd had quite a day myself. I had just hung up my coat in the hall and flopped down in an armchair in the sitting room, looking forward to putting my feet up.

He marched over to me and grabbed my arm. "Not Alicia!" he insisted, referring to a discussion we had begun two weeks before about baby names. Alicia was my choice for a girl's name, if a girl arrived. I could instantly tell from his breath that he had been knocking back the whiskey. I pulled my arm away. "In my family," he went on, "it's bad luck to give a baby the same name as someone who's committed suicide."

I didn't reply, but went to find some peace in the kitchen, leaving him slumped on the sofa. I wasn't in the mood for an argument – wasn't in the mood for much of anything. If he wouldn't accept Alicia, perhaps I could persuade him to go for Alissa. I had three months to change his mind. All the same, it was the first time his drinking had really concerned me. I'd noticed he had a penchant for whiskey, but it hadn't ever bothered me. That evening, I found out he could be aggressive.

At seven months pregnant, I was in fine form. I had put on less than thirty pounds – not bad for twins! – although, I have to say, my tummy felt like it was going to burst. It didn't stop me racing around from one property to the next. In fact, my doctor, fearing premature labor, told me to slow down.

Slowing down wasn't really an option; as I soon as I stopped working, I was overwhelmed with memories of Wei, and an awful feeling that something was missing. I tried to do as I was told by the doctor, and decided to treat myself to a shopping trip one afternoon.

I had made a few purchases for the twins, and still had a good part of the afternoon ahead of me before I was due to meet Manuela at around seven, when her antiques shop shut for the day.

It was a beautiful late-September day, the sort we dream about in the middle of a bleak winter or a baking-hot summer. The last few shafts of pre-winter sun fell and warmed us gently. I sat down on a bench in Green Park and contemplated the small clouds that had formed all sorts of weird and wonderful shapes, trying to let go of my worries. Easier said than done. My mind wandered to my marriage, and suddenly , I was anxious. Since the wedding, Badji often got home late, and occasionally didn't show up at all for days at a time. Just before his most recent absence, he had flown into a rage when my stomach got in the way of his desire. That had shocked me. But thinking about it, I had to admit that my pregnancy was one of several excuses I found to avoid sleeping with him.

The truth was, I just couldn't fill the gap that Wei had left in my life. I thought I had forgotten him, but time had proven me wrong. Too many things reminded me of China: my conversations with

Leo, or keeping my journal in Mandarin. I couldn't help myself: each and every entry was addressed to the person I still thought of, deep down, as "the man of my life." I couldn't stop comparing the memory of his gentle touch with my husband's aggressive approach. Sometimes, a little voice would whisper that Wei wasn't dead. But if he was still alive, how could he leave me with no news?

Now and then, I wondered if my constant state of preoccupation prevented me from leading a normal married life. Perhaps that was what made Badji so distant to me. For someone who always looked for the truth, I didn't know what to believe anymore.

I got up from the bench and continued my walk until I was strolling down Bond Street. At one point – and I have no idea why – I turned my head toward the opposite side of the street. I was shocked to see my parents crossing the road. They were right in front of me, and hadn't even noticed I was there.

I walked quickly towards them, calling out, not inconspicuously: "Daddy! *Maman!*" They couldn't hear me. My heart was pounding. I tried again, louder this time, just a few yards from them. "Daddy! *Maman!*"

My father turned around. I saw his look of surprise, then warmth. It was another shock to see how he had aged, and how thin he was. My mother, typically, feigned a casual glance and tried to drag my father away by the arm. Gordon broke away forcibly. "Let go of me, Sarah!"

My mother looked astonished, and removed her hand. Gordon came toward me. He clasped both my arms, and gazed at my tummy.

We were smiling and crying at the same time, until my mother's brittle voice cut our embrace short.

"Stop it, Gordon. You look ridiculous! People might see us… if you've finished your public outburst, I'd like to get on with my shopping."

I swallowed my disappointment, galvanized by my father's affection. "*Maman*, come on. Why don't we have a cup of tea together?"

No chance. Her face froze over, and she shot me a look of disgust.

"I see your sweet tooth is stretching you to bursting point. My poor daughter. You look hideous. When I was pregnant, people barely noticed. Oh, but I forgot!" She slapped her forehead with the palm of her hand. "I forgot you're having a black baby."

That cynical smile: I knew it so well. I attempted, rather clumsily, to counter her, taking deep breaths, trying to steady my voice so it wouldn't tremble. No good; I was in a state.

"*Maman*, you're going to be a grandmother. Can you, for once, be happy for me? I'm expecting twins." As I was saying it, I knew it was pointless. I sounded like I used to as a child, trying to justify myself. It only bolstered my mother and weakened me.

"Perhaps you've forgotten. I no longer have any children." She paused to see the effect her words would have on me; then, adopting a deliberately breezy tone, she said to my father, "Right. Are you coming?"

My father's "No!" resounded like a gunshot. For the first time in my life, I heard him openly stand up to his wife. Incredible.

"I'm going to have a cup of tea with our daughter." He gripped me by the arm, and abandoned my mother on the pavement. We set off. A few streets later, we came out in Carlos Place and entered the Connaught Hotel.

We spent two delightful hours together, possibly at the same table where my mother and Oliver used to sit all those years ago. My "father" bombarded me with questions about his future grandchildren, our lives, and Charles's work. He had not seen his son for such a long time. I gradually got a grip on my emotions. I still hadn't dared to ask about his health. He looked so tired.

As if he had read my mind, he took my hand. "Kim…I have cancer. Please, don't say anything. Let me tell you. The doctors aren't optimistic. I have one wish, and that's to meet my grandchildren before I head off. I've often been a coward, but I've always loved you. With your permission, I would like to come and spend a week with all of you; perhaps more, we'll see. I want to make up, talk to my son, meet my daughter-in-law. I haven't got a lot of time left, and I want to make the most of it." He paused. I was terribly upset. "I was intending to write to you and your brother, but good fortune has brought us together first."

"Our door is wide open to you. Come whenever you like." Suddenly, the drama of the last few hours caught up with me; I started to feel dizzy and get stomach cramps. I pretended to be fine so as not to distress Gordon.

"I'll call your brother tomorrow," he said. "Would you be kind enough to tell him? I'd rather he didn't hang up on me." He seemed quite befuddled, and I found that touching. I wanted to ask all sorts of questions about his illness, but thought better of it. We would have plenty of time to talk things over during his stay.

"And what about *Maman*?"

"As usual, she doesn't want to know. She's decided to go off 'round the world when I've passed on...." He evidently wanted to say more, but couldn't. He quickly composed himself. "What do you say to a little glass of champagne to celebrate our reunion?"

"Excellent idea!" My tummy was rock hard; I thought it might relax me a bit. We drank a toast and continued to catch up with one another, relieved to be on the same side at last.

Then it was time to say goodbye. We promised to speak on the phone the next day. I stood on the corner of Carlos Place with a lump in my throat as I watched my father walk off into the distance. Night was falling, but when I looked at my watch, I saw that I had a solid hour before I was to pick up Manuela. My head was awash with thoughts. On one hand, the joy of seeing Gordon again; on the other, the misery of finding out he was ill and of seeing my mother more determined than ever to cut us off completely. And to think she was denying herself magical moments with her family....

I was suddenly exhausted.

Luckily, my car wasn't far away. I had parked it in front of a little house we had just bought in the Green Park end of Hay's Mews. Why not drop in to see how the renovations were coming along? The idea perked me up a little.

A short while later, I was standing in our latest property. The work was coming along; girders had been put up to support the walls. The floorboards creaked underfoot, but I didn't realize anything was wrong until it was too late. On my fourth step into the room, the planks gave way under my weight.

I landed in the cellar. I was so lucky; my fall had been broken by a pile of old carpets that had been ripped out, but not yet taken away. For the next half-hour, I felt groggy. When, at last, I summoned the strength to get up, an intense pain shot through my ankle. I couldn't move without it hurting.

I tried to get over to the stairs. It was dark down there; only a tiny bit of street lighting penetrated the partially-blocked basement window. There was a small shaft of light filtering in through the hole in the ceiling, too. I slowely groped my way along, so the pain wasn't so intense. When I got to the foot of the steps, I sat on them and began to pull myself up backwards, as I couldn't put any weight on my foot.

If I could manage to get outside, I tried to reassured myself, I was bound to come across someone who could help me.

Then, mid-climb, I felt a stab of pain in my back, and got short of breath. A warm liquid flowed between my thighs. I knew what that was. Whatever happened, I mustn't panic. I gritted my teeth and continued my climb.

At the top of the steps, I pushed the cellar door. It wouldn't budge. The builders must have locked it.

A wave of adrenaline swept over me, but again, I made myself concentrate. When I felt a second stabbing sensation in my back, I had to look facts in the face: I was going into labor in a cellar, and nobody knew I was there. Why had I refused Margaret's offer to come up to London with me? I tried crying out: the rather pathetic noise that came out of my mouth couldn't be classified as shouting. And who was there to hear me, anyway? I began to pray that my children wouldn't be born in that gloomy place, and went back down the stairs, still on my bottom, so I might lay myself out on the ground. My only hope was that Manuela would raise the alarm when I failed to turn up.

For the next few hours, I remained flat on my back in the rubble, lost in the pain of contractions and oblivious to time passing. I was alone, battling to ignore one black idea that was looming larger and larger. My children were going to die. Through the pain, the sweat that was stinging my eyes, and the tears, too, I called out into the darkness:

"Alicia! Help me please, Alicia!"

Silence.

Then a voice.

"Kim! Where are you?"

It was Edward. Her brother's voice. I heard my brother's voice, too.

"In the cellar..."

They broke down the door and came down the steps. I was trembling with fear and pain. Edward pointed a huge flashlight, blinding me. Charles crouched over me. I moaned, "Call an ambulance, they're coming!"

"There's no time. Come on, we're going to get you out of here. Climb onto my back. Margaret is waiting in the car."

But with my huge stomach, it was an impossible task. The only answer was for Charles to bend over so I could lie back-to-back on him, with Edward holding me by the calves. Somehow or other, their human stretcher got me out. The two men laid me down on the back seat of the car. What a relief to see my nanny. She took my hand and squeezed it tight. Edward drove, while Charles kept an eye on me. We made for St. George's Hospital, five minutes away.

Between contractions, I managed to tell Charles about my chance meeting with our parents, and the phone call he should be receiving from our father; but the pain was getting worse and worse, and I ended up talking gibberish in English, French, and Chinese.

I held onto Margaret's hand. She told me not to push, but it was no good; my first baby came into the world on the leather upholstery. I could just make out Charles's voice telling me it was a boy. The car door opened, and I was slid onto a stretcher. We had reached the corridor of the emergency ward when the contractions came again. The nurse stopped just in time to deliver a little girl.

Everyone was rushing around me. My son and daughter were taken from me. I would learn the next day that they were four-and-a-half pounds and three-and-a-half pounds, respectively. Just lighter than I had been twenty-six years earlier. They were immediately taken into intensive care under the expert eye of Margaret Black – this was familiar territory for her. There was no time for me to hold my babies. I was wheeled, bewildered, into a room in the main body of the very hospital where I had been born.

Edward and Charles left my side at three o'clock in the morning. No one could get a hold of Badji. As for my nanny, she refused to leave me by myself, and found a bed in the hospital to sleep in.

∿

"I think we can say we're lucky to be here," declares Vittorio.

"Marsie, I don't know how you coped. Weren't you scared?" Kenya asks.

"Yes, very! But my babies' survival was more important than anything, and I was preoccupied with trying to find a solution."

∽

The next day, the doctor asked me for my children's names. For my daughter, I couldn't look further than Alissa. I changed two letters so as not to get into a fight with Badji. For my son, I had come up with various names; but, whether consciously or not, the letter W popped into my head, and out of my mouth came "William."

Towards the end of the morning, Oliver and Leo arrived, weighed down with presents. I took my father's arm and hobbled with him to the premature baby ward. Oliver saw my two little bundles in a glass box, labeled with blue and pink bracelets and connected to an array of tubes. He was so moved that I, in turn, was overwhelmed. He turned to me and asked simply, "Where is your husband?"

My look said it all. I rested my head on his shoulder. In his own inimitable way, and shrouded in mysteries as his stories always were, he told me about his first visit to the hospital twenty-six years previously. He described the night he spent cuddling me when I had no other visitors, and how he had slipped the silver rattle into my cot the following morning. Then, with a flourish I had come to recognize, he took a little folded-up piece of tissue paper from his pocket, and handed it to me.

"You can add this to your collection. It goes with the blue sapphire I gave you when you left for China."

Gently pulling apart the paper, I found two little diamonds; one pink, the other blue. I couldn't contain myself any longer, and fell into my father's arms.

Back in my hospital room, I found Manuela, who had brought the two things I needed most: her friendship and her maternal touch. She spent the whole day with me, shepherding my numerous visitors. Just before teatime, Gordon poked his head through the door, armed with a present and a large bouquet of flowers. I introduced him to his daughter-in-law, and was surprised to hear them launch into a conversation in Italian. Did she say what I thought she said?

"Are you pregnant?" I asked.

"Yes, I was just about to tell you, Kim – sounds like I don't have to, now."

Gordon gave her a hug. What a happy meeting that was. I would never have imagined they would hit it off so well.

That evening, the nurse took my temperature and announced it was much too high. Alone in my room, I realized for the first time exactly how lucky I had been. I could have lost my children. I felt sick just thinking about it. I was also wondering where their father had gone off to. Was he in the middle of one of his marathon poker sessions? How many times had he promised me those would stop? It was our most common bone of contention: often, he would lose large sums of money and come to me, begging for help. I wasn't furious or worried. Just confused. And exhausted.

Badji turned up the next day, bewildered. I decided to let it go. My reproaches wouldn't change him one bit. And I was too eager to share my joy with him.

We went to see our babies hand in hand. We were even allowed to touch them. Unexpectedly, I saw my husband melt at the sight of Alissa, who looked much more like him than William. He turned to me with loving eyes.

"How about I take a week off? Do you think the doctor will let me sleep in your room?"

I'll never forget those five days we spent at the hospital. Badji turned back into the man I once knew, the tender man who made me laugh. He pampered me and looked after the little ones, carrying the milk I expressed six times a day, as they were unable to breastfeed. It was Badji who alerted the doctor to the fact that Alissa looked weaker than her brother.

"Sadly, she will always be more fragile," the specialist told us with an apologetic smile.

It was soon time for me to be discharged, and for Badji to go back to work. Although the swelling had gone down, my ankle still stopped me from getting around. Manuela and Margaret came to the rescue.

The first time we were alone, the day before my departure, Manuela shut the door and sat down beside me. I could tell she was upset about something. "Is he being kind to you?" she asked. She wanted to talk to me about Badji; she, for one, had still not forgiven him for missing the birth.

"He's been the most adorable father ever. And husband!"

From the look my friend gave me, I knew that whatever nonsense I chose to tell myself, she would always be there to put me back on the right track.

"And Wei?"

"I need to turn the page and live a proper family life," I replied defensively. "I've only got one priority now: my children. They're my true love; the rest is just a dream."

"But you're not a person who can compromise, Kim. I know you. Sooner or later, you will crack. And the thought of Wei will only get stronger."

"I must forget him. For my children."

"Perhaps that's not what life has in store for you. Remember that Chinese legend you liked to tell…."

"*The Seamstress and the Cowherd.*"

"Who knows if one day you will be reunited?"

I didn't reply. Just then, the nurse entered the room with some papers for me to sign before I could be discharged.

The next morning, it broke my heart to leave the hospital without my babies. They had to stay in the incubator until their weights increased. For the next two weeks, I brought them my milk every morning, and spent as much time with them as I could. That way, the bond between us stayed strong. On November 2, I was allowed to take them home at last.

I barely noticed the countryside flash by on our journey to Little Wittenham. It was cold. Thin, piercing rays of sunshine spread out across the land. Just before we reached our hamlet, the babies woke up. I stepped over the threshold carrying Alissa, just behind Margaret and ahead of Manuela, who had William in her arms. My nanny immediately set about tidying the kitchen, unpacking a baby-bottle warmer, packets of this and that, and bottles of water, scrubbing everything as she went.

Manuela and I headed straight upstairs to the nursery with the little ones. I walked into the room and was bowled over to see the children's names written in Chinese calligraphy on two silk scrolls hanging on the wall above their cribs.

"Did you make them?" I asked Manuela. By way of response, she just smiled. She knew what calligraphy meant to me. "When did you find time to put them up?"

"I asked Charles to hang them today at lunchtime. I wanted you to be the first to see them in place."

"They're gorgeous. And in the wild grass style, my favorite. What a lovely present. Thank you." I held her close.

I *was* incredibly grateful, but felt a familiar pang of anxiety, too. In a flash, Wei's spirit had invaded the whole room.

The twins began to cry; and at that, I was back in the real world. Manuela helped me to change and feed them. And then I settled down in a *bergère* chair, a little one in each arm, surrounded by cushions. Manuela slipped quietly away. I hadn't noticed it had gotten dark outside. Badji still wasn't home. My eyes were drawn to the calligraphy hangings once more; then I turned to look out the window. It was an extraordinarily clear, starlit night. I nestled my two angels close to me and quietly told them the story of the seamstress and the cowherd.

~

"Oh, Marsie," Kenya exclaims, throwing her arms around me. "You went through so much."

Vittorio nods, obviously moved. "And you were so brave."

"Well, I had to be. And also, I wasn't alone."

As I say these words, I realize just how true they are. I wasn't alone. It's true that I never had the mother I longed for. But there were my dear friends, who became my family. There were my fathers—the one I knew growing up as a child, and the very different person he became when I had children of my own; and of course, there was Uncle Oliver, steadfast through all the brightest and darkest times. There was Wei, whose love gave me strength even when we were apart. There were my children, and how I knew from the start I would give them the kind of love and the kind of childhood that my parents were unable to give me.

And now, there are my grandchildren. Their kind, sweet faces, the way they listen on the edge of their seats. They want my story to turn out well, but they also love me enough to want to listen to me talk about my pain, not just my joys. They are full of hope—for themselves and the adventures that await them ahead. And, I can see in their eyes, they are also hopeful for me. I have to be brave for them, as I was for my children. My grandchildren still need me. And there's so much more of my story yet to tell.

∽

Thanks to Virginie Michelet without whom this book would never have been born. Working together was a great happiness.

I would like to thank Marcel et Giselle Croës, whose life in Peking in the sixties was a considerable source of inspiration. I thank my Chinese friends who helped me enormously by sharing their experiences and carrying out valuable research: Lawrence Wu, Frida Liu, Emma Guo, Seuyin Wong, and Riu-Tchen Zhang. For the English chapters I am grateful to Rachel Roberts, the archivist at Cheltenham Ladies College, and the team at the Connaught Hotel in London.

∽